HER LAST SUMMER

Also by Emily Freud

My Best Friend's Secret
What She Left Behind

HER

LAST

SUMMER

EMILY FREUD

QUERCUS

First published in Great Britain in 2024 by

QUERCUS

Quercus Editions Ltd
Carmelite House
50 Victoria Embankment
London EC4Y 0DZ

An Hachette UK company

A CIP catalogue record for this book is available
from the British Library

PB ISBN 978 1 52942 904 6
EB ISBN 978 1 52942 905 3

10 9 8 7 6 5 4 3 2 1

Typeset by CC Book Production
Printed and bound in Great Britain by Clays Ltd, Elcograf S.p.A.

MIX
Paper | Supporting
responsible forestry
FSC® C104740
www.fsc.org

Papers used by Quercus are from well-managed forests and other responsible sources.

For Lola

When you are in the middle of a story it isn't a story at all, but only a confusion; a dark roaring, a blindness, a wreckage of shattered glass and splintered wood; like a house in a whirlwind, or else a boat crushed by the icebergs or swept over the rapids, and all aboard powerless to stop it.

Margaret Atwood, *Alias Grace*

Sweat trickles down her sunburnt face. A cackling monkey jumps across the vista. Vines like ropes dangle from above. Fear reverberates through her. This nightmare has to have an end point, she tells herself, as she pivots on the spot. Why did they come? So stupid and reckless. She's going to be eaten up by this place. By the sun, or whatever terrifying beasts are out there. Or by him. The boars or white-handed gibbons will chat happily as they munch through her bones and flesh. Red dripping from their hairy chins. A bloody hand offering their young a bite. She remembers someone telling her about Malayan sun bears and thinking what a friendly name. But now, as she twists and turns, vulnerable in her stinking clothes, she wonders if beady eyes are watching her through the thick undergrowth. Will her last moment be the terror of realisation just before the attack?

BOYFRIEND OF MARIGOLD CASTLE FOUND ALIVE

British teen rescued after spending months in snake-infested Thai jungle

October 9th 2002, *The National Mail*

One of the two teenagers who've been missing in Chiang Mai, Thailand, since separating from their guided tour over two months ago has been found unconscious by a local fisherman. Heavily dehydrated and malnourished, Luke Speed, 18, has been taken to hospital and will be questioned by the authorities once deemed fit. His girlfriend, Marigold Castle, is still missing. Police say they will make a statement in due course.

The largest rescue operation ever employed in this region failed to find the teenagers, and after a six-week recovery effort, it was scaled back considerably. It had been thought unlikely they would survive in the jungle alone. The evergreen rainforest of the Khao Soon National Park is older than the Amazon and reaches across five hundred square kilometres. Hidden within the expanse are deep valleys, lakes, looming limestone mountains, caves, and a thriving ecosystem of wildlife including snakes, wild boars, lizards, monkeys and bears.

We have contacted the family of Luke Speed for comment. Marigold Castle's parents have requested privacy at this time.

THE TRUE CRIME

1

My fingers grip the microphone tightly as lights glare. Squinting slightly, I smile out at faces obscured by drifting motes of dust. The auditorium is full. I only know because it was whispered over my shoulder for encouragement as I waited to go on. Blushing, I listen as the woman sitting to my right lays on a thick, overembellished introduction. She lists the accolades of my short but accomplished filmmaking career, and I'm left to wonder how I'll live up to it for these rapt onlookers. Usually, I am the one shuffling a pile of carefully curated questions in my lap.

'Ms Chambers. We're honoured to have you here. Really, very honoured.'

I bring the microphone up. 'It's great to be here.' Feedback rings around the space and I move it an inch away, feeling foolish. 'Thank you for inviting me.'

'The students here at the London Film School used your documentary, *Missing*, as one of our seminar films last term. It is obviously a very sensitive piece, with a little girl abducted and a family traumatised – can you tell us about your process of finding stories, and approaching the victim's loved ones?'

I collect my thoughts, before placing the mic back beneath my chin at the optimum distance. 'When investigating this type of crime, you must be mindful of all the people involved. They never chose to be victims of something like this – it chooses them. I wouldn't make a film if the families weren't willing to take part, or without their permission. They've had hopes dashed many times, and we certainly don't want to add to that pain. But at the same time, these are horrific crimes, and shining light on them can result in peace – in the case of *Missing* and Molly-Ann's parents, it was finding her body so they could have some finality in their grief. It can also, as we saw here, take a dangerous criminal off the streets, and stop the spread of further pain – the pain that violent crimes cause. But we do need to look at the bigger picture, questioning the system we assume will protect us if the worst should happen. So, when researching and developing, I'm looking to tell an intimate narrative with a big-picture angle that says something about our justice system or the society we live in. I want to access a story's inner and outer worlds. From the police station to the kitchen table. And ultimately seek the truth, and hopefully get some answers.' Feeling I've rambled, I stop. I could talk for days on the subject.

She smiles supportively, and I note her eyes scanning her sheet for the next question. '*Missing*, which I should mention has been shortlisted for a Grierson Award, congratulations—' Applause interrupts her, and she pauses to allow it room.

I hold her gaze, fighting the urge to look down, away from the compliment. 'Thank you,' I say, as the enthusiastic clapping peters out.

'The film resulted in new evidence being uncovered and the correct perpetrator behind bars. How does it feel as an investigative journalist to be an active participant in a story like that?'

'This film was years in the making but what initially drew me to this case was an article I'd read about Molly-Ann's stepfather. He'd been in prison for a decade at that point for a crime he was adamant he didn't commit. The circumstantial evidence was huge, but a body was never recovered. At the time, there was new evidence, but the Crown Prosecution Service were refusing to reopen the case. We spent a few months looking into the story, and decided the untapped leads were worth exploring. We approached the family and his lawyers, and they gave us access. We had no idea at the time it would lead us to Max Barber, a construction worker the family had on their property the year before she was taken.'

'And he's now been found guilty of her murder,' she says knowingly.

'We approached witnesses who were finally willing to speak. As is often the case, as years pass secrets no longer bear the same weight. Those revelations resulted in the police finally agreeing to reopen the investigation.'

'And we all know what happened next . . .' She leans forward. 'They found Molly-Ann.'

My smile fades at the memory. 'Yes, well.' I look at my

hands. The memory of Molly-Ann's mother sobbing, the pain in her eyes seizing the camera lens as I caught my breath. 'Yes. And after testing the DNA samples, her murderer was confirmed to be Max Barber.'

'What an incredible moment! Because of you, an innocent man is free, and a murderer is off the streets. How does that feel?'

'It's overwhelming, if I'm honest. All we ever set out to do was to tell the story of how a miscarriage of justice can still happen in this country, even with all the checks and balances we have in place. It's an unexpected, but extremely pleasing, by-product of doing my job.'

'You tell it incredibly well, I must say.' The audience murmurs in agreement. 'I've not had such an array of emotions as a viewer for a long time.'

'We had a lot of texture in that film which helped. Recorded phone calls, psychiatric reports, police interviews. Telling these stories in the UK where you're not permitted to film in the courtroom can be challenging. But we got lucky.'

'That plot twist . . .'

I nod, agreeing. And with a wry smile I add, 'Sometimes the truth is stranger than fiction!' The audience laughs.

'What compels you to tell these stories? You seem to be a dog with a bone once you start.'

I hesitate and look out across the crowd. As I open my mouth to reply, a solitary figure stands up. A flash of recognition and my stomach plummets. Memories clutter my mind and I close my eyes briefly, ordering away the darkness. When

I open them, I realise it was just a harmless student, taking a photograph. I clutch the mic harder. 'I just really care about the truth. And telling stories.' She looks at me as though she knows there is more. But I purse my lips and cock my head to one side with a generic smile, waiting patiently for her next question, and she moves on.

2

I head back to the production office, rushing from platform to train. I walk quickly, as always. Companions often ask me to slow down we are so out of step. The interview has taken it out of me, and I feel as though I'm being chased by confusing emotions, and whispering echoes from words left unsaid. I know the only way to stop my skin crawling is to work. Once inside, I hop into my seat, opening my laptop and placing headphones on so I can ignore the bustle of the media company. Focusing instead on the treatment I'm writing for what I hope will be my next film. My shoulders slowly lower as I get lost in the research calls and court transcripts, body-cam footage and news articles.

I'm completely sucked in. The next time I look out the window, evening is settling across the roofs of Soho. A muddle of aerials and chimney stacks stick into the silvery sky. Inside, desk lamps are turning off and bags are dragged up from the floor. Huddled end-of-day conversations. I watch from my bubble, thinking of where they are off to now, and who will be waiting for them at home.

I hear Cleo, my assistant producer, stand up and stretch. Next the sound of her bum bag clip. Her slender frame reaches the corner of my eyeline before she speaks. 'Cass?' I stop typing and turn my head, fingers frozen above the keyboard. 'A few of us are going for a drink at The Ship, want to join?' she asks, leaning on the corner of my desk, and I begin to shake my head. 'Come on, it'll be fun. It's the perfect summer's evening to get jostled about on the pavement with a cold beer. Cass, you deserve it,' she attempts. I gesture at the document on my screen. It's really starting to look like something pitchable.

'I want to get this over to Raef before his meeting in the morning. I think he might say it's ready. You go, have fun.'

She gives me one of her looks. 'Cass, you work too hard.' My stiff, determined smile causes her to relent. 'Okay. Want me to stay and help?' I shake my head as she places a hand on the top of her swivel chair, ready to jump back in.

'No – you go. All these calls you made really helped. Enjoy yourself.'

She's pleased. Just like me at that stage of my career: hungry, ambitious. Desperate for praise. She begins to walk away, calling, 'Don't stay too late!' I watch as she joins Mo by the black grid glass doors; he's an edit producer she's been spending a lot of time with recently. They grin at each other and start chatting; the sound of Cleo's high-pitched laugh makes me smile. I'm glad. Too much of this job is long hours and weeks away – an expectation that you can drop everything and jump on a train at a moment's notice. There isn't enough time for a personal life. I've given up having one. I wasted my twenties chasing a good story. Was it a waste? I doubt I'd be in this position – barely thirty and one of the youngest female directors with a Grierson nod under my belt. Only a few years older than Cleo. They treat me like another species around here. They can't work out how I've pulled it off, like I must have cheated somehow. But it's just sacrifice. You must choose. And I did.

A few hours later and I stifle a yawn. My slouched back feels tight and sore, and I pull my arms behind me so my hands meet and gently rock my head from side to side. Then I lean towards my screen again, double checking the cover email, ensuring all integral elements are front facing, as Raef skims when in a rush. I chew my lip as I attach the document and hit send. I hope he'll be pleased with it. Songbird Productions is the new kid on the production company block, and even though Raef's the founder and owner, he still takes the lead on all new developments.

Satisfied, I close my laptop and secure it in my bag.

'Hi, how are you?' I ask the cleaner as she empties the bins.

'You're always here,' she teases. 'On your own!'

And I laugh. 'Work shy, the lot of them.'

She smiles, but I think I notice a flicker of pity in her eyes. The noise of a hoover wails from one of the meeting rooms. I like being the last one here. It makes me feel as though I've eked out every possible moment of productivity from the day. Wrung it dry.

I stride across the open-plan office, thinking of what I'll

have for dinner. Another takeaway most probably, or a ready-made soup. I need to stop and get some food for Herzog, my cat.

The phone rings from the unmanned reception desk. It echoes shrilly around the empty foyer. Ignoring it, I continue towards the lifts. The ringing stops as I pass, but begins again immediately. I pause and stare at it, and then across to the lifts.

I sigh before making a U-turn. Leaning over the high bar of the reception desk, I reach down and pick up the handset. I've been at the company from its inception so feel it's part mine anyway. My first job in television, over ten years ago, was on reception at a large company where Raef was the creative director. As I went up the pecking order, we became friends, and he took me with him when he started up on his own.

'Songbird Productions,' I say. Grabbing one of the branded notebooks and pencils off the desk to take a message.

'Can I speak to Cassidy Chambers, please?' I blink at the sound of my own name. The man's voice is throaty and carefully paced.

'Who's speaking, please?' I ask, intrigued. I make research calls from the office for the various projects I have on the boil, hoping to get one over the line and commissioned, so it could be anyone.

'My name is Luke Speed. I . . . I . . .' He pauses. Unsure how to explain. But he doesn't need to.

'I know who you are,' I reply, my voice rising with surprise.

'Is that you?' The way he says it makes me feel as though I've been lost.

15

'Yes. I'm Cassidy.' I pull at the strap of my bag and let it slump on the floor before hiking the phone cord over, so I can make myself comfortable in the desk chair. 'What can I do for you, Luke?'

'I finally got round to watching your film, *Missing*, last night. It . . . it brought up a lot of stuff for me.' I flick through the filing cabinet of missing persons cases in my mind, having researched hundreds on my hunt for a new project. I know Luke's story. I was in my first year of secondary school when the teenagers went missing while backpacking in Thailand. I remember my mum watching the coverage on the news through a haze of cigarette smoke. They were on the cover of every newspaper for weeks. It was one of the big missing persons cases of the noughties and was never fully resolved.

The story is on my list to do some deep-dive research into, but I got distracted by something else and haven't had time. It has all the tropes of a successful true crime series: a love story, a suspect, a young woman whose demise has never been uncovered. The did he/didn't he? The nostalgia of that time. Backpacking in the region had been propelled into the zeit-geist because of a recent film adaptation of *The Beach* starring Leonardo DiCaprio, and when this story exploded all heads turned to the Asian continent. There was an outpouring of grief for the beautiful couple. But when Luke was found he became the lead suspect. Last I heard he'd got addicted to hard drugs and vanished into the underworld. Another victim? Or the guilty party? Gripping.

What is he doing calling me?

'Your film, it made me think. It's been twenty years since Mari went missing.' He pauses, and I resist the urge to butt in. 'Everyone's had their chance to tell the story, all built on accusations and assumptions. It's time to set the record straight. It's time to tell my side.'

I stand up, needing to move somehow. This never happens. 'Luke. Let me get this straight. You are approaching me because you'd like us to make a documentary about what happened to you and to Mari in the jungle?'

'Yes,' is his simple reply. 'No one . . . no one believed me . . . They still don't believe me . . .' His voice cracks.

'Luke,' I say gently. 'You must have been through a lot.'

'I'm sick of hiding.' There is an anger now, a raw frustration. 'Of people deciding who I am from dribs and drabs of information the media skewed. I've finally got myself out of the mess I was in and need to regain control of my life. It's *my* story. Not theirs.' His anger rising. I am surprised how yanked by sympathy I feel. 'And the only way I can do that is by laying down the past, in my own words.'

I clear my throat. 'Luke. This will be a big story. It will take its toll . . . They'll come for you, you know that, right?'

'Let them. I can't live my life with it hanging over me. Something needs to change before I can move on. I don't know what else I can do. I'm stuck. And . . . I want to find her. I want to be able to say goodbye.' The desperation in his voice is haunting.

I realise my hand is balled into a tight fist and I let it go. 'You need to understand, Luke, just because you've come to me doesn't mean I'll let you off lightly. I'm going to ask you the tough questions. Everyone will want to know exactly what happened in the jungle between you and Mari.'

'I want the tough questions,' he says, almost exploding with frustration at my reticence. 'I want people to see me as a human. Not as a . . . murderer.' He pauses. 'Because I didn't hurt her – I loved her. I still love her.' The tenderness in his voice causes me to blink.

'You know they may not think that, right? You may tell your story. And they still may not believe you.' I want to be honest with him right from the start before this has a chance to snowball. I don't want him running to me down the line saying he didn't understand the consequences.

'I want to, Cassidy. I know you'll do it justice. I trust you with my story.'

I feel a lick of pride and take a deep breath. 'Okay, Luke. Let's do this.' I take down his details and tell him I'll call first thing once I've spoken to Raef. I already know this will sell quickly. Stories like this, with a contributor still under suspicion willing to be the focal point of a film, don't come around often. The streaming services will all want a go at it, a lot of the traditional broadcasters too.

This is the big one I've been waiting for. And I can't quite believe how it has fallen into my lap. Luke Speed is my next obsession. I already know it.

3

Raef is jittery. He's doing that annoying thing with his leg when he's rushing with adrenalin. Rocking it subconsciously as he inhales thickly on his vape. Since I phoned him a few evenings ago, full of heady elation, he's been gushing about the possibilities of the project – who he's going to pitch to, what it could look like stylistically. The scope. The awards. I'll get random voice notes day and night with thoughts far too premature for the stage we're at.

Luke is due to come into the office today. I can tell by the angst haemorrhaging off Raef that he's nervous, having built it up in his mind that Luke won't be what he's hoping: a strong character who'll be able to carry a film. This meeting will, hopefully, expel those fears. I'm not worried. Over the last few days, I've spoken to Luke for hours. He's desperately likeable and brilliant at articulating himself. I just know it will transfer onto screen. I have good instincts for this sort of thing.

I've been busy writing up the cold case as a treatment using my research calls with Luke, and news articles and interviews that have accumulated over the last two decades. Meeting him is one of the final hurdles; after this, Raef wants to start the ball rolling selling the series, and at least get some development money.

After completely immersing myself in the story, it's even more compelling than I remembered. Mari and Luke were high school sweethearts. All A stars at A level; captains of the sports teams. They were beautiful, sultry and wholesome. The real deal. When they went missing the whole country was on tenterhooks. Vigils were held. The Archbishop of Canterbury mentioned them in a sermon. The prime minister talked about their plight in parliament. People donned purple ribbons, to match the colour of their school uniforms. There was collective euphoria when Luke was found, and then grief when Mari was officially declared missing, presumed dead. That united grief turned to united anger when Luke's story came out.

He was no longer a victim, but a culprit.

Luke's outlandish claims of being followed by a maniac in the jungle were simply laughed at by Thai police – even more so by the British media. He described this crazed man as having wild hair and his body covered in mud; he'd stalk them day and night. One outlet did a mock-up of his description which travelled across the internet before the term 'going viral' had even been invented.

In 2002 Luke gave a shambolic interview to the police after months of near starvation and disorientation so severe, he was half crazed himself. He said that one morning he woke up in their makeshift camp, and Mari was simply gone. Poof.

No one believed his theory the perpetrator was this chilling figure in the jungle.

Then, more evidence came to light which painted a different picture of Mari's boyfriend. CCTV emerged of them arguing during their trip. Travellers came forward, saying they'd witnessed the pair fighting. But what really went against Luke was the fact the police could not find one shred of evidence there was anyone else in the jungle. The fabled man Luke talked of was dismissed as utter rubbish. The rescue service never recovered her body. So, a definitive answer has eluded everyone since.

Raef flicks through the treatment I'd printed off for him. 'Right. You okay leading? We need this to go well.'

I nod, trying not to let his anxiety rub off on me. 'Sure. It will be fine, Raef.' I flick him a look.

'I'm seeing Sangeet from Channel 4 and Felix from Disney+ this afternoon,' he says, as if to underline how important this initial meeting is. 'I've got more tomorrow. It wouldn't look good if I cancel.'

'I know, Raef,' I say with a sigh. I told him to wait until we'd done this housekeeping before he got everyone excited. But he couldn't help himself. Raef seems to thrive under pressure, and I think he assumes others do too. 'I told you. Luke can carry this, I'm sure of it.'

He looks at me intensely, as if checking for cracks. 'Well, I hope he doesn't back off once we go through everything for informed consent.' Part of this meeting will need to include what the project could entail, and all negative repercussions that could come from it. Then he'll need to sign a release form, confirming he understands and agrees to take part in the film.

'Let's just take it one step at a time,' I reply calmly. Raef nods. I've got a good track record of coming up with the goods.

The phone rings in the middle of the meeting room table. We look at each other. Showtime. He nods at me to take it, and I lean forward and snatch it up.

'Luke Speed is here to see you,' the receptionist tells me.

Thank goodness. I was half terrified he wouldn't turn up.

'Great. Send him over to meeting room three.' I tighten my ponytail and brush down the front of my shirt, before turning to look out the glass wall.

The first thing I notice is everyone in the office stops what they're doing, and looks up, transfixed. The women especially, but the men too. There is a shift in the atmosphere. Heads are tilted, backs arch and lips part. When he comes into view, I understand.

He's tall, with a broad chest and toned arms. Although bald, this suits his chiselled face. He has a slight tan and a fresh-out-the-gym-shower glaze. He's wearing a crisp white T-shirt and khaki trousers with white Converse, a bag slung confidently over the back of his shoulder. There is a mid-century vibe about him. Incredibly well put together.

He catches me staring through the glass and smiles, and dimples form on his cheeks. I return his smile warmly, feeling like I've got to know him well during our long research chats, some of which have lasted hours. But I've been picturing the

22

Luke from twenty-year-old photographs. Not this Luke. I wasn't picturing him like this.

I open the door for him and Raef jumps to his feet, holding out a hand. 'Luke, great to have you here. Thank you for coming in.' He gestures to a seat at the other side of the table and picks up the phone. 'Tea? Coffee?'

Luke pulls out the chair and begins to sit. 'A glass of water would be great. It's so hot today,' he says, gesturing to the window and the vivid blue sky.

'Can you bring a coffee, one of those herby things Cass likes, and some cold water and glasses to meeting room three?' Raef tells the runner at the end of the line. 'Thanks.' He puts the phone down and takes the seat across from Luke. His extra charming smile plastered, which he saves for people in need of impressing.

'So, Luke. Thank you so much for choosing to trust us with this,' he says, rubbing his hands together.

Luke nods, glancing at me. 'It was more because of Cassidy than anything.' I feel myself flush. This isn't me at all. I'm trying not to look at him directly because I'm afraid he'll sense something.

'Yes, well. She's ours so it all works out,' Raef replies jovially, swivelling his chair in my direction, and I take my cue to jump in.

'Yes, thank you for coming in, Luke,' I say, looking up at him with an assured smile. 'We wanted to get you in here to go through the process, so you really understand what you're committing yourself to before we start.'

'I appreciate that. But I've already made up my mind,' he says, leaning back in his chair, poised and relaxed. The runner bursts in, the mugs and glasses knocking together as he nervously puts the tray down on the table. We wait for him to leave before continuing. Raef terrifies the younger cohort of the team. He is the king of factual television, and the long list of critically acclaimed hours of television that precede him are intimidating. His eye for detail in the edit is unrivalled. He pushes the limit ensuring nothing has been left unanswered and the very best is eked out of a narrative before it hits the screen. His storytelling is emotive, newsworthy, and often a national event discussed around water coolers up and down the country. I doubt I'd have done so well, so quickly, without his guidance and relationships to piggyback on.

I pour Luke some water and place the glass in front of him. 'So, at this point we are gauging interest from the channels. Pitching the idea and how we see the series. They may want tweaks as we go, which we'll discuss with you at every stage. But currently, we see your part in all this as master interviews. They may go on for a few days. We might leave them for a while as we work on the case and come back for more.' He nods as I speak. 'We'll also take you back to your home town, do a bit of filming where you and Mari grew up. As there is limited archive, no footage of your trip, just grainy photos from twenty years ago, the channel will probably want a bit of reconstruction to add visuals to the film.'

Luke leans forward with a confused look. And I explain further. 'A blend of your interview and a dramatisation of the events from your interview. Shots of you sitting down talking would get boring for the viewer after a while,' I explain. 'We need something else to cut into that. These days we record everything on our phones. I'm sure there will be a heyday of retrospective documentaries in about twenty years' time – with all the self-shot archive people will have accrued.' I smile at the thought. 'But for now, to tell your story, it is important for us to do some extra filming to really give the audience insight into what happened out there.'

Luke nods at me. 'Okay, I understand.' His deep blue eyes bore into mine confidently, like he's not scared of looking directly at me. As if he has nothing to hide.

'We'll also try to interview primary and secondary sources. Family members. Old friends. Travellers you met during the trip. Police, embassy workers.' I note a line of worry cross his brow and I add, 'We must tell a balanced story from all perspectives. We wouldn't be doing our job properly if we didn't.'

He shifts around in his seat. 'If you can get anyone to talk.' He shakes his head sadly.

I lean across the table. 'Luke. We wouldn't want to do any more harm to Mari's family by bringing this up again, without their permission. It wouldn't be fair.' I look over at Raef and he nods. 'We wouldn't want to make this film unless Mari's parents, Elsie and Charles, are happy for us to. They don't have to necessarily be in the film. But it is something Raef and I feel strongly about.'

Luke looks at his hands sombrely. 'Yeah. I get that. They've been through enough.' He thinks for a moment before speaking again. 'I hope they understand that I want answers too. That's why I'm here. To find out what happened to her once and for all. None of us have been able to move on, surely they'll see that.' The sentence collapses into a whisper.

I notice his eyes tear up, but he blinks the emotion away quickly. I feel an unusual sense of protectiveness over him. Over his future. The weight of responsibility in my hands is unwieldy. 'We're going to try and do that, Luke. We're going to try and find out what happened to her.'

He smiles softly. 'I know you will, Cassidy.'

4

At the lift, I give Luke a final wave. The doors close on him leaning back on the mirrored wall, his hands in his pockets, casting me a last wry smile. I watch the numbers descend to the ground floor on the digital display, as I reflect on the intensity of the last hour. Crossing my arms in a tight hug, I stroll back to the meeting room, slowly for once. Cleo catches my eye. She does a thumbs up/thumbs down sign, and I reply with the former and she grins. I close the glass door softly before turning back to Raef.

He's standing by the window, looking out at the sky, haze rising into a simmering blue. 'Excellent, Cass. Really good,' he says, taking a drag from his vape. The smoke curls up around him as he turns to me. 'Do you think he killed her?'

I blink at the forthright question. 'Raef, I have no idea.' I sit down on one of the padded leather seats, and lean on the table, my chin on my palm. 'But it would be peculiar he comes to us, wanting to do this, if he did. Wouldn't it?'

He takes the seat opposite and taps his pen on his moleskin

notebook. 'Isn't that a psychopathic trait? Wanting the lime-light. The infamy. All that.'

I nod. 'Yes, I suppose. Although I didn't get that from him. Did you?'

He looks up at the ceiling for a moment, thinking. Then shakes his head. 'No. But it could have been for show, a manip-ulation. Couldn't it?'

I sigh. 'Yes. That is something we need to be wary of.'

'That could be an interesting film in itself, I suppose,' he mutters. 'A character study.' I watch him enjoy that thought, irritated by the speed with which Raef has labelled Luke. There is something about Luke, boyish and vulnerable under-neath his exterior. There is a desperation for validation; and a guarded hope that comes with being mistrusted and dismissed for years. It doesn't feel calculated at all.

Raef ruminates further. 'We should do a background check on him – find out if there is anything in the last twenty years we should know about. Proper, thorough due diligence. Any other skeletons in his closet, we need to know about them.' I give him a pointed look at the phrase he's chosen.

'Of course.' I hold up my pad to show him the note I made myself earlier, underlined twice.

'Never miss a beat, do you, Cass?' He chuckles. 'This is going to be good. I can feel it.' He stands with a flourish. 'Right, I'm going to head to my meetings, fill them in on what we've got on the boil. You're going to speak to Mari's parents, right?'

I nod. I'm not looking forward to the phone call. The tidal wave of emotions as soon as they realise the reason for my call. It will inflict pain. But hopefully, it will be worth it, and they'll get answers. I can't imagine the horror of not knowing what happened to a loved one for twenty years.

Raef hurries out the office, ignoring the receptionist's call for attention, a notepad jutting from her hand. 'Email me!' he shouts over his shoulder, placing his Ray-Bans on the bridge of his nose, his perfectly worn leather satchel bopping as he strides away.

I go back to my desk and stare at the number for Mari's parents I managed to negotiate from a contact at a national newspaper. I peel off the yellow Post-it note from the corner of my screen and stare at the digits. There is no point putting it off.

I hear giggling and look up. Cleo is talking to Mo in the little kitchenette. It is obvious they fancy each other. All beaming smiles and shining eyes. I'm distracted by their movements momentarily. The way he's touching her arm when he talks, and how she leans that extra few inches when trying to hear what he's saying. An invisible pull. The beginning of a game they will play until they build up the courage, after a few drinks at The French House most probably, to kiss. Maybe they already have. And then the early pink cloud of a relationship will turn into the comforting mundanity of a long-term coupling. Before they grow tired, and have learnt enough from each other about themselves, or the type of person they should be with. And move on. Performing this dance with various people before eventually settling down.

I prefer to watch than take part. There is something about

being part of a relationship, another person's story, that scares me. You can't control the narrative once you're inside it. You're lost to your emotions and reactions. I prefer to document from afar. It's safer. Mo and Cleo are moving into a new space together. This initial patter, full of laughter, touch, the way they are reaching for a connection. It's chemical. It's older than time. One day she'll come into the office looking sad with tear-stained cheeks. And I'll have to comfort her and try not to get annoyed that she can't focus on her work.

'Cass?'

I turn. The runner is standing in front of me, his phone in his hands. 'Want something for lunch or are you going out?' His thumbs held rigid above the screen waiting to take a note.

'I'm fine,' I say, reaching into my bag and plonking some Tupperware on the desk to answer the question. He nods and moves on to another member of the senior team.

I lift off the Post-it and insert my wireless earphones, and walk towards the long corridor which runs alongside the meeting rooms. Pacing during tricky calls helps me think. I press the call button, and take a steadying breath. It rings three times before an older-sounding gentleman picks up. 'Three-nine-zero, five-six-nine-seven,' he says. My grandmother used to answer the phone like that, and I smile at the memory of her.

'Is that Mr Castle?'

'Who is this, please?' His voice worn and tired, and I feel guilty to be bringing this to his door. I have seconds before he makes a snap decision and hangs up.

'My name is Cassidy Chambers. I'm calling from a television production co—'

'No thank you. Have a good day,' he replies swiftly.

Before he has time to move his ear from the phone I edge in a sentence. 'Luke Speed wants to be interviewed for a documentary.' The dull sound of the dialling tone doesn't materialise. Just silence.

'Luke,' Mr Castle croaks. 'How is he?' A calmness settles over me as I realise he isn't angry. But most of all, I'm surprised by the first question he's chosen to ask.

'He's in a good space, Mr Castle. He's ready to talk about what happened, in the jungle.'

'Where were you calling from again?' he enquires.

'I'm a producer/director from an independent production company called Songbird Productions. I recently made a film called Missing. It was about a girl that went missing a long time ago. During filming we came across new evidence, meaning the guilty party has been jailed, and an innocent man freed.' I pause. 'Her body was recovered.' I know where I want his mind to go. 'Luke wants to finally tell his side of the story, Mr Castle. He wants to refresh people's memories, open new lines of enquiry. Hopefully even galvanise another search.' I let him ruminate. I wish I was sat across from him so I could gauge his reaction. He hasn't hung up which is a good sign.

'We haven't had a call like this for a while.'

'I understand this is hard to talk about, to consider going over it again. But this is a huge development, don't you think?' More silence.

And then he asks, 'What do you want from us?'

'Nothing, at this stage, Mr Castle. I just wanted to let you know what was happening. Nothing has been commissioned yet, but most likely it will be. And we wouldn't want to continue without telling you what was going on ... or without your permission.'

There is a long pause.

'I see. I will need to speak to Elsie. She finds this very difficult. I doubt we would want to be on film.'

Small steps, I think. 'That is completely up to you, and not something you need to decide now. As I say, we haven't even got the film commissioned. We're in the very early, preliminary stages of this project.'

'Luke wants to be interviewed. Really?' He sounds incredulous.

'Yes. He feels he can't lead a full life without an attempt at closure. Which is understandable.'

'I always liked Luke. Very much,' he mutters. Again, I am taken aback by the fondness in his voice. 'He was an excellent student,' he adds, almost as an afterthought. Mari's father was the headmaster of their public school. 'If Luke is willing to tell his side of the story, that's not something we would want to get in the way of.' Relief swells through me, and I'm already itching to tell Raef. 'I will speak to Elsie. Though I doubt she would want to be filmed.'

'I understand.' There is no point pushing that right now.

'You get yourselves sorted. And then come over for a cup of

tea. And we can discuss it further,' he offers, kindly. He seems pragmatic, and I've warmed to him instantly.

'Thank you, Mr Castle. I just want to say that I am doing this with the best intentions. It's an important story to tell.'

'Yes, yes,' he says, waving the comment away. 'Once you have a film in production, call again. Goodbye, Ms Chambers.' He hangs up.

I stare at my phone in shock. That went far more smoothly than I was expecting. I stride back over to my desk allowing a little smile of celebration as I open my Tupperware box and stuff a sandwich into my mouth. Chewing, I turn to Melissa, the development production manager, who deals with logistics. 'Mel, I think you need to start a new spreadsheet,' I say, grinning.

5

The next few weeks pass in a blur of activity as we get the series off the ground. In the end, one of the traditional broadcasters commissioned the film. Initially, I was exasperated by the decision. They won't pay as much money as the streamers, but Raef has the last word. I know he was steered by the fact he has a highly profitable returning series on the table with them and felt this could sway that project too.

Raef is always thinking of the bigger picture. I've come to terms with the fact there'll be a constant fight over money, but there isn't much I can do about it. I just need to get on and do my job the best I can.

I now have a section of the office dedicated to the production. Melissa has carefully jotted down shoot days on the whiteboard above our small collection of desks. Schedules have been drawn up, budgets signed off and crew hired. I obviously wanted Cleo, the assistant producer who I've worked with for a few years now. There's not a safer pair of hands, and she is excellent with contributors. I've hired Jamal, a researcher, who was recommended to me by another producer. And Melissa

34

has been seconded off development and onto our production at my insistence.

'Has anyone got back to you?' I ask Cleo, who's been calling around the other pupils in Mari and Luke's class.

She looks at me, eyes wide and despondent, and I know she hasn't had a bite. 'They will, it's early days,' I tell her kindly. No point stressing about it yet. We'll get there, it just may take a bit of time. I may need to get more involved with that side of it, although I know that will make Cleo feel incompetent, but better bruised egos than a flimsy film.

That evening, I'm home drinking a glass of cold white wine staring up at the cork board newly adorned with research from the case. Flashing lights of emergency vehicles bounce around my living room, and I can hear loud bangs from motorbike exhausts as they thunder past. I live in east London near Old Street roundabout, just behind the drive-thru McDonald's, in an ex-council block. I'm on a relatively good wage these days, and could probably move, but I'm settled here. It's convenient and Mary, the elderly lady next door, feeds Herzog while I'm away for work. Besides, I don't need any extra space. One bedroom is plenty for me.

I look up at the information pinned on the board. There is so much out there in the media, not to mention the reams of conspiracy theorists on numerous Reddit threads, about Mari and Luke. Before I'd laid it out like this, I'd been a tad over-whelmed. Little lines of red cotton map my thoughts. I take a few steps back to get a bird's eye view. The photo of them on a beach on one of the islands leaps out. And I lean forward, untacking the pin, holding it in my hands.

They were unbelievably young and beautiful. Luke was smaller then, less muscle, leaner. He had a full head of floppy hair, and sand flattened on one side of his face as if he'd been sunbathing. That same distinctive mole by his smile crease, those sparkling eyes wincing slightly at the bright sun. His arm slung casually over a petite Mari wearing a red triangle bikini. Her long hair is white blonde and streaky, and her button nose squidged up slightly with mischief, with a snorkel dangling from one hand.

The scene in the background is the backpacker's dream: white sands, turquoise water. Palm trees slinking into the sea. If only they'd stayed down south on the islands and never gone to the jungle, none of this would have happened. I wonder where they'd be now. They had their pick of a future and could have been anything they wanted. Opportunities would have been thrown in their way.

I want to jump into the scene and warn them. Tell them not to get lost that day on the trek. To stay closer to their guide. Never miss a step.

My mobile phone vibrates on the glass coffee table. I walk over and look down. My sister. I contemplate allowing my voicemail to kick in, but then I'll have to deal with it later. 'Hello there!' I say, looking around for my wine. I rescue it from the sideboard and take a sip. 'What excuse have you got to check up on me this time?'

Rebecca makes an infuriated sound before replying, 'Well,

you never bother calling me, and when I want a chat, I get accused of meddling.'

'Well, that's because you're on the lookout for things to be judgemental about,' I tease.

'That's not fair!'

She's right, it isn't fair. I get comfortable on the sofa, scooping my legs under me. Herzog saunters over and hops on, and lifts his chin onto my lap, his eyes closing into a snooze. He seems to just sleep all day when it's hot like this.

'Sorry, let's start again. How are you?' I ask.

My sister is the opposite of me. She's a primary school teacher, and chose the career because she enjoys a routine, and the excessively long holidays which she can plan for a year in advance. Everything could be the same for her year in, year out, until she retires. She recently got married and had her dream honeymoon in French Polynesia. Her husband, Eric, is exactly what you think of when you say 'banker'. Nice watch, convertible. Lovely house in Dulwich. A cottage on the Deal seafront for weekends. Safety. Everything she's ever wanted since growing up with hardly anything, having to learn life's rules on our own. I am five years older, so really, with our mother incapacitated most of the time, I was the only person she had to rely on. I sort of feel like she is my biggest achievement. But would never tell her that. And the pressure of looking after her, and hiding the chaos of our childhood, is imprinted firmly onto me. But that's because I didn't have anyone to rely on, like she did. Maybe there is a little residue of resentment. And guilt, too, that I kept our mother's secrets.

I don't have the energy to be that person for her any more. But she doesn't need me these days. She's fought in her own way for everything she's got. Plus, she's madly in love. Which is all I've ever wanted for my little sister: to be happy. I'm prouder of her than she'll ever know.

I bet she's pregnant.

'Cass, I have something to tell you!' she says with an excited squeal. Here we go: 'I'm pregnant.'

Wow. Quicker than I thought. 'Oh, Rebecca, that's wonderful!'

'Obviously don't tell anyone. It's very early days.'

'Of course I won't.'

'Especially not Mum.'

My smile falters a bit. 'No. Of course I wouldn't. That's wonderful news. When are you due?'

'Mid-February. I'll have to finish halfway through the year which is sad. My year twos are so precious.' I wonder if she'll ever go back. Or if this is just the beginning of a string of children. It's good. She's breaking the cycle. Just like I am, in my own way.

'Have you . . . have you gone on any dates recently?' she asks tentatively.

'No,' I say. I knew it was coming but it still irritates me. A heavy sigh from her end of the call. 'I like my life. I like my own company.' I've told her this before, but she doesn't understand. It's as if she can't imagine a future if no one loves you. As if that's why we're all here and what's the point of anything otherwise? You are no one unless you belong to someone else.

'Did you look at that list of therapists I sent you?' she asks. I stroke Herzog and take another sip of wine. He purrs and lifts his head in appreciation. He gets it.

'Rebecca . . .' I warn. This is turning into an interrogation.

'Please, Cass. Just hear me out. I just want you to be happy. And everything you went through . . . I mean . . . don't you want to be free from that? Really free from it?'

'Rebecca, I am happy,' I state.

She makes a little sound of deflation. 'I was reading this article about how post-traumatic stress can stay with you long after—'

'Rebecca,' I say firmly, and she stops.

'I know why you work so hard all the time, Cass. I understand. It's some sort of distraction technique, isn't it? But can't you have both? Maybe not a man or is it . . . a woman? Whatever you . . .'

Oh god.

'Listen, can we just stop having this conversation?' We sit in silence for a moment. Then I tentatively add, 'I can't wait to be an aunty. Look, why don't we go for lunch and a swim in the lido or something to celebrate?'

'I'd love that – this weekend?' she asks hopefully.

My eyes fall on the cork board. 'I can't this weekend. I'll send you some dates, I promise.' She makes a sound, like she knows that's rubbish, and I pretend to have another call and make my excuses to end the exchange.

Why do people always expect you to want what they want?

I carefully remove the snoozing cat from my lap and

walk over to the thick manila folder on the sideboard, containing the translated police report. Charles Castle sent me over a box of research he'd accumulated from all the years searching for his daughter. I've read Luke's initial interview a few times now.

No . . . no. You have to listen to me. I didn't do it. The man – there is a man in the jungle. Please. You have to believe me. (sobbing) Please, you need to go back out there and find her. She could be alive. She could be waiting for us to save her. (sobbing) Why is nobody listening to me? You're wasting time!

I pick up the photo of the teenage couple I discarded on the sofa. It's taken from the actual negative, from Charles's collection, rather than a newspaper clipping. I look down at Mari's playful face, and frown as I notice something. There is a mark on her neck. I swipe the photo with my thumb to check there isn't anything on the shiny surface and hold it up to the light. Maybe just a blur on the coating of the photograph or something. Could it be a love bite? Or a bruise? I walk back to the cork board and pin it. Tearing the cap off a pen with my teeth, I slide a sticker onto the corner of it, drawing an arrow and a question mark. Then I take a few steps back and stare. A hollow shot rips through me, tingling at the edges, getting bigger, like plastic burning. There is something dark here, more than just a lost teenager. Everyone knows it. No one bought Luke's story from day one, and they could be right. He could be a sociopath – a liar. He could be playing me. Sometimes the answer to a question is the most obvious one. I may need to come to terms with the fact the protagonist in all of this isn't the good guy I feel he is after all.

6

280722_THE JUNGLE_LUKE SPEED_MASTER I/V

'Let's start at the beginning. Can you tell me how you and Mari became an item?' I ask. Luke nods, wincing at the light. He begins to speak but I hold up a hand. 'Sorry, hang on.' I turn to the cameraman. 'Duncan, can you tone that kino light down a bit?' As it dims, Luke's narrowed eyes blink with relief. I check the shot in the monitor set up by my feet: that's better. I admire the location. An old warehouse, partially crumbling, with big steel beams. And this big slab of a man just to one side of the screen. It looks great. Raef will love it.

Luke scratches his head and frowns. A corner of his lip escapes between his teeth for a self-conscious bite. All this pre-interview stuff is good, and I like to introduce characters like this. Not with a perfectly cut piece of interview, but the preamble. Before they've begun to put on a show. With these intimate incidental moments. Like the way he is shifting and looking around uncomfortably, as if he's been coerced into this interrogation. And if what happened twenty years ago was nothing more than a series of unhappy accidents, he has been forced into all of this. But if it is all a lie – is he acting? Are these nerves something he's practised in front of the mirror, perfecting them in a calculated rehearsal of all he is about to divulge?

Once I've strung those adjustments out a little, I sit up straight in my chair, casting my eyes down the list of questions gripped in my hands. I've a pen slotted into my ponytail, ready to grab and make notes on the hoof. 'Okay, you and Mari – how did the relationship start?'

Luke looks pained for a moment, as if ambushed by memories. He leans forward, his hands together, resting his forearms on his thighs, before building the courage to sit up and look directly at the camera, like I've asked. I want this interview fully down the barrel. Like he's talking to *you*.

'Mari and I.' A sigh. 'Mari and I were best friends.' A sadness falls over him, and I lean in sympathetically. 'We hadn't always been close. The first few years at Ravensbourne we didn't even speak really. I was involved in all the extracurricular stuff. Music and football mostly. Kept me busy. I knew of her, saw her about. Heard people whisper. They weren't very nice to her those first few years. I always seemed to be late to the party on all that social politics stuff. I didn't really get involved.'

'Why didn't people like her, Luke?' I ask him. I know all this; he knows I do. But I need to have it on tape to capture the building blocks of this story for the viewer.

'They picked on her because Mari was different. She was the headmaster's daughter. Teenagers don't like that, do they? Mr

43

Castle was a good guy but quite strict. I guess people thought she might get them in trouble, if she came to our house parties or hung out and did what we were doing.

'She acted like she didn't care when people threw bits of paper at her in class or didn't choose her when pairing up. Looking back now, I think they took that coolness as a kind of superiority.' He shakes his head. 'Which it wasn't, not at all. But I guess I only know that because once I got to know her, I realised she was only protecting herself. She was hurting and found it upsetting. She could have told her dad what was going on, but she never did. She didn't want to be seen as a snitch or whatever.' He laughs lightly. 'God, it all sounds so trivial now.' I give him a supportive smile, and he continues. 'One day I was cycling home and I passed her. She was crying so I stopped. One of the idiots in my year had stolen her bus pass, and she hadn't wanted to tell her dad. I got off my bike and walked with her. I think she thought I was messing with her at first. But I just chatted away about my day. Told her a few funny stories. And she finally laughed. Spoke back. And we just talked and talked, and I found out how funny she was. How different she was outside that building.' A smile dances on my lips when I think of a young, kind Luke jumping from his bike to help her. And Mari – finally having a friend. How hopeful she must have felt.

'So, you went against the peer pressure of everyone in your year – at fourteen that's quite brave, isn't it?'

He laughs, embarrassed. 'Ha, I suppose. I didn't really think about it like that. I just liked her. I can't explain it. She just lit up – she lit me up. We were like this magnetic force that charged each other. And once we took it public all the crap she'd endured stopped. And she became friends with my friends.'

'So, you saved her from teenage purgatory?'

'I don't really see it like that,' he says, dismissing my comment.

'Everything I've read from that time, about you both, says you were the most popular kids at school. Is that how you'd describe it?'

He goes a little red and scratches his head. 'Um ... I guess that's a good headline. I get why they picked up on that. "Most popular kids at school get lost in the jungle."' He pauses, thinking. 'So much of who we were has been pulled at and shaped to be palatable for others. Sometimes it's hard to remember the truth at all.' His voice wobbles at this. 'We liked school, it felt easy. Like I said, I was into music, football. I understood the system and seemed to flourish – it wasn't hard for me. It was all the stuff that came after ...' He swallows. Then he smiles at a memory. 'Parents liked us. They trusted us. Teachers always said we were a good influence on others. No one had any doubt we'd do well after school.'

'How did Mari's parents feel about her having a boyfriend?'

He sniffs and clears the emotion from his throat. 'I always got on with Mr Castle. Even before Mari and I started seeing each other, we had a rapport – because of trips I'd gone on with the school. Trophies he'd handed me. I guess it wasn't ever an issue. I think her mum liked the fact that I brought

45

her daughter out of her shell. Before me, Mari didn't really have a social life. We could do both. Party and school. We were nerds, but I guess you could call us cool nerds.' He grins, embarrassed at the label he's given himself. 'If that's a thing.' He stops, caught up in the memory of it. 'We had our whole lives ahead of us . . .' His voice cracks and he looks down at his hands, fascinated for a moment. As if he can't believe he was the king of his life. And now there he is, staring at an almost forty-year-old's hands, with absolutely nothing to show for them.

He looks up. 'We had our whole lives ahead of us. We would talk about for ever. We just had no idea that our time together would be so short.'

7

I down the dregs of my coffee and slip the last corner of toast into my mouth before checking my backpack for my laptop and headphones. I pull out my worn filming bum bag and review its contents: spare batteries, pens and a mini notepad, gaffer tape – all the little accessories that can prevent a faff and avoid breaking the momentum of a shoot when on a roll. I've carried one since I was a young runner, and it's a hard habit to shift. I know Cleo and Duncan will be on hand, but when you're busy filming, and someone has to run off to get something sorted – in my experience, having a back-up is never a bad thing.

Herzog scoops around my legs, his tail arched, and I bend down and stroke him. 'I'll be back later, little one,' I sing as he purrs, before zipping my bag shut and yanking it over my shoulder. I head out the door.

It's our first day filming on location with Luke. We're heading to his home town near Cambridge to visit the school I've heard so much about: Ravensbourne. It's an important element of the film – setting up the backdrop to how this whole sorry saga began. I want the audience to understand where these two kids came from, and the expectation on their shoulders when they left for this pre-university trip of a lifetime.

I didn't go to university. I worked. I worked and worked until people took me seriously. I didn't let on that I was sleeping on friends' sofas when I got my first internship, or that I had second jobs to help pay the rent until I became a researcher. I would never have dreamt of an extended trip abroad, wasting my hard-earned cash, when I knew I had an uphill struggle to make it in my desired career. In some ways, I think it's given me an edge. My work ethic is intense and boundless. When you have no safety net, sometimes you have determination that others just don't.

I join the rush-hour footfall heading towards the tube station and think of Mari and Luke packing to go to the airport. Excitedly texting each other on their mini-Nokias. I don't really understand this need to go around the world to 'find yourself' – as a teenager, is there anything to find? You can only do that by years of trying and failing. Not by buying a plane ticket and running away. *Running away*, I think to myself. But Mari and Luke didn't have anything to run from, did they? They had the perfect lives waiting for them back home. More likely they were chasing that hollow promise of a brand new enlightened 'them' at the end of it. Or maybe I'm giving them more credit than they're due; they were probably just looking for a good time.

*

King's Cross station is hectic. We arranged to meet under the departure board and as I approach, I set my sights on Cleo who's pacing with a phone to her ear. As she turns, she notices me and performs an exaggerated eye roll to let me know she's having some sort of irritating call, most likely about kit. Luke hasn't arrived yet and I stand near Cleo, looking around for signs of him. Once she's off the call she turns.

'It's not like you to be nervous.' There must be something about my stance giving me away.

'I'm not nervous,' I say. It comes out in a snap, and she looks stung. 'Well, maybe a little. He's late,' I concede with a sigh, and she gives a supportive smile and looks down at her screen.

'Only two minutes.'

Then I see him. His head bobs above the blur of faces. He's hard to miss, and it's as if the hordes part as he moves through them. Slow motion. Seeing me, he smiles and waves. I raise my hand.

'Hi, Cassidy.' He stops in front of me, scratching his head, looking nervous.

'Hello, Luke. How are you doing today?' My tone is formal. I feel like I'm overcompensating for my reflex to be too familiar with him. 'Can we get you an iced coffee or something? I think we have time before the train.'

'I'm fine – thanks, though.'

'I know today is a big deal for you,' I say kindly. 'It's the first time you've been back for a while, isn't it?'

He nods. 'Not been back for years.' He swallows.

I squeeze his arm supportively. 'We'll take it easy, okay? Just let me know if you want a minute. We're not in a rush.'

He seems to relax at that. 'I can't believe we're going back to my old school. The last time I was there was my final exam. I didn't even pick up my results because I was . . .' – he swallows – 'away.'

Cleo takes another call; I can tell it's Duncan, the cameraman, and she lets him know our train is slightly delayed. He's meeting us on the other side with the kit and a hire car, as he lives outside London, and it made sense. I listen as they discuss a meeting point. Luke has shoved his hands in his pockets, waiting patiently. 'So, are you happy with what we're doing today? Is there anything you're unsure of or want to talk through before . . . ?' I begin.

He shakes his head. 'It's fine. I get it. You want to start peeling back the onion,' he says. 'Peel away,' he adds, attempting a joke through his obvious apprehension.

I smile. 'Great. But do let me know if anything makes you uncomfortable. It's one thing doing all this in the quiet space of an interview room. But filming out in public can feel very different.' I take a few tentative steps towards him. 'Have you spoken to your mother?'

With that he looks away, and clenches his jaw. 'She's unsure. She understands why I want to do this and is supportive. But nervous. I don't want to push it. You must understand she was pulled into all this too. The thought of raking it up again . . . She's scared what it will do to me . . . I obviously haven't been able to deal with my feelings around it very well, in the past. And she's nervous it may set me back.'

I nod, trying to hide my disappointment. 'Okay, no problem. I could speak to her if you think that will help?'

'Sure,' he agrees. 'Let's maybe give her a few weeks to come around to the idea.'

I'd love to interview her. What must it be like – the mother of a son tipped for greatness, suddenly having all that pride turned in on itself? It must have felt like a sort of grief, too. Dealing with the accusations of your precious boy killing a girlfriend. You can never underestimate the knock-on effect of a case like this. Life-changing for so many.

It's still early days, I remind myself. It will all come together. It always does.

We file onto the carriage and take our seats; it is hot and stuffy. I hold my hand underneath an air vent, but nothing comes out. I pull out the small camera I brought along for incidentals. As we set off, past the mash of reflecting skyscrapers and old brick walls covered in graffiti, I record Luke, staring out the window. Light travels across his face as we traverse through the city and into the countryside. I stare at his image on the screen of the camera, trying very hard not to look directly at him for fear he'll see my curious gaze.

I put the camera away and sit back in my chair. My phone buzzes; I have an email notification. MARIGOLD CASTLE, the subject says. I open the app – the email address makes no sense. Full of numbers and letters. Intrigued, I scroll further.

Little girls get hurt if they meddle in things they don't understand.
Especially little girls like you, Cassidy Chambers.
Anon.

I look up, stung. There's a high-pitched ringing in my ears. A lick of dread plummets through me. I drop my phone and fish around for it on the floor.

Cleo notices. I must have gone pale. 'You okay?' she asks, her tone a blend of amusement and worry.

I nod quickly. 'Yes. It's nothing.'

Luke gives me a concerned look and I force a relaxed smile. Heart pounding, my finger hovers – I should forward this to Raef. Report it. But I don't. I press the little rubbish bin icon and tell myself to forget all about it.

8

Our cameraman, Duncan, is waiting for us when we arrive at the station, and once we've all piled into the hired people carrier, he yanks the sliding door shut. The raspy, slithering noise of metal on metal makes me shudder. During the drive I zone out. Duncan's moaning about not getting the exact camera model he requested. He is a strapping man in his fifties with a sing-song Welsh accent, who has travelled the world with a camera on his shoulder. He can be irritatingly obsessed with getting the shot he wants, and sometimes doesn't understand the delicacies of dealing with a contributor, but I'm always pleased for this once I'm searching through footage in post, often lingering on the picture to admire its beauty. I look out the window, making the odd noise of agreement as he goes on and on. The green landscape is wilting under this oppressive heat and we pass large, gated houses as we make the drive out of town towards the school. I glance occasionally at Luke. His eyes are glued to the window and his hands are cupped in his lap, shaking from his restless legs unconsciously drumming. I think what it must be like for him, having not made this journey to Ravensbourne since the summer he left, in 2002.

The current headmaster wasn't keen on the filming, as he didn't want the good name of the place associated once more with such a torrid story. We explained we were planning to talk about the school anyway, so having a few shots of Luke walking down the corridors wouldn't make a difference. Besides, nothing bad happened on campus – the opposite, in fact. He relented as it's the summer holidays, so the building is empty of students and faculty. Cleo had worked her magic and she'd proudly emailed around the signed location release form.

'Here we go,' Duncan says, indicating as we approach the turning. I sit forward in my seat as we leave the country road and join the main drag. Turning past a manicured hedge, the building comes into view. The sun hangs bare, scorching the steeples of the Gothic Revival building. I've seen photographs and promotional videos online, but it's different being here. Evocative of a stately home or university with its turrets and fierce moulded gargoyles. It sits on acres of land filled with every type of sports field imaginable.

The caretaker lets us in, and I look up at the ornate stone carvings as we march through the arch of the main entrance. It is noticeably cooler in here. Duncan and Cleo set down our equipment at the top end of the looming corridor. Every clatter and pleasantry ricochets.

'If you need anything, give me a shout. My house is on the grounds so I can be here in a few minutes,' the caretaker says, giving Cleo his mobile number before leaving us to get on with it. I watch as he swings his battered old golf buggy back down the grit path.

'It's like Hogwarts,' Cleo murmurs, craning her neck to look around the main corridor which is covered in wallpaper, all twisting vines and thorned rose stems. The glossy red clay floor tiles shine as if newly buffed.

The online video I watched beforehand helped me get an idea of the layout and build a shot list of locations for today's shoot. But being here ... I can't believe this is a school. My own secondary was a drab old pre-fab hangover from the fifties. With rotten windowsills and an aggressive rodent problem. You could see your breath in the science lab on a cold winter's day.

I imagine what it must have felt like wearing the coveted purple emblemed uniform and walking down these halls. Did they realise how lucky they were? I doubt it. At that age, you can only really know what you have if it's taken away.

Duncan kneels on the floor carefully unpacking the equipment, as Cleo mics up Luke. I can't help but notice how her cheeks go red as she passes the little wire up the inside of his T-shirt. 'Sorry,' she mutters.

I step forward. 'Okay, Luke. We've discussed the main areas to focus on. Are you happy to take the lead and show us around a bit? Any short anecdotes about your time here as we go would be great. I might interject with a few questions here and there, depending how we get on. We'll play it by ear, okay?'

He cranes his neck, looking anxiously down the hall. He

seems to be having trouble regulating his breathing. I touch his arm to get his attention. 'Luke?' I question quietly.

'Sorry. Yeah.'

'Are you sure you're okay? We could take a minute. Have a walk around without the camera first?' I suggest.

He nods, wiping a hand over his forehead. 'No – it's fine. Let's just get on with it.'

'Okay. You go, we'll follow.' I gesture down the hallway. And he takes a deep breath and begins to walk away. His footsteps rebound on the glossed surface, and his shadow extends back. I grab Duncan's arm as he begins to follow, forcing him to hang back. 'Wait till he's out of shot, this looks great,' I whisper in explanation.

Once he's exited through the double doors at the far end, I let go of Duncan's arm. 'Okay. Let's go.'

Luke guides us around the interior of the school. At first, he's stilted, overly conscious of every movement, every word. He gives the camera sideways glances of apprehension. But as the day goes on, he relaxes, and begins to point things out, answering questions about the house system and trophies he won in cabinets with more enthusiasm. I think he actually begins to enjoy himself.

When we arrive at the door to the sixth-form common room he peers through the glass at the top of the door. His hand enclosed around the handle, reticent to open it. 'Luke, are you okay?' I ask softly. He nods, then builds up the courage and pushes it open.

The room is different to the rest of the school. Painted bright colours with student art splashed against the walls, alongside a tapestry of posters and timetables. There is a little kitchenette and, in the centre, a large square of tables to study on. On one side is a chill-out area with sofas and beanbags. We film Luke walking around, taking in the space, scratching the back of his head, in that way he does when he feels overwhelmed. I stop myself asking questions, and just let the look on his face do the talking.

'It could have been yesterday,' he says softly, his voice cracking a little. 'We didn't have these beanbags over here – there was like a giant L-shaped sofa.' He walks to a fire exit, and I almost shout at him not to open it, worried the alarm will go off and irritate the caretaker. But he clicks the bar, and nothing happens. 'We'd go out here for sneaky cigarettes. This sticker has always just been for show.' He flicks the 'alarmed door' sign and inspects the ground. 'Looks like it's still the unofficial smoking area.' His grin dissolves as he remembers the camera. 'Maybe leave that bit out. I don't want to get them in trouble.' I smile, and nod.

Next, we head into the grand hall. He swallows thickly, and walks directly to the centre, his head tilting up at the large, curved ceiling. 'It seems so much smaller,' he mutters to himself, his voice clear through my headphones, which pick up every breath on his mic. He walks over to one side of the room and looks up at the names carved on wooden plaques. 'I think we're up here somewhere,' he says, searching. 'Twenty years ago,' he mutters, as he navigates back through the years.

Then he points. 'There.' I follow his finger. In gilded lettering: *Head Boy – Luke Speed, Head Girl – Marigold Castle.*

'It's funny, you would have thought people would cry fix at the headmaster's daughter being head girl. But no one did. They knew she was the right person for the job.'

I step towards Duncan, and whisper, 'Make sure you get some good GVs of the board.' He gives me an exasperated look. He doesn't like to be patronised, but he does occasionally miss things and I'd be fuming in the edit if we didn't have it.

My eyes drift to the grand stage and imagine the debating societies, the assemblies and elaborate productions. I hear a piano note, the sound strident against the empty space, and turn to see Luke standing by the large grand piano, tinkering. He closes the lid and strokes the glossy black surface sombrely. I hang back. Letting Duncan shoot these quiet, telling moments.

Next, we head outside to the sports fields. Luke stands in the middle of the football pitch. His hands on his hips. A far-away look dominating his face. Then, he begins to run. 'It was the final match of the season against Garratt High, and I had the ball,' he pants, kicking an imaginary football. 'There was this kid we all called "Touch" because he was so damn good. And I'm running towards the goal, with a clear field ahead. The pressure is immense, we just need one more in the net to take the season. Garratt High were unbeatable, so far. I'm charging towards it. But then Touch comes into view on my right and I think, *Faack, he's going to ruin it for me.* He tries this crazy tackle' – Luke looks up at the camera, a grin on his face – 'and I just think, *No. You're not ruining the last game I'm ever having*

58

with my school, with my team. The goal was miles away – too far to try it really. But it was my only chance before he went for another tackle. And I managed this perfect strike.' He kicks the imaginary ball towards the goal. 'And *bang*. Pooof!' he cries, running in circles, lifting his T-shirt over his head. 'Yeah! The crowd went wild. We scored. We won the league.' He falls onto his knees. 'It was perfect.'

The celebration is over. He stands up, lifting his hands behind his head, pacing in circles as the anguish settles in. The rest of us watch from the sidelines. 'At least I had some good times,' he calls over, a grin masking what he must truly feel, being back here, reliving all this.

We walk back into the building. 'Are you okay?' I ask gently.

He's quiet again. 'Yeah.' He nods quickly. 'Fine.'

'You're doing really well,' I encourage.

We're heading to the canteen next. I'm feeling good. We've got more than I could have hoped for on a shoot day like this, where there isn't much action and it's all very reflective. I'm itching to get on with interviews and meet the other people involved. There is a lot to do before we can really begin tying this together. The more time I spend with Luke, the more I feel like this story is about how he is another victim in all of this.

Maybe there *was* a man out there in the jungle. Could there have been some sort of police cover-up? I make a mental note to check in with Jamal how his outreach to the Thai police is going.

Once we're halfway up the corridor to the canteen, I realise Luke, who was trailing behind, hasn't joined us. I walk back the way we came, into the hall, and hover at the door. Luke takes the small stool behind the piano. The sound of the cover lifting and knocking on its back reverberates. He shifts the stool forward, and the legs screech. Then, he raises his hands, and lets his fingers gently fall onto the keys. The delicate sound fills the cavernous space like a flower opening. I check Duncan has caught up, and smile with relief that he's in place, capturing this.

The song he plays is classical. But contemporary. I recognise it. It's so familiar, but with this arrangement, completely new. I mouth words, trying to come up with the ones that go with this tune. Then I get it. Red Hot Chili Peppers, 'Under the Bridge'. I swallow thickly. It's bittersweet and rousing. Music is such a time capsule. It takes me back to my early teens in the early two thousands. Pastel shimmery make-up, low-rise jeans and mini-disk players. Giggling at a friend's house as we spoke to some random guy over MSN Messenger. Crying when my mum slapped me around the face for coming home late.

I look up and around at the decorative ceiling, the thick green velvet curtains, then down at the rows of dark mahogany chairs. Imagining it full of kids in their ironed uniforms, staring ahead at Mari's father giving assembly. All that money. All that privilege perceived to be the most successful route to adulthood. GCSEs, A levels, a gap year around the world before arriving home and heading straight into one of the top five universities. Having a blast and then landing a job offered by someone in their vast black book as soon as their feet hit the ground. They only knew a world where doors opened, and people said yes. They only knew success.

I stare at Luke as he plays. Thinking of all the chances he had. And Mari too. And how they both lost it all over one misadventure.

Then I think if the opposite is true – if Luke did have something to do with Mari's disappearance – how does one go from head boy and football star to murderer? What happened between him scoring that goal in the summer of 2002 to them getting lost in the jungle to make him do that?

Luke finishes. The last note rings around the space and fades to nothing. He looks over at us, slightly abashed. 'Sorry, I couldn't help myself.'

I shake my head. 'Thank you for playing for us.'

And he sits there a moment. His shoulders down, head forward.

We decide to get a few shots of Luke outside the school sign on the main road. His hands are in his pockets. All the confidence he built up with the camera has faded now we are outside the safety of the building, and he's nervous. I look at the impressive sign, the coat of arms, the swirling gold writing against the purple-painted board.

I'm lost in a train of thought as Duncan steps around Luke, filming. A spot of rain, and I look up at a wisp of cloud. I don't think we brought an umbrella. We should put the equipment in the car. If we leave within the next half hour, we'll make the four o'clock train.

Then, out of nowhere, a car comes to a screeching halt. A door opens. And I gasp as a man charges over to Luke and grabs him by the neck.

'Hey!' I call, adrenalin pumping. 'Hey!' I walk forward to intervene.

'You cock – how dare you show your face around here . . . ? Where is she? What did you do to her?' the man spits, and I put my hands over my mouth to stifle a scream as he punches Luke in the face. Luke falls to the ground, groaning. It all happens so quickly.

Duncan drops the camera to step in, but the man has already turned and stormed back to the car, slamming the door and speeding away.

9

'So, how did the idea of Thailand come about?'

Luke clears his throat and shifts about again. 'That September I had an unconditional place at LSE and Mari was hoping to get the grades she needed for Oxford. We'd already discussed our relationship – whether it could weather that storm. We were quite grown-up really, talking things through. People used to call us Dawson and Joey. We made a pact to make it work. This wasn't a puppy love thing. We were in it for ever.' He peers at me. 'You think that's stupid, don't you?' I shake my head. 'Everyone seems to think that I did her a favour, but really, it was her doing me one. I had no idea how lonely I was until I met her.'

A pause. I let it run, feeling there is something he's willing himself to say.

'I had a lot going on at home, that I never felt I could talk about with any of my peers. As a teenager, back then especially, you always had to pretend you were cool, you know.

Unbothered by stuff. But really, my dad was dying. He was diagnosed when I was twelve. It went on and on. Remission and then it came back. My mum went insane with the uncertainty of it. Home became this emotional torture chamber. I thought that if I didn't tell anyone else, I could keep the pretence going in my head that it simply wasn't happening.

'While my classmates were focused on all this trivial stuff, I found out my dad, my favourite person, wasn't going to make it. He was the one who played football with me. Encouraged me with my music. Built me. He *built* me. He was wasting away at home, every day getting just a tiny incremental bit worse. And then finally, during my A level year, he died.'

I give him a sympathetic look. I'm so sad for that young man, and the one sat in front of me now.

'But . . . I still got four As. That's what I did back then, I distracted myself with work. All the years above were doing the gap year thing. We heard about full moon parties, tuk-tuks, ferry rides and jungle treks. It sounded really transportive, like, I could never be stuck in my head if we were somewhere like that. That Alex Garland book, *The Beach*, had been turned into a film and we'd watched it about twelve times. It felt like the ultimate freedom, packing a bag, not making any plans, just getting on a plane and leaving it up to destiny. There was no question who I would go with. It would always be Mari. Every day, every moment. She made life bearable. I don't know what I would have done without her when my dad died.

'So, the plan was Southeast Asia for the summer. We had three months until uni started. Then we'd take turns in each other's accommodation on weekends. Afterwards, she'd move to London, and we talked about getting a flat in Clapham or something. The trip was going to be the beginning of the rest of our lives. The first step to independence. No rules, no one to answer to. It was going to be magical.' He sighs. 'I was worried about going because of . . .' – he pauses again, choked; he looks ahead at the camera, his eyes bloodshot – 'my mum. I felt really torn about leaving her. But she wanted me to go. She told me that Dad wouldn't have wanted me to miss out on my future because of her. I wish she'd stopped me. I wish she'd begged me not to go.' He pleads at the camera, as if trying to distil an understanding to the people who will one day watch this and judge him.

I look down at the monitor I have at my feet. He looks so vulnerable, so in need of help. I have the urge to stand up, discard my notes and hug him. I shake it off. Remembering what he could have done. What is it with him? I must constantly remind myself that I've only got one side of the story so far.

10

On the way back to London I look up from tapping down notes to check on Luke. He's staring out the carriage window, lost in thought, a deep line across his brow as he processes the day. I haven't said much to him, I can tell he's embarrassed. And all the ease between him and us seems to have been knocked out of him with that punch. He moves his jaw back and forth a few times, grimacing.

To be honest, I'm still in shock. It was so sudden and unexpected. In the aftermath Luke tried to brush it off and shouted at Cleo to hang up when she called the police to report it. He begged her, not wanting the police involved who'll make it bigger than it needed to be, he said. Maybe he has an element of distrust in law enforcement, because of what happened in Thailand.

I look down at the WhatsApp from Raef asking how today went. I've not been able to bring myself to reply. I can't deal with his attempt at hiding glee when he hears of the drama that unfolded. He'll have to bite his tongue to ask whether Duncan managed to cover the punch. That's the thing about telly. Shock and awe will equal a bingeworthy series, with high ratings. But that means the journey your contributors go on is tough.

'Are you okay?' I ask. He purses his lips, leans back on the headrest and sighs. 'Did you know him?'

He shakes his head. 'Could be anyone really,' he mutters. 'Everyone loved her. Or decided they did once the story blew up. Even if they'd never met her.' He sniffs. 'I mean . . . I get it. If I thought the guy who had something to do with her disappearance was back in town, I'd have done worse, probably.'

'Must be hard never being able to go home?'

He looks out the window again, pained. 'I feel like home vanished when my dad died. It's not like my mum even lives there any more.' He blinks quickly, staring at the countryside as it rushes past. I curse myself; this would have been great on camera. I wait until he's distracted to make a note to have this conversation again during one of our master interview sessions we have scheduled across the next few weeks.

We arrive back at St Pancras and Luke hikes his bag onto his shoulder. 'Bye then,' he says, his neck craning to look for the underground sign.

'Thanks for today. Are you sure there isn't anything we can do . . . ?' I gesture to his jaw and he pulls up his collar and shakes his head quickly.

'See you later, Cassidy.' He begins to turn around.

'Oh, Luke. Before I forget . . .' He pauses for a moment and turns back. 'That release form I gave you, did you get a chance to sign it?'

'Oh right, yeah. I was just going to get this lawyer I know to take a look.'

I smile. 'No problem, no rush.'

He turns, nodding bye at Cleo, rushing through end-of-day crowds. Why do I feel like he's stalling getting it back to me? What if we get to the end of filming, and he still hasn't signed it? I shake my head. *Stop it, Cassidy. He's just being cautious.* Besides, he called me. He wants to tell his story. I stare at his figure as he strolls through the busy terminal. Dread hanging all around.

What if he's innocent and I can't get that across in my film, and it only makes everything worse for him? What if he's guilty and I'm helping to propagate a lie?

'Want me to do these?' Cleo asks, shaking the Ziploc pack of memory cards we shot over today. We need to download them and save them onto the project file on the shared drive on the main server. They are the most precious things we own right now. Especially as we shot stuff that we'd never get again. I look at the bag, thinking about the punch, and what a nightmare it would be if we lost that action sequence. It says so much about the life Luke is forced to live now. It makes him sympathetic, and the viewer feel conflicted.

I trust Cleo, but I trust myself more.

'I'll do it.' I take them from her and begin to unbuckle my bag, placing them inside.

'Okay, if you're sure,' she says, wounded.

'I want to watch some of the rushes tonight,' I tell her, hoping to quell any fears that I don't have confidence in her. I look towards the exit; the loose dusk of a summer's evening has emerged since we got off the train. I feel tight and sweaty after the sticky heat on the airless carriage. 'We've had a full-on day. Come in a bit later tomorrow, okay?'

'Cass, I don't need to—'

'Just say yes, and go grab a beer with Mo.' I know she's been messaging him all day. She blushes slightly, and nods. 'See you tomorrow, Cass.' She joins the crowd, her steps quickening with excitement the further away she gets.

I come out onto Euston Road and cross onto Pentonville. It's busy out; people crowd at pedestrian crossings waiting for lights to change, looking red-faced and bothered. I'm about to pass a bus stop and crane my neck back, a leap of triumph as I see one approaching. I decide to jump on and get home to a cool shower as quickly as possible. 'Thanks,' I mutter to the driver as I wave my phone on the contactless point. I walk to the back of the bus. A seat! I'm in luck tonight. I rest back, and enjoy watching people on their daily commute home, wondering who they are and what they've been through, what every frown and bemused smile has been triggered by.

What a day. I feel elated and fretful for everything more there is to do. I get out my phone and scroll through the emails I've missed. I stop. A tiny drop of fear worms its way through my body. That email address again. My eyes drift over the sparse sentences.

I told you to STOP. Little Lady, I know where you live. All alone in her little house. Playing with all her dolls.

I sit up in shock, turning to look around the bus, but all I see are bored, vacant faces. Nausea overwhelms me. Who is doing this? The channel hasn't circulated a press release about the series yet. I force the practical side of my brain to intervene with the other which is desperate to catastrophise. It's nothing. Cleo has been doing research calls about the series, so it's not completely under wraps. Someone bored with a chip on their shoulder and too much time on their hands. They want me to react, they want to stir something, just for kicks. This is the very reason I'm not on Twitter or any social media. They find you. They always do. There is always someone thinking it would be funny to press your buttons. Just because they want someone to feel worse than they do.

'All change,' the driver calls, ringing the bell. I frown; we're still a few stops away. I just want to be home. Moans ring out from other passengers before they begin trooping out the doors. I follow, stepping onto the pavement, still engrossed in the email I've just received. As the bus turns to go back in the opposite direction, towards King's Cross, I hug myself, walking at speed towards my home.

Then I realise, I don't have my bag! I pat myself mechanically, praying I'm just having a moment. But no – I don't have it. I've left it on the bus. The memory cards! The film! I turn on the spot. Eyes fall on the red double decker ahead and I sprint towards it. My arms in the air waving.

The traffic is worse the other way. And I manage to follow

it, between a run and a light jog. When I finally catch up to it, we're back on the King's Cross end of Pentonville Road. My fists smash down on the doors, and once I have his attention, I wave my arms around, pointing to the seats at the back, trying to explain. Finally, understanding, he releases the doors. 'Thank you,' I pant as I scramble on, rushing to the seat. There it is. Untouched. Relief! I pick it up, undoing the clips, praying.

The external drive and memory cards are still inside. 'Oh, thank goodness,' I cry. I walk back down the aisle hugging the bag into my chest, still heaving from the run. I can't believe what I just nearly did. How would I explain it to Raef, or my team? Or to Luke?

I walk into the nearest pub I can find and stride straight to the bar and order a pint and a shot. The tequila burns down my insides. My irregular breathing calms. And then I take a less frenzied sip of beer. Someone places an empty pint glass on the bar next to me and I look up. Luke.

He smiles knowingly. I've been caught. He turns, leaning back on the bar. His arms crossed. 'Well, Ms Chambers, you surprise me.' I lick the remaining bubbles off my top lip.

'What are you doing here?' I ask.

'I needed a drink after today.' He assesses my state. 'Why do you look as though you've just run a desert marathon?'

I don't want to tell him I nearly lost the footage for the film he's trusting me with. 'I left my phone on a bus – had to chase after it.'

He nods, looking at the empty shot glass. 'You're a hard

one to work out, Cassidy,' he says, eyes narrowing. 'I usually think I'm good at reading people, but you . . .'

'There is nothing to work out,' I state.

'I'm sure that's not true,' he says, as if he knows. And I feel validated in a strange sort of way. I spend all this time trying to understand other people. No one has ever tried to work me out. But I've never really wanted anyone to.

I change the subject. 'Has anything like that happened before?' I say, pointing to his jaw. His demeanour changes, and he gestures to the barman for another drink. Then he rests his hands on the lip of the bar. 'I've never been punched before.' A look at me. 'I guess I have you to thank for that,' he teases.

'I think you're very brave doing this,' I tell him.

He gets the pint and pays. Then points at a table in the corner, and I nod, following him over. 'I suppose it's selfish. People are hurting. And my need for resolution is the reason for that.'

'Pain will be there anyway. This way, Mari's family may get answers they crave. They're old. They must want a degree of finality before . . . before . . .'

'These answers . . . are you expecting to get them from me?' he asks, an eyebrow raised.

'There might be something you say that might spark something for someone else. Often witnesses who weren't ready previously, after long periods, decide it's time to come forward. Time is a healer – relationships change, and what stopped them once may no longer exist. With new evidence, the police may even try another search. They may even find out who the man you saw out there is. Track him down, wherever he is now. Someone must know something. They always do.'

'Or I might confess?' he says, a smirk forming. 'Is that what your boss is hoping? To catch me in the bathroom with my radio mic on? Whispering what I did?' he says, teasing still, but a note of gravity in there too.

'No,' I say. This is a tricky space to move into with him. Because of course, if Luke is guilty and if that were to happen, that would be good. 'I don't understand why you'd be guilty and want to do this.' Beer catches the back of my throat and I cough. 'Unless this is an elaborate ploy to finally confess?' I wrap the comment in a jokey tone, and gauge him for reaction.

He gives none, only moving his glass in small circles on the surface of the table. He continues in a more sombre tone. 'Why do you cover stories like this? Isn't it depressing being embedded within such sadness all the time?'

I think of the email on my phone. Someone who knows my history is messing with me. 'I just want to find the truth.' I look up at him, deciding how far to go. He's telling me his story. I should tell him some of mine. Sometimes the truth is an exchange.

'When I was six, I was taken by a man off the street. My mum was sleeping – well, sleeping something off. It was a sunny day, and I wanted to play and crept out. I was in his basement for a week before I was found. Day had turned into night. And another . . . another.' A caustic shudder runs through me. I blink away the image of the dolls, each with perfect pouted

73

lips, long stiff lashes and shiny synthetic hair. 'Finally, the police burst in, and I was bundled out.'

He wasn't expecting that. I see the shock. Eyes wide. Pity that I want to run from. I don't want sympathy. 'Cassidy, I . . . I had no idea. I'm so sorry.'

I raise my chin, clear my throat. 'The only reason I was found was because of a local news reporter. She questioned the man while he was out buying groceries. He seemed shifty, some of what he said was odd. She took the tape to the police – which was when they looked into his background and asked some local neighbours about him . . . and that's how they found me . . .'

I close my eyes briefly, trying not to get emotional. *Keep it down, Cassidy. You're tough enough not to let it affect you.* 'You see, if we don't have independents out there seeking the truth, things get missed. People get missed. If no one is out there means-testing the justice process. Prodding it, looking for cracks. I mean, who knows what would have happened to me? I could still be there.' I swallow. 'I'd be another person lost, never to come home . . .'

He wipes his face, never imagining this is what I had to tell him. 'Cassidy . . . I'm so sorry that happened to you.'

'I want to put that experience to good use. I want to find the other lost girls and make sure they get home. Stop their murderers and kidnappers before they have a chance to spread that pain further. You've given me access to this story. I want to do it justice. I want to help.'

'I don't want that punch in the film,' he says quietly.

74

An oppressive silence hangs between us. 'Luke, it's important that people understand what your life has been like since the jungle. That you can't live how you should be able to. Because I think you're still stuck there too, aren't you? Like Mari – your life ended in the jungle.' He ponders that a while.

'Cassidy, do you believe me? About the man out there?' he asks, peering over. His voice small, as if he's been scared to ask.

I wonder how to tackle this. I have a gut instinct that he's telling the truth. A strong impulse – is it real? Am I blindsided?

'Luke. I'm not going to lie to you just to get you on side. I'm always going to be honest with you. That's what you want, right?'

He leans closer. 'Yes. Of course. I know you don't know me well enough or haven't really interrogated this yet. But you'll see. You'll see who I really am.'

There is a hair of tenderness between us. Delicate, but strong. As if we have this innate understanding of one another. A bond.

'I should go.' I stand. This is getting too intense.

'Stay, finish your drink.' He gestures at my half-full glass.

I shake my head. There is something about this interaction which is making me want to run. Feelings I have no control over are spinning. 'I have to go do some work.'

As I walk to the door I hear his voice. 'Cassidy, wait.' I turn around and see him standing, a white folded cluster of A4 papers in his hand. He offers it to me. 'The release form, I signed it.'

I take a few steps over. 'Great. Thanks.' Trying not to let him see how much it means that I have it in my hands. Calmly, I take it.

'Bye, Cassidy,' he says softly.

'See you soon, Luke.'

I leave, and burst into the pollution-drenched muggy air which settles on my hot mottled face. This strong connection I feel to him. Is this a game? Is he playing me? Is he trying to reel me in and manipulate me, so I don't tell the real story?

But the one he wants to be told?

11

100822_THE JUNGLE_LUKE SPEED_MASTER I/V

'I'd been away without my parents before. Me and the guys went to Majorca after our GCSEs, but this felt different. Getting on that plane, changing in Doha, boarding another plane exhausted – it felt as though we were impossibly far from home. We were excited but I remember we were quiet too. Looking at each other checking we were okay. The loud tannoy in the airport barked places we'd only ever read about or seen on TV. Repeated in languages we'd never heard spoken out loud. We were sheltered, suburban teenagers. This was wild. It was scary. I look back now and think how young we were. Just kids really.

'The first flight we'd been alert. Upright, looking around, scanning the magazines we'd bought. Starting the books we'd carefully selected for our hand luggage. But we couldn't concentrate on anything. The next flight we were knackered. Emotionally, and physically from the stale air con and jittery apprehension. We half slept the whole way, our limbs draped over one another. Occasionally I'd stroke her hair and just stare out the window at the clouds.

'I get it, we were lucky. A trip across the world – time to be free. "Find ourselves" was the mantra people kept saying. Which now, at nearly forty, I know that sounds naive. But we'd been in this completely closed community our whole lives. Ravensbourne was the only world we knew. Going to Thailand, doing this trip was our way of breaking free from that. I know it sounds entitled, stupid, but we saw it as a rite of passage. Like passing our driving test or sitting our A levels. It was expected.

'We came out in Bangkok airport totally bewildered. Angry-looking men at border control interrogated our plans and made us feel guilty. The rush of the airport. The signs with squiggles of writing we had no way to decipher. We'd whispered between us when negotiating the taxi. Wondering if we were getting ripped off. Eyes wide, looking out the window as we sped through the chaotic traffic.

'Our parents had paid for this plush hotel just off the Khaosan Road, in the backpacking district, for our first night while we got our bearings. Mari was in her element – we had a bubble bath and ordered room service. Feeling halfway between grown-ups and rock stars. I remember her jumping on the bed singing "Dilemma" to a clutched fist, pointing a finger at me as she sang "*my boo*".

'We couldn't believe our luck. We'd arrived. No one to answer to. For the first time, we were totally free.'

12

When people say they didn't sleep last night, they're lying. They slept. Maybe not much, but at least a few hours. Last night, I didn't sleep for even a second. The nursery rhymes he played on a loop goaded me. The dolls. Oh, the walls of dolls. His dirty hands fingering them before he handed them over – telling me to play as he stood shaking with joy. I get a sickly, nauseated feeling, like when you've eaten something you realise is out of date, when I think of how I enjoyed the attention. I didn't get much at home. Then the growing discomfort when he said it wasn't time to leave when I asked. And asked. And asked. It slowly dawned on me I was somewhere very bad indeed.

I feel underwater as I try and focus on my screen. The office is busy, and the sounds of booming phone calls and laughter are muffled. I look up at the whiteboard showing the master interviews completed so far. And then down to the photograph I have stuck on the wall. The same one I have at home of Luke and Mari on the beach with the red bikini. They look so happy – but everyone knows photos lie. I remember a gallery

I went to recently; the exhibition displaying the final photographs of people before they died by suicide. They looked so normal. Bridesmaids grinning, teenage boys sitting with happy birthday badges. A shot of a glamorous young woman pouting for an Instagram post. All we're ever doing is showing people what we want them to see. It's my job to find out what was really going on beneath the surface.

'Cass?' Cleo prompts.

'Yes?' I ask. She looks at me strangely. I sit up straight in my seat, realising I'm slumped. 'What's up?'

'The train?' She points at the clock on the wall which shows London time, next to New York, LA and Tokyo.

'Shit.' I grab my bag. 'Let's go.'

We make the train by a few minutes, and I relax back in the seat still reeling from the dash to make it on time. Today we are meeting Mari's parents. No filming – just a preliminary gathering to discuss the film and allay any concerns they may have. I'd love to interview them. I'm sure they know that. But I'm not going to push it. They're an elderly couple who've dealt with extreme sadness, and I want to tread carefully and give them all the time they need.

I try to focus on the articles I want to refamiliarise myself with before we arrive. Charles Castle, Mari's father, was interviewed for *The Times* five years after her disappearance. He was attempting to revive a search party, which never materialised. At the time of the article, he is in his seventies, a photo taken in an upholstered armchair in their living room. Years of intolerable sadness etched on his face. He holds a framed photograph of Mari in his hands. In the piece, he describes his daughter as having everything to live for. His only child, lost. They were both quite old when she was born. Mari's mother, Elsie, was forty-three. She was their miracle baby, apparently. Just when they thought it would never happen for them, Mari arrived. Then eighteen years later she was gone. Devastating.

'Here.' Cleo hands me a Red Bull out of her backpack. 'I grabbed a few this morning,' she says. She must have noticed how tired I've been. 'Anything you want to discuss beforehand?'

'Let's just take their lead. Build bridges.'

She nods, sipping her drink. Biting a corner of her bright pink acrylic nail. 'What do you think then?' she asks, after a while.

'About what?' I reply, my eyes moving away from my screen.

'Do you think he did it?' A perfectly plucked eyebrow arches. I smile. I can tell she has been dying to ask.

'Well, if he's innocent, then there was a crazed man stalking them in the jungle. Maybe the Thai authorities didn't want that out there? Maybe there was a cover-up? It happens, especially when there is intense media scrutiny involved.' Cleo frowns, she thinks that's a reach. But sometimes the truth is out of our comfort zone. 'But I don't know. I think there is something else . . .' I let it hang in the air. 'It would be great to find that Dutch couple they met, the ones who were interviewed by the police, especially Astrid. Any news on that?'

'No. I've gone through every person with the same name on Facebook, and no one looks right. She probably got married, changed her last name. I can't find any record of her in Holland. Maybe she moved.'

I nod. We need more. This is starting to feel flimsy and one-sided. I've got a meeting with Raef tomorrow and he's going to want an update.

'Want to know what I think?' she asks, her head cocked to one side.

'Sure.' Cleo has good instincts, although her lack of experience lets her down occasionally.

'I think he's lying about something. I mean, all that stuff about the jungle and that guy – it sounds so far-fetched. It's like something made up for a horror film. He must have done it.'

For some reason, this riles me. 'Really? I don't know. He's braved it coming forward. I don't see why he'd be doing this . . .' I realise she is staring at me strangely, and I wonder why I feel so intent on defending Luke. I tone down my rhetoric. 'But we don't know enough yet. Either way. We're just at the start of this.' I sigh. 'I've got a lot to catch up on before we get there,' I say, turning back to the article on my screen.

13

100822_THE JUNGLE_LUKE SPEED_MASTER I/V

'That first evening we went out to get dinner and check out the infamous strip we'd heard so much about. The Khaosan Road is the central point for backpackers in Southeast Asia. Everyone ends up there at some point, organising visas, train tickets and ferry journeys. If you're going to bump into anyone you know, it would be on those 400 metres of tarmac. This was the gateway to our adventure.

'We were eager to get out and explore. Walking out the automatic doors, the muggy heat hit me like a tidal wave. We must have looked like such tourists straight off the plane clinging on to our open travel books, stopping occasionally to check the map. I remember feeling this big intimidating whack of culture shock at the noise and the fetid smells, the beetling tuk-tuks that came out of nowhere honking horns, causing us to spin on our heels to get out the way. It was overwhelming.

'I didn't like the Khaosan Road at first. I found it too much.

We had this moment where we stood at the top of it holding hands, staring up. It looked exactly like the pictures I'd seen. But being there, the attack on the senses amplified all of it. Music pumped, stalls cluttered the street and big lit-up signs ran up sides of buildings in a confused muddle with streams and streams of wiring which looked very unsafe. Its every pore crammed within it some sort of service or something to sell. Bugs on skewers ready to eat. Nightclubs, restaurants, massage parlours or some place to sleep. A man selling floral garlands pushing a buggy full of monkeys. Street vendors with food, trinkets and bongs. Westerners everywhere wearing fisherman trousers or Chang Beer slogan T-shirts. Petite Thai girls in tight dresses tried to lure us into bars.

'I'd never been anywhere so colourful or chaotic. Once you'd been there a while you realised how uniform the disarray is. But in that first glimpse, all I saw was a big mess. It was exhilarating.

'So that's the night we met that Dutch couple, Sander and Astrid. Mari loved them. She'd talked a lot about making friends backpacking. Wondering if anyone would talk to us. It wasn't something she needed to worry about. Everyone chatted to everyone.'

'Astrid and Sander – the ones who were interviewed by the police?'

He sighs. 'Yes. They had this vibe towards me right from the start. I think they assumed I was trying to clip her wings or something. I was just trying to look out for her. Mari could be a bit too trusting, naive – assume nothing bad could happen to her, take things too far because she couldn't see the risk. I guess . . . I guess they thought I was a bit controlling. But they didn't know Mari like I did.'

'Tell me about that night.'

'I'd read the Lonely Planet back to front. I was quite diligent about it. I guess I was the organised one out of us two. I'd circled some good evening spots in the area. Mari made fun of me for it. She'd joked that travelling wasn't about having a plan, we weren't retirees on a cruise. She wanted spontaneity.

'This bar we ended up in had this wide balcony, like a mezzanine level, which overlooked the street, great for people-watching. *Buckets! Buckets!* a sign in neon writing shouted. We'd heard a lot about these. Cola and little bottles of undiluted Red Bull – rumoured to have speed in – poured into brightly coloured sandcastle buckets heaped over ice with cheap plastic straws poking out. Mari wanted one. I tried to suggest keeping it mellow with beer for the first night. She wasn't having any of it. Fuck it. Let's party. Those buckets, we must have drunk a hundred. Before . . . before the jungle, that is.

'I noticed Mari eyeing up the people at the table next to us. They were tanned and had a relaxed, slightly feral look about them. Like they'd discarded their money belts a long time ago. The guy had dreads and the girl was wearing those dumb fisherman trouser things. They irritated me, to be honest. They seemed try-hard. Mari couldn't stop staring at the blonde girl. I could tell she was impressed by her and how comfortable she was in that environment.

'I made the order and said thank you in Thai, "*khob khun*

ka", like we'd practised on the plane. The ice cubes made a clinking noise as they sloshed around. We each took a straw and sucked. I remember it so vividly – impossibly sweet, almost syrupy. She'd tugged on the straw. More and more. I grinned at her and followed. We were in it then.

'The CCTV footage of her dancing, off her face on the balcony . . . I have no idea if my memory is from that video, or from it really happening. Everything is such a weird tapestry now. Stuff I've read, footage. Other people's recollections – I find it hard knowing what I knew back then, and what I've picked up along the way. Does that make sense?'

I nod. It does completely.

'Anyway, yeah, that's when we met Astrid and Sander. We sort of hung out with them for a bit. I could tell Mari was into them. They annoyed me, if I'm honest. I remember Astrid asking if we'd just arrived, then she said something patronising to Mari about working on her tan. Mari didn't seem to notice. She kicked me under the table when I told them our parents had paid for a room at the four-star up the road.

'Astrid told us that with the full moon party only being a month away, we should go island hopping and get to Koh Phangan before the accommodation filled. So that really cemented our plans.

'I can't help thinking, if we'd gone to the jungle first, before the islands, like I wanted, everything could have ended so differently.'

14

Cleo gets out the taxi and opens the heavy iron gate, and the car inches into the drive and swerves to one side of the two-storey limestone manor house. I've spent the short drive pepping myself up; I need to be on form for the Castles, I owe them that. It will have taken them a lot to prepare emotionally for today, and I want to walk away feeling like I've given them the full picture, and they feel confident to have entrusted us with this. If we mess this meeting up, it could mean early doors for the whole project. Even though they've assured us they are happy to proceed, the worry has taken root and sprouted in the run-up to this first delicate meeting.

Crunching gravel underfoot, I look up at the stretched Georgian windows, and the blue sky reflecting off them. Cleo and I walk to the impossibly large front door. I've seen photographs of the exterior of this house. One in particular springs to mind. It is of Mari in her early teens, leaning against the wall sticking out her tongue. Charles, old enough to be her grandfather, with a happy, lopsided grin, wearing a bow tie. In the background, her mother, Elsie, in a floral dress, a strained expression. Even then.

We ring the large circular doorbell; it makes a draconian shrieking noise. We wait. Cleo smiles at me nervously. Her clothes are smarter than usual. A short-sleeved blouse and high-waisted jeans. Our office, like every other production house, has a very informal dress code. Her usual attire is ripped jeans and biker boots that jingle. Ever since I began working with her a few years ago, I've been impressed with her ability to read the room and act accordingly.

The door opens and Charles Castle stands there, not quite smiling. This isn't the usual social call. He will have to talk about things that hurt. Stuff buried deep to keep him able to manage day to day.

I hold out my hand. 'Mr Castle, I really appreciate you having us over.'

He nods, taking my hand. 'Welcome to Holly Manor, Ms Chambers.' Then he ushers us inside. 'I thought we could have tea on the patio as the sun's out.' His back is stooped, his pace slow. He must be ninety by now.

The house smells musty, and most of the curtains are drawn. Curls of dust glimmer in cracks of light. A moulded figurine of Jesus on the cross hangs on the wall, between framed photographs and paintings. We pass an office, piled high with papers, a large map of Thailand on the wall and an ancient-looking desktop computer on the brawny dark wood desk. 'My war office,' he explains gruffly, pointing it out. 'There isn't anything I don't know about that part of the world.' Pride in his voice. It must be helpful to have a focus. He used to go back every year to keep the story alive. The journey must be too much for him now.

We enter the living room where large French doors reveal the garden. Mr Castle opens the door; the handle sticks. It is an elderly couple's house gently declining as maintenance is foregone. He walks through, and we follow. It's like walking out of a cave and into a manicured pleasure garden. I take in the beds overflowing with multicoloured flowers. 'My wife is a far keener gardener than a housekeeper,' he quips, as an explanation for the huge disparity in upkeep. 'I'm amazed how she keeps it so vibrant, even in this heat.' Over a circular hedge, to one side, is a stunning rose garden. Each a different pastel in bloom, twitching tentatively into the blue sky. Heads of petals raised like pompoms shaking in the light breeze.

He motions to a collection of white-painted iron garden chairs, and I take one. The turned metal pokes into my back. I try to get comfortable. I notice Cleo having the same problem. The sound of a shaky tray and I turn to see a little old lady walk out onto the patio. I recognise her from the television interviews and photographs instantly – Elsie. In everything I've seen she's in agony, unable to look up, so deeply turned inside herself.

She's aged, obviously, but still looks younger than her husband. 'Hello,' she says, setting the tray on the table. Not able to look me in the eye. Wiping her hands on her apron with a look of dissatisfaction.

'Your garden is breathtaking, Mrs Castle.' She flinches. I

hope she didn't take the compliment as trite, a cheap way of gaining her trust, because I mean it.

'Tea?' She breathes as if every moment of this is an effort. And I feel drenched in guilt that we are here.

'That would be lovely, thank you.'

She pours from the old-fashioned pot; it shakes in her hand, and I must fight the urge to stand up and help her. There is a plate with a circle of chocolate Bourbons she passes around. Then takes her own seat, perched on the edge, hands on her lap, as if waiting for a train.

'I hope you don't mind we have been apprehensive in taking part in your project,' Charles says. 'We have been let down so many times by production companies who've spent a lot of time with us, and then their project came to nothing.'

I shake my head. 'It's understandable. Every time you get a call like mine it must take its toll.' They look at each other. Elsie shakes her head at Charles. I wonder what kind of conversations they've had about us in private.

Charles clears his throat. 'As you said, after your documentary, *Missing*, a . . . body was located. The family had a funeral.'

'Yes.' I hate to give false hope. 'It was extraordinary. I'm not saying anything like that will happen here. In a similar way to a new police appeal, visibility can help. But it's hard on those close to the case.' I pause. 'I know Molly-Ann's family found it extremely difficult dealing with the uncertainty of whether she was still out there. Or whether she had died, and they could allow themselves to grieve.'

'Yes,' Elsie's small voice pipes in, and I look over to her. Her eyes are on her lap and her hands twisted in fabric.

'It must have been so terrible for you both. You must miss her awfully.'

Elsie stares out to her garden. She doesn't reply.

Mr Castle gets up and walks to the corner of the patio. Hands in pockets, jingling some coins in there. 'I suppose Luke comes across well on camera. He was always a very charming young man.'

I nod. 'He is very articulate.'

'He was one of the smartest young men we had at the school.' His face fills with pride. 'I had a lot of time for him.' He turns to me swiftly. 'Do you believe his version of events?' There is a pleading quality in his eyes, a desperation.

'The story out there is rather . . . I can understand why many have found it difficult to digest. But to me, he seems genuine. He'd have to be a pretty good actor – because there is no doubt in my mind he cared deeply for your daughter.'

'I knew his father; did you know that? We played golf together. Very sad what happened to that family. I had a soft spot for Luke. He was always so trustworthy, an excellent student. And Mari was . . . for that period, she was very happy. Wasn't she, Elsie?'

Mrs Castle looks at him sharply. Shaking her head, refusing to get involved, staring at her hands.

'Mari wasn't always easy,' he admits.

'Charles,' Elsie mutters. As though reminding him of something.

91

'Who is easy at that age?' I say, full of empathy.

'I was around fifty when we had her. She was our only child.' His voice thickens with emotion. 'Luke was a good influence on her. We were pleased with the match. He brought out the best in her.'

Elsie cuts in then. 'Marigold was a wonderful daughter. Bright, and charming. She was head girl; did you know that?' The longest sentence she's uttered since we arrived. It comes out like a jingle on an advert, easily memorised. Charles looks back at her and presses his lips together, sadly.

'We were maybe . . . overly protective of her. You must understand we never thought we'd have a child. She was a gift from God. We could never shake that feeling we'd lose her . . .' The sentence lingers. The irony hard to ignore. Charles coughs. 'There was this idea of Mari in the press. One we probably had a hand in steering. We didn't want them . . . twisting anything. Overanalysing things that didn't have anything to do with the case.'

'What kind of things?' I ask, confused.

'People care more about girls who fit a certain mould, don't they?'

'What . . . ?' I say, breathless.

'Charles!' Elsie says sharply and he frowns.

I sense a tension between them. 'No one deserves what happened to them out there. Every missing person is important, no matter what kind of person they are.'

'But that's it, isn't it? If they don't fit that ideal, they don't

92

count, not to the media, not to people buying papers,' he spits. 'And that's a fantasy if you think so,' he adds roughly.

Cleo shoots me a look. I give her a slight frown. I don't know what's going on either.

'What does Luke want to get out of this? I heard he'd hit the sticks, was rather down and out,' he asks, changing the subject.

'He's okay these days – he's back on his feet. Clean, for a long time now. He says he's stuck, he can't move on, still. He wants to make this film to have closure. Try to reclaim his story a little. While also finding out what happened to Mari.'

'And you think he's innocent?' He looks at me stiffly.

'I think that's one possibility. I wouldn't be doing my job if I didn't see the others. Mr Castle, I'm trying very hard to get as many points of view as possible so I can get to the truth. And one of those outcomes may be that Luke had something to do with Mari's disappearance – whether it was an accident he couldn't own up to, or something more sinister.'

He flaps his hand away, to stop me talking, irritated with my reply. 'Yes, yes. We know. We stopped seeing Luke after it became apparent there was some ambiguity around his involvement.' He opens his mouth to speak but closes it again. He looks me dead in the eye. 'I don't think he had anything to do with it. I just know it, in my gut. Luke was a good lad.'

He paces onto the lawn. Looking out at the roses. 'You know we still hope she might be out there somewhere. We haven't touched her room . . . Just in case. Silly really.'

93

I lift out of my seat slightly at this. 'Would you mind if I had a look?' I ask, trying not to sound too keen.

Elsie looks at her husband nervously. 'What could you possibly need to look in there for?' she asks, gripping the fabric of her skirt.

'It would just be good to get an idea of her. See if there is anything that was missed.'

'I don't think it will help,' Elsie says dismissively. Charles gives her a look.

'Obviously only if you are happy for us to.' I don't want to upset her. Charles crosses his arms and sighs. The silence is unbearable. Cleo looks over at me.

'Elsie, this might be the last chance,' he says simply. And she looks down. Finally nodding her approval. He turns to us. 'If you think it will help.'

Charles walks very slowly up the stairs, his hand on the banister, pulling himself up, step by step, heaving the whole way. 'I don't come up here much these days. I have a room on the ground floor now.'

I look down at the hallway below. Elsie is standing with Cleo, her eyes narrowed up at me.

'This photo is gorgeous, Mrs Castle. Is this your wedding day?' I hear Cleo ask as I move onto the landing.

Charles stands at the closed door a moment before his hand clasps the knob and turns it. 'Take your time,' he says, leaving me to it.

Inside is just like I would have imagined. In fact, it is very

94

similar to my room at her age. The posters – Leonardo DiCaprio in *The Beach*. The Red Hot Chili Peppers' album cover that year, *By the Way*. A huge wall-length Gwen Stefani from her No Doubt days. Mari's revision chart is still on the wall with faded biro and highlighter colour codes. I study her photos, which are displayed as a collage on a board. Mainly of her and Luke at various places. At prom, parties, a school trip abroad, huddled on sofas at friends' houses during gatherings. I take various shots using my phone, hoping to pick out some of the faces from the class photograph we have back at the office.

I flip a chewing gum in my mouth. My stomach gurgles, full of caffeine and anxiety. I wait for the sound of Charles's footsteps to shuffle down the stairs before opening drawers and fingering through sketchpads. 'Come on, Mari,' I whisper. 'Tell me something I don't know.'

I fall on one sketchpad – and take it out and open the pages. The intricate drawings are a lot to take in. It's very dark. Black pen and red crayon. Blood. Red like raw meat. She was very talented, but it's all so bleak. Not really what I would have imagined from the preppy-looking blonde girl in the photos.

I turn a page – a mess of doodles. Writing and notes. Lines of poems. *Deep in the mud. Replant me . . . Ring-o-ring . . . I am ready to fall . . .* I feel uneasy and look at the door. It's not a great feeling creeping through someone's private things. Then I see it. An email address. But it's crossed out. Like she didn't want anyone else to see it. I turn my head, trying to work out the letters. In the end, I take a photo.

My two fingers walk across the dusty desk, encountering

a little rolled-up piece of paper. I pick it up. A Boots receipt which has gone sepia over time. The print faded. I run down the list of items. It must be the toiletry shop she did before the trip. Her money belt is on there and plug adaptors. Suncream and mascara. A twin pack of disposable cameras. I look at the date and time she was handed the receipt and feel sad. She must have been so excited picking out her things for the trip. No idea what would come of it. I take a photo and leave the receipt to curl back into itself on the desk.

Later, I sit back in my office chair. 'Why would someone have two email addresses?' I ask out loud to the others on the team. Cleo and Jamal swivel to face me. Melissa ignores the question, as usual. Too stressed with logistics and call sheets.

'Porn,' Jamal says knowingly.

'Maybe she set it up and never used it?' Cleo shrugs.

'Jamal – think you can break into it?'

'I'm not a hacker just because I'm twenty-three.'

'Can you find out more about this email address? Call the company? See if we can get access to it?' I ask him.

He takes the Post-it off me. 'Call Silicon Valley? I'm not sure it works like that.' His patronising tone deflects off me. 'It's probably defunct. I have a friend who might be able to help, though.'

'Great. I want the emails – all of them to and from this address.' I'd spent a good hour deciphering the code.

'They've probably been deleted . . .'

'Just do what you can,' I say, irritated by the negativity.

'We've done the background check on Luke,' Melissa says, her back still turned. Her desk a clutter of papers and Post-it notes.

'Oh yeah?' I look up, intrigued. I've been waiting to hear what has come up about our protagonist.

'He's never been in trouble with the police for anything violent, not that we can find, anyway. But we have been incredibly thorough. A few petty crimes years ago – stealing, that sort of thing.'

'Okay,' I say, thinking. He was a drug addict for years; petty theft goes hand in hand with that lifestyle and doesn't surprise me. If he'd been violent, that would be a mark against him, so this firms up his story. But it also means no new leads.

We need a breakthrough. Maybe there is something in those emails that will show this whole tale from a perspective we've not seen before. People who aren't on our radar, that she was talking to at the time. Maybe open a new line of questioning I could try with Luke. Because we really need a turning point for the film.

Something big.

A cliffhanger.

97

15

100822_THE JUNGLE_LUKE SPEED_MASTER I/V

'No one's ever asked me about the good parts of the trip before. Because that first month, island hopping, was some of the best times of my life. Everything we'd been promised on a plate. White sandy beaches for days. And everything was so incredibly cheap; we could live like kings and queens for less than ten quid a day. We'd spend our time lounging around on the beach, nursing hangovers with a smoothie and reading over-thumbed books discarded on free shelves in bars. Going for a Thai massage and then getting the beers in. We stayed in huts on the beach, which were sparse, but we didn't need much. We were out all day anyway. Sometimes we'd be more active, play volleyball, or go on a trek to find waterfalls. Mari loved skinny dipping in the moonlight. But one thing that was a given, we'd always, always party all night.

'The initial journey down south was exciting. We took the night train and then a ferry over. It wasn't the sort of travelling I was expecting: hanging out of open-sided trains, chickens on

98

buses with locals putting up with us as we wilted without air conditioning. It was far more organised than that.

'We waited outside the travel agent's with a gaggle of western kids. This guy with a clipboard put different coloured stickers on us, for our various destinations, and we were sort of herded around, like sheep. We were both tired, hungover and overheated. Mari got out her sketchpad and drew the various characters around us. She was talented. Have you seen her work? She got into Central St Martin's; did you know that? But decided the smarter thing would be to take the place at Oxford, to read English. I think maybe her dad influenced that.

'But anyway, it did feel like an adventure. Mari slept on my shoulder, we'd mutter things to each other. You know – just one word was all we needed to explain a whole thought process. It was more than finishing each other's sentences. Just a nod or an eye bulge would set off a private joke that had been brewing for years and we'd laugh.'

'So, you never argued? What about that day on the Khaosan Road?'

'Look, we bickered all the time. Like an old married couple. Find me a couple who doesn't – I'd say *they* were abnormal, wouldn't you? I know that travel agent said we had this big argument in the street. Everyone jumped on that, especially the police. It was just this stupid spat we had about whether we should go up north trekking first, or down to the islands. It wasn't a proper fight – I mean, we'd had far worse! I don't think I gave it a second thought. They said she cried, which wasn't true. No shouting. Nothing. I think when people find something out, like what happened to Mari – she went missing, right? – they start to interrogate every little thing they saw. An upset girl in the street with a boyfriend, gesticulating wildly. Well, he *must* have killed her. Do you know that seventy-five per cent of wrongful convictions are caused by inaccurate eye-witness statements? And every sharp word shared between us was overanalysed and blown out of proportion. It makes me so cross people thought of us like that. It's like my memories have all been fiddled with and ripped apart.'

'It must be intense travelling as a couple, on your own like that. It's understandable emotions flare up.'

'It honestly wasn't that bad. At some point, on the islands, we made friends with these two French girls. They'd been around South America and had been in Thailand for a few weeks. One of them told us she'd had enough of her friend. And she couldn't work out how to tell her she didn't want to travel together any more. After they'd gone, Mari and I couldn't stop talking about how glad we were that we were there together. Because nothing like that would ever happen to us.'

16

We're on Harley Street, in central London, filming an interview with the psychiatrist who treated Luke once he arrived back on home turf. That period is so full of hysteria, and is hard to pick through. There are photos of Luke emaciated in the Thai hospital, skeleton thin. Once discharged, he was placed under house arrest in a local hotel while another search was performed using the information given in his statement. But Mari wasn't found – dead or alive. And following further inquiries, the police case against Luke fell apart.

After some wrangling from the British consulate, he was brought back to England, and the next chapter of his nightmare played out. Landing back to a hostile British media, his life was irreversibly altered. He'd missed his place at LSE, and they refused to allow him to defer, relieved, most probably, to find a loophole to having him there. He couldn't leave his house without someone shouting at him, or a camera in his face. He was the nation's favourite villain – a photograph of him doing anything, even relatively normal, was splashed across covers, with headlines like: MONSTER ON THE LOOSE.

Finally, Luke had a breakdown. Unable to cope with the accusations and profound rage against him. He ended up under Dr Ackerman's care. And after Luke spoke to his old doctor, and gave permission for this interview, explaining he'd like his professional perspective on film, Dr Ackerman has agreed to discuss Luke's time under section in an on-camera interview.

'Are you comfortable?' I ask.

'As I'll ever be,' he replies. He has a naturally relaxed demeanour and I already feel like this will go well. We've set the shot up at his desk, and he quickly shuffles things around, neatening them up. He slides his pen cap up and down with his thumb, absent-mindedly. 'If you could direct your answers to me, not the camera, and it would be helpful if you could include my question in your answer, as it's unlikely we'll use my voice in the edit, sound good?' He nods. 'Let's give it a go.' I clear my throat. 'So, can you tell me what sort of state Luke was in when you first met him?'

Dr Ackerman nods, as his thoughts go back in time. He's fifty now but was a young doctor back then. 'Luke was heavily sedated in A&E before he was taken by ambulance to a place of safety and then admitted to a ward. I remember he was incredibly thin, dark bags under his eyes. Rapid blinking. He was in a bad way. He looked like he'd been to hell and back, and to be honest, Ms Chambers, he probably had.'

I hold up a finger. 'Sorry, Dr Ackerman, it would be great if you didn't use my name so it's slightly more generic – is that okay?'

'Sorry, yes.' He pauses, before repeating, 'He looked like he'd been to hell and back, and to be honest, he probably had.'

I give a thumbs up. 'How long was Luke in your care?'

'Luke was with us a few weeks. He went back out but found it tough, and so I got him admitted under a section three. The first few weeks back were some of his worst. He had nightmares, displaying psychotic symptoms. Shrieked the whole place down.'

'Psychotic symptoms? Like hallucinations?'

'Yes, they could be characterised as that.'

'Is it normal for people dealing with the aftermath of extreme events to hallucinate?'

He raises his eyebrows. 'Yes. Especially when dealing with post-traumatic stress. He told me they were flashbacks of what happened to him in the jungle.'

We haven't got to the jungle in Luke's master interviews. He chokes up when it is mentioned, and I don't want to lose any revelations to off-camera research. It will be an important moment to capture on film.

'The man he said was following them. What do you make of that? Do you think he was hallucinating?'

He closes his hands together in front of him on the desk. 'Yes, he could have been hallucinating – they were starving, heavily traumatised – but' – he pauses – 'he also could have been followed. We just don't know for certain. What we do know is the police never found any evidence of anyone else out there. I felt, after knowing Luke for a good few months, that he was an incredibly likeable, lovely boy – man. But possibly, he could have done something to Mari and his brain wasn't able to process it. So, he invented this man to deal with the trauma. To . . . to replace his own actions.' I lean forward. I've not heard this theory before. 'I'm not a police officer. And no one's ever asked me. But I think that's a real possibility.'

'That's fascinating,' I say, looking down my list of questions. Disregarding them now I've heard this.

'You think he hurt her, couldn't cope with that fact, and created this man to cover for his own actions?'

Dr Ackerman nods. 'He was in survival mode, so his brain did something to help him deal with it. He could have been having a psychotic episode.'

'Would he ever remember the truth of what really happened?' I ask.

He pauses, before explaining, 'Often the brain blocks the memory. Because the truth would be too hard to handle. And these false memories can feel as real as day. Usually, we'd be able to eventually counter these imaginings with the truth.' I look confused and he explains. 'A man under psychosis thinks his next-door neighbour is the devil and hits him – we can then, as practitioners, together with the police, and family and friends, counterbalance this with the truth – that his neighbour is not, in fact, the devil – once he's come out of the psychotic episode. But no one's ever been able to one hundred per cent ascertain that was the case here, with this man Luke says he saw. No one was out there with him, apart from Mari.' He strokes his chin. 'I mean, he may not have hurt her in the way people think he did. Maybe she broke a limb, for example, or a cut went septic. She was in agony, with no way to get to medical help. And he had to make a decision to put her out of her misery. They were in hell out there on their own. Two suburban teenagers. Imagine.'

I swallow at the thought. Terrifying.

'It wouldn't have been difficult for his brain to malfunction in that extreme environment. It's a possibility.'

'And he would be innocent if he'd done something under psychosis?'

'It's complicated, and many people would need to be involved in that decision. It would be a long and lengthy process. But I'm sure my initial assessment would come into play. And I'd certainly agree that he wouldn't have been in his right mind if that's what a post-mortem suggested.'

'How could a post-mortem suggest that – it's been twenty years?'

'Say Mari had a broken a limb that she'd been hobbling around on for weeks – a post-mortem would show an unhealed, untreated fracture, for example. There are many clues left behind on a body, even twenty years after the event. There could be other forensics, or evidence left behind, that prove there was another person out there. If they found Mari, it could help determine what part Luke had to play in all this. But it's hard to see that happening. The Thai authorities have refused to reopen the search, year after year.'

I log the interview with Dr Ackerman. This is great. A theory that offers an alternative way into the case. Something that could explain everything. I try to put myself in Luke's shoes. A teenager, barely legal drinking age, stuck in the worst possible situation. With a choice in only his hands. The worst decision anyone would ever have to face. A person you love, screaming in agony. No way out.

What would I have done? That is the question I hope my viewers will be challenged with when this interview comes to light.

I think about the concern on Dr Ackerman's face when speaking of Luke, and the huddled chat before we left about how he was getting on, and how pleased he was that he had found his feet. Another person deeply affected by my protagonist. Nearly everyone I've met on this journey is quick to say how much they liked him. Even the ones you'd expect to hold a grudge. Charles roots for him still. And having got to know him, I understand why.

Unless he *is* just a master manipulator.

'Cass,' Cleo says, and I look up and she nods at Raef who's beckoning me over.

'*Urg*,' I say under my breath, before getting up and walking across the office.

Raef shuts the door to his office. 'So, how's it going?'

'You do know *Making a Murderer* took ten years to film, don't you?' I remind him.

He clicks his fingers. 'We need a good title. *In Plain Sight*. As in hiding in—'

'It's early days, Raef. There's always the chance he's a victim too, and it's not fair to pigeonhole it yet. We have months, at least, to go.'

He looks at me, thinking. 'Okay, Cassidy – and how do you think it's going?'

'Good. I'm happy. It feels like there is a lot to uncover. It feels . . . it feels rich. The story is extraordinary, Luke is extraordinary.' I wonder if I should mention the evening drink we had. Raef would probably like it – slap me on the back and congratulate me on my 'handling' skills. But it wasn't like that. And besides, I don't like the idea that Raef may think the only reason I've got Luke to open up is because I'm a woman. I got this story on merit, nothing else.

'So, anyway, there is something going on behind the scenes I hadn't wanted to discuss until it was for certain.'

'Really?' I reply, annoyed. I am the one, after all, that knows every detail about this case. Raef just knows the top line and he's the one having spontaneous big-picture catch-ups with his mates at the channel. 'I've got some news for you, Cassidy.' He leans forward dramatically. 'They want to take him back. Isn't it great?'

'Back?' I repeat.

'They want him to return to Thailand with us, with the cameras, and retrace his steps. Interviews and reconstructions are great and everything. But they're worried there won't be any big revelations in your interviews, like we hoped. We thought, if you were out there, with the brilliant relationship you've fostered, he might remember something. He might *say* something. Whatever it might be, and—'

'Dig his own grave?' I state flatly.

'If he doesn't have one to dig, that shouldn't be a problem,' he replies confidently.

'But I thought this series was bought with a reconstruction element? Not with Luke . . . *there*.' I could scream. I feel control slipping from my fingers.

'It's great, isn't it? They think with this we can get three eps, instead of just two parts. They want him to take you to all the spots he and Mari visited and describe his version of events.'

'Even . . . to the jungle?' I blink, my voice filled with disbelief.

'You think he'll go for it?' he asks. I stare out the window, across the haphazard roofs of Soho, thinking. He'll be stressed at first. Then he'll pragmatically ask if it's important to the film, to get his story across. And I'll say yes, immeasurably. And he'll agree to it. I could get him to do it. But do I want to?

'But Raef . . . he lost his mind out there. What if he has some sort of panic attack or—'

'We'll get the psych to do a report. Everything above board.'

I try to imagine the scale of this. Trudging through the jungle, with him. Then I think about the film. The imagery, the possibilities of his reactions caught on camera when confronted by his past. I saw how going back to the school affected him.

'So, you'll speak to Luke?'

'Can I think about it?'

He gives me a look. 'This is the film the channel wants, Cass. I can put someone else on it.' This is an empty threat.

I already know Luke won't do this film without me. I could fight it. I could ward Luke off the idea and tell Raef he simply won't do it.

Then I think of what Dr Ackerman said. Maybe Luke will remember something he's repressed. Maybe that is how this can finally end for him, for Mari. I imagine the film with that moment in it. It could be remarkable. Instead of a lingering ending, leaving the audience to make up their own minds, it would be unequivocal. There may be an opportunity to find her body, open a search in a focused area, like in *Missing*. Luke and Mari's families would be able to come to terms with what happened and move on. It would be hard for him, but at least there would be a finish line, rather than the constant buzz of uncertainty he, and they, must live through.

'We'll have crew? I can't do it all on my own, not on another continent with logistics and permissions and everything. And I won't do it without a green light from the psych. Luke's obviously in a very different place now, but I don't want him out there if he can't handle it.'

Raef holds up his hands. 'Of course. I'm not going to send you to the other side of the world on your own with a murderer who could spin out.'

'A suspected murderer,' I remind him and he nods, *whatever*.

'Let me know what Luke says.' He drums his fingers on the table. 'Great work, Cass. Brilliant.' His phone rings and he shoos me out the door. I stand outside his office bewildered and invigorated by the new scale of all of this.

17

200822_THE JUNGLE_LUKE SPEED_MASTER I/V

'So, Koh Phangan is the main party island in Southeast Asia. It's where the full moon party takes place every month. Nearly every backpacker between eighteen and thirty in that part of the world will head over to the small island for one hedonistic night. Part of me felt it was just a tick-box excursion on this trumped-up package holiday we were all on. But you couldn't deny the atmosphere. The build of it. Like blood rushing to a heart.

'We'd been on Koh Samui and got the ferry over a week before the big night. People were arriving in droves. Temporary structures were erected on the beach. Along the main strip, hair salons, internet cafés, restaurants and bars were all open and packed. Music pumped. Scooters whizzed past with stuff tied to the back like a storm was coming.

'We were staying in a little complex of huts called "BooBoo Bungalows". Little dirt paths between palm trees, and bamboo porches where we'd drink beer and play cards. It was loud, we could hear the party beach even when we'd finally get to sleep in the early hours. There was no air conditioning, just a stand-up fan that barely worked. But we didn't complain. We were just happy to be there, and to get a sought-after room. We'd go lie in the many restaurants that had decks that jutted out onto the beach and read, lounging on each other, eating and drinking whatever we wanted. Chatting to other travellers that had just arrived. Feeding off each other's excitement, feeling like we were part of something.

'The night before the full moon we bumped into Sander and Astrid again. They invited us to this place up the hill the next evening, said it had the perfect view to drop a few ecstasy pills, which they'd managed to get their hands on. We told them we'd think about it. We weren't really into drugs. We didn't need them. We could have fun on our own, together, we didn't need something chemical enhancing it. That night we danced till dawn and dived into the sea as the sun rose. It was magical.

'I could be quite disparaging about it all, but this was fun. But we'd been fooled into this false sense of security, thinking we were protected in this well-travelled bubble, and nothing bad could ever happen to us out there.'

111

18

The next evening at home, I stand on the balcony, high up, watching the sweltering restless city rumbling past, lost in the story of Luke and Mari and everyone touched by it, even me. I neck the dregs of my wine and turn inside to find the bottle for more. I pick it up. An inch of liquid sways at the bottom. There is more in the cupboard. I hike myself onto the counter and pull one down from the shelf. Jumping back to the floor, I fish around for the corkscrew in the drawer, and without thinking, begin to open the bottle. Before I push the arms of the corkscrew down, I come to my senses. What am I doing? I'm already tipsy. It would be reckless to carry on. I'm exhausted from weeks of limited sleep, and the unremitting noise in my head.

Drinking to oblivion is not the answer. I put the bottle down and take a few steps back. Wiping my face, a shower of belligerent thoughts heckle me. I'm falling apart, just at the moment I need to be at my most stable.

The anonymous emails keep coming. Every time one shoots through, the notification turns my stomach. I received one last night, just before I went to bed.

I see you're not taking my threats very seriously. More fool you, little girl.

All I could think of was him. His pursed, saliva-covered lips as he watched me in the bath, a hand shaking as he passed me a dirty rubber ducky that looked as though it was found in the street. The water lukewarm, turning icy as my little fingers pruned. Too scared to ask him to help lift me out.

He died years ago. I went to his funeral. I was the only person there. I'm not sure why I went. It was an odd thing to do, I suppose. I thought it might help me, in some way. So I had unequivocal proof that he was gone. And . . . I felt sorry for him. I can still hear him weeping as I was taken away. Shouting a name that wasn't mine. His daughter died, many years before. Decades of being on his own and building his doll collection. He just needed one more to finish the job: me.

I changed my name years ago, so I didn't have to keep explaining myself all the time. I don't want a profile; not one like that, it might confuse things professionally. People might think I'm weak, or fragile. Which is a label I would never have placed on myself before.

With a sigh, I check my phone. A message from Rebecca with a photo of her three-month scan. I smile and attach a heart emoji to the image and tap:

Looks like you x

Her reply is fast. **I hope they look like YOU x**

I focus in on the grainy black and white image. There it is.

The next generation of us. I doubt I'll have kids, so this child will be the closest I'll get.

I scroll back through my messages and my smile fades. Luke still hasn't replied to the text I sent a few days ago, after my meeting with Raef, asking when would be convenient for a phone call. I flick back through the weeks of messages, with his usual prompt replies. This silence is unnerving. I chew my thumbnail. He's gone cold on me.

I hate this part of the job. The low-level anxiety that a contributor could drop out and months of hard work would be gone in a second. All those people, disappointed, in me. All that money, wasted.

I walk up to the cork board of information, which I've been adding to since we began this. It's so haphazard it wouldn't make a jot of sense to anyone else. I look at the photograph I have of Luke. It's recent. A screen grab from our interview rushes. I've written a little bio. Age thirty-eight, a data analyst, a job he can do anonymously, from home. He lives in a rented apartment in Balham, alone. His life is lonely. Gym, microwave meals and work. Not many friends, or girlfriends. He's been burnt too many times for that. I can't help but feel unbelievably sad for him.

Then I realise, we live very similar existences really.

How are you going to frame it, Cass? The question Raef has asked me repeatedly. Are we building a film about a narcissistic sociopath, on the hunt for a news cycle to bask in? Or is this a poor innocent man the world has been holding to account for twenty years? Getting punched in the face by strangers whenever he dares to rise above the parapet.

My phone rings. My chest bursts with relief when I see his name flash on the screen. I take a gulp of water, to sober up. 'Luke. Hi,' I say, trying to keep my voice calm, at a level.

'Cassidy,' he replies softly. I like how he says my name – the full name every time. Not 'Cass' like nearly everyone else. 'Sorry, I've been on a deadline.'

'That's okay. I know you've got other stuff going on outside of this.' I try to sound breezy, and not like I've been checking my phone every five minutes, catastrophising the consequences of him dropping out with every hour that's passed. 'How are you, Luke?'

'I was followed by this huge ginger cat on my lunchtime walk. Made me think you had Herzog trailing me.' I can't help but smile. I've told him all about my rather large orange cat. 'Then through all my meetings I realised I hadn't got back to you.' I swallow, enjoying the attentive tone. The photo of him on my cork board catches my eye.

I shake my head, reminding myself of the reason we need to speak. 'I've got some exciting news I wanted to float with you, actually.' I take a breath, trying to smooth over the wobble in my voice. 'Feel out any concerns you may have.' I pause, waiting for him to respond, but I'm met with silence. I was hoping he'd chip in with a level of excitement I could then sail through. 'Luke, are you there?'

'Yes, I'm waiting to hear what this exciting news is,' he replies, with a note of intrigue.

I stiffen. 'Oh, right. Yes. Well, they looked at some of the rushes from your interviews. And they're excited. Really excited. They want us to go back to Thailand. They think in the same way a police re-enactment can result in new leads, you there, retracing your steps, could really help bring this to life.'

'They want you and me to go to Thailand, together?'

I swallow. 'Yes.'

A long pause.

'That's not something we've ever discussed.' His words cool.

My stomach plummets. I rush to repair this. 'I know. But as we said in the initial meeting, plans may change as we uncover the story. Sorry I hadn't prepared you for this . . . It's . . . it's not something I ever considered they'd want.'

'Can I think about it?'

'Yes, yes of course.' I think about what Raef said. About the episodes and the money, and I rush to add, 'We'd have a crew – a cameraman, a soundie, an assistant producer and a researcher to help with logistics. A local fixer. It wouldn't just be *us*.' My sentence ends on the word, and I feel an awkward silence.

'I don't know . . . going back there . . .' A sharp intake of breath. 'What if . . . *he's* still out there?' His voice trembles. I am immediately reminded of the skeleton-thin eighteen-year-old rescued from the jungle.

'Luke, there will be a whole crew of us. And it was twenty years ago. That man . . . there is no way he's still there,' I say, going along with it. 'And we'd get you to speak to a psychologist before you went, to make sure you're fully prepared, and talk

116

you through the trip. Go through all the pitfalls. Make sure you are mentally prepared and able. They'll also be on hand for any phone calls along the way if you need extra support.'

'My nightmares . . .' he tells me, stammering.

'What happens in them?' I ask gently.

'That he's . . . he's still following me. Standing outside my window. Waiting for me at the door. Sometimes I'm back in the jungle. When I wake up, I'm so relieved I'm not really there . . . I . . .' *Oh god.* 'You know what the worst thing was about being there?'

'What?'

'Just knowing no matter how far we walked, we could be going in the wrong direction. Even at a vantage point all you can see is just the endless heads of trees. You have no idea if you're walking towards or away from civilisation. Or if you're simply going in circles. You have no idea whether to be hopeless or hopeful with each step.'

'I can't imagine,' I say, closing my eyes for a moment, lost in the image of Mari and Luke depleted, in muddy ripped clothes, completely disorientated and terrified.

I hear him shift around, standing up or something. 'I'll – I'll think about it, okay? I've got to go.'

'Of course, Luke, I understand.' I fight the urge to push him further. He needs to make the decision, or it's never going to work.

'Cassidy, do you think it's the right thing to do? Will more people watch the film and hear my side of the story?'

I swallow. What else can I say? 'It might even make them

117

reopen the case, search for her, Luke. That's what you want, isn't it?'

'I'll think on it.'

I nod into the receiver as he hangs up the phone.

A few hours later I get a text: **I'll do it. Because it's you, I'll do it.**

And I can't help but feel like I've just set a trap.

I turn over in my sleep. I slept! I hear a tapping and open my eyes, leaning over to check the time on my phone which is charging on my nightstand. Three. Damn. If only it were five, that would count as a full night. The tapping continues and I decide to get up. Herzog dances around my feet as I enter the kitchen. Rain is battering the windows. It hasn't rained for weeks; that must have been the noise I heard. But then I hear it again. It's very different from the sound of the storm.

I walk towards the balcony. A flash of lightning surprises me and I gasp, stepping back. *Crack!* Lightning illuminates the space. A man covered in wads of mud with crazy hair and even madder eyes. I scream. The nursery rhymes jingle in my head. And I scream and scream.

Until I wake up, clawing at my sheets, my mouth open and still shrieking as the room moves around above my head.

19

'So, the night of the full moon party arrives. We're full of this intoxicating excitement that has been building since we arrived on the island. Mari bought this neon body paint and dabbed these pink, green and yellow lines on either side of my cheeks. She'd gone to the hairdresser's and got an updo and wore this skin-tight white Lycra dress she'd bought from one of the shops on the strip. She looked incredible with her tan. We wore these white and purple flower garlands an old lady was selling on the beach.

'That photo they used of us in the papers – the one from that night. We got one of the guys in the hut next to ours to take it. We'd screamed "Full moon!" with our arms in the air instead of "Cheese".

'We decided to take the others up on their offer of the Es. Mari said if we were ever going to do it, it should be that night. I went along with it.

'So, we go out for dinner – we couldn't eat much so ditched

the food and got some watermelon shakes on the strip and put some vodka in them and sat watching the water holding hands, staring out at it glowing with burning wooden torches. The flames reflected into the lapping water. Music pumped into the stars. Then we joined the throngs. Jumping and twirling along the heaving beach – the dance floor extended out into the sea.

'Sander and Astrid danced over to us excitedly. Popping these tiny white pills into our hands. I looked over at Mari and asked her, are you sure? She had this glint in her eye. I knew we were doing it. And we grinned as we placed the tablets into each other's mouths.

'Nothing happened at first. We looked around at each other expectantly. It was Astrid's idea to go for a walk while they took effect. Along the way we lost the others. And suddenly we were on our own at the quieter end of the cove.

'I'll never forget it. She turned to me, and she held my hand and she said: You know what, Luke? If we weren't eighteen and we were standing on a beach like this one day, and you asked me to marry you, I'd say yes. And she kissed me. It was this really long, passionate kiss. "Marry me," I said, half high, half not. I just wanted to say it out loud. I just wanted to tell her I was hers for ever. And she whispered, "Yes," into my ear. I don't know if she meant it, or if she was just high too. I guess we never got to find out.

'I've never told anyone that before.

'Then she sank to her knees and her whole body began pumping. Up and down, like she was fitting or something,

120

thrashing about in the shallows of the water. I knelt next to her, tried to hold her still. Kept her head above water as her arms flailed about. Then her eyes sprang open. She was okay. The relief was unsurmountable. Next thing I knew Sander rugby tackled me away and I watched on as Astrid helped her up, shooting daggers. Mari coughed, blinked, and stood there. Confused. They thought I was hurting her. I tried to explain what happened, but all I saw were these horrified looks on their faces. Mari kept saying she was okay, but I'm not sure they believed her.

'I have this image of her flower garland floating, broken, in the water. Real clear. Like I knew then something really bad was written in the stars or something. I know Sander and Astrid still questioned what happened that night, because of what they told the police. But it's like I told them in my interview, she had a fit. It wasn't what they said, I'd never ... I'd never hurt Mari. Never.'

20

It's about a week since Luke agreed to go to Thailand. I'm still having trouble sleeping, and the apprehension around the trip has only exacerbated the insomnia. Cleo places a coffee next to me. 'Thanks,' I say cheerily, masking the turbulence within. I look back down at Luke's psych report and reread the last paragraph.

> Having assessed Luke in a one-to-one consultation,
> I'm confident he has been provided with all the
> relevant information to give informed consent
> contributing to the film he is pursuing with
> Songbird Productions. We've discussed at length
> the various outcomes of going back to Thailand,
> where he experienced a very traumatic event.
> We also discussed coping methods when it comes
> to backlash and he understands the pitfalls of
> putting himself back on a public platform, and
> how the perception of him may be adverse. He's
> had therapy, he isn't on any medication, nor do I

```
think he needs any, and he's been sober for some
years. He tells me this is his way of taking back
control of his past.
```

'Hey – Cass.' I look up. Raef motions me over. 'A word.' And I follow him to his office.

'All okay?' he asks, nodding towards a chair. I sit down.

'The psychologist green-lit him.'

'That's brilliant news!' he says. 'I knew you could do it,' he adds, as though I had something to do with that decision, and I frown.

'Now, look. I didn't want to bother you with this, but I've just heard they aren't giving us more money for the extra hour.'

I blink. Anger rises. 'What?'

'They've done their sums and think we can do it on what we've got. I've worked it through with the head of production, and we've done a bit of streamlining. This overseas shoot needs to be a two-weeker – in and out. We can't go back and get pick-ups and we can't extend. Okay? I've got three more shows in the pipeline with them, and I know they're not giving me the answer until they see how we perform on this. It needs to be on time, and on budget.'

'What . . . exactly do you mean by streamline?' I ask, trepidation rising. All the promises – were they just to get everything lined up? Just to change the parameters once we were all set up? 'Raef . . .'

'You'll still have Duncan, Cleo and a fixer. More than enough feet on the ground. I just can't get the extras – Jamal will have to work from here, and we'll need to cut back on extra crew out there, and the timings need to tighten up a bit. But it's still all very doable. More than enough!'

I try and find the fight to push this, but I'm too exhausted and frustrated, and I know the decision has already been made.

'Cass, you're doing a great job. The interviews are brilliant. All that loved-up stuff. Great. Dr Ackerman is tremendous, adds a lot of shade and mystery. But look, also, we're never going to get three parts out of this if we don't get family members on tape. Friends. People they met travelling. We need to up the ante on that side of things.'

I flail slightly on the spot, anger and resentment boiling over. Heat reaches up my neck, and I narrow my eyes at him. He threw this trip at me, refocusing the shoot and all our resources on it. 'We're getting there, Raef. We'll have to cover that on the other side of Thailand.'

He nods. 'Great. What about Luke?'

'Luke?'

'You've spent a lot of time with him now. You must have a gut feeling.'

'Maybe he imagined this man. But maybe we're all wrong and there really was someone else out there, following them.' I stumble on my words.

He gives me a funny look and sits back in his seat. 'Cass, I . . . Look, be careful out there, okay? You need to take a step back – be the collector and observer. Don't get too emotionally involved. Okay?'

124

'I never get emotionally involved,' I reply. But I know that's not true here. I don't think I've ever cared about anything so much in my life.

21

200822_THE JUNGLE_LUKE SPEED_MASTER I/V

'We both had terrible comedowns after the full moon. Mari was worse, she vomited for two days straight. I did my best to look after her. I have no idea what was in those pills and I'm convinced there was something in hers that caused her to react badly. We were trapped in our tiny shack, stinking of puke, on this huge, depressed lull after the massive high of the previous few weeks, and all I could hear was the dregs of partying around us. I felt like it was all some joke. No one cared about the culture of where we were. All they cared about was partying and their next shag.

'In those two days, I watched my beautiful girlfriend, normally so spirited, elegant – wonderful – turn into a puddle of despair. I felt some responsibility. I should have protected her from this.

'Most of all, I just had this overwhelming urge to get away. I'd had enough of chasing the fun. I wanted to do something meaningful. I thought the jungle was the answer. I wanted to see what it was like trekking in one of the hardest places to survive on the planet.

'The jungle was something my dad had done – he told me about it when we'd discussed possible travel plans before he'd died. He'd done a lot of travelling in his twenties, proper pioneering stuff. He'd lived on a kibbutz in Israel, an ashram in India. He was a true traveller. This wasn't that, not one bit. I thought up there we'd have time to reflect – and have a real adventure. Maybe afterwards we could go over to Myanmar, or Laos, and really do some hard, spirit-changing travelling. Not this.

'We needed to get out of that dressed-up wasteland and start again.'

22

It's several weeks since Luke was given the all-clear by the psych, and Raef forced me to take a long weekend before Thailand. I took a box of Mum's favourite chocolates to her care home. She now has Alzheimer's – the kind brought on by excessive drinking. Sometimes she's nice to me when I visit. Other times she gets stuck in the rhetoric that kept her drinking, that I am, like everyone else, the enemy.

That visit she was neither. She just looked out the window, barely even registering I was there.

I often think now how much I covered for her as a child when the social services visited. She had the ability to snap into this character they could approve of. Even after I was taken and red flags were waving, she managed to rein it back in. What if I hadn't lied when they asked me about my home life? Why did I feel I had to protect her?

I thought about that as we stared out the window, in silence, watching a sparrow pick at a cage of nuts.

I then drove to Deal, to spend the weekend on the beach with my sister Rebecca, her husband Eric and his family. She'd wanted to have a party and announce the pregnancy. I didn't tell her about my secret visit to Mum. She's so happy, and I didn't want to tarnish that. I ended up only staying one night. Eric's family dynamic is a perfectly oiled machine, Rebecca fits in so well. I felt as though I was on the outside, looking in.

I'm relieved to be back at work, and we've been busy organising logistics and rustling up contributors we may be able to interview while we're in Thailand. Melissa had already begun the process of obtaining the filming visa because of the re-enactments that were due to take place with the director who'd been brought on to shoot the dramatised element of the film, which is no longer needed. So, we can get out there quickly just by changing the crew on the paperwork. And because Luke isn't technically working, he can walk through without even needing a visa. We've let the local authorities know what we are filming and who we are with, but I was nervous that if we put Luke's name through the system, there might be a 'computer says no' situation which might hold up the whole shoot.

I rub my eyes; they feel gritty and dry. My phone makes a little buzzing sound and I realise I have a call scheduled. Cleo managed to get hold of one of Mari and Luke's old classmates and she's agreed to have a chat over the phone. I dial her number and take a sip of cold coffee as it rings.

'Hello?'

'Alice, hi. Thank you so much—'

'Cassidy Chambers.' She cuts me off, her voice sharp and full of scorn. 'The only reason I'm speaking to you today is so your little researcher, or whatever she is, will stop emailing me. I think it's rude. I've said no. I'm not going to change my mind so please leave me alone.' She sounds quite tearful by the end of her sentence.

'Alice, I'm so sorry you feel hounded.' Cleo turns and glares at me. I ignore it. It's my fault. I'm the one who told her to give it one more try, even when she protested. I stand up and walk to the corridor to continue the call.

'I'll have a word with Cleo about that. But she's very passionate about this. We all are. And, well, quite a few people have mentioned your name and how close you were to Mari, and we just want a few words from one of her peers. About what she was like. To help the viewer see her as a three-dimensional person. You know? Not just a photograph in the papers. But someone who cared about things. Who loved drawing and reading and laughing. That she was real. Otherwise, there'll be something vitally important missing from this whole thing: Mari.'

There is a quiet lull at the end of the line, then, 'That wasn't her,' she says stiffly.

'Pardon?'

'The way you described her, drawing, reading, laughing.' I frown. 'Mari . . . she could be quite . . . scary.'

'Scary?'

'She could be quite manipulative, really. People found her tough. We were all quite irritated when she got her hooks into Luke. I've got to go,' she says suddenly, like she's said too much.

130

'Wait, Alice – what do you mean?'

'I've got to go. Please respect my wishes and don't call me again.' And with that she hangs up. And I stand there. Blinking. Surprised at the animosity directed at Mari. Maddened by the haste with which she ended the call before I could find out more.

I walk back to our group of desks. 'Argh!' I cry, tripping over a camera case that wasn't there when I'd left. The others look up at me. Around our desks, boxes are piled high. Camera equipment we can't hire out there, kit for the jungle – walking boots, mosquito nets, rain macs, packets of Imodium and first aid kits.

We leave in three days. I feel this building pressure around me, like glass walls squeezing in on either side. I notice Raef peering at me through his open door, as he talks to someone on the phone. He can tell something's up.

I feel like I've got a big fat nothing. A story about some teenagers on a holiday that went tragically wrong. An accident, a mystery. Big woo-hoo. I bite my nail. *They're going to find you out*, my head taunts. *You're not nearly as talented as everyone says you are.* My nostrils flare at the thought. I think of the trail of anonymous emails that have been following me around since I started this. Slowly eroding my senses.

I fall into my desk chair and look up at the photos on the cork board. The picture of them at the full moon party, all dressed up and covered in neon paint.

Something . . . something occurs to me then.

'Hey, Cleo. How many disposable cameras did they find?'

'Huh?' she asks, spinning around in her chair.

'The police – how many cameras did they recover from Luke?' She looks blank. 'Well, how many photos do we have?'

'I don't know, I never counted them,' she says sarcastically. I've been pretty rough on her in the last few days. I deserve a bit of sass.

'Can you?' I ask and she huffs, spinning back around to her computer where she has a file of them.

I open a cardboard box with my new hiking boots in and begin to try them on. They are heavy, stiff and restrictive. 'Are you sure that these are right for the jungle? They're not snow boots or something?' I ask Melissa with a groan. She gives me a look. 'I spent half a day researching those for you. You should walk home in them, break them in,' she says in her matronly voice.

'Twenty-seven images. That's exactly one disposable camera. I googled it.' Cleo says. 'Why?'

'There were two when she bought them, it was a twin pack,' I say, thinking of the receipt.

'Maybe they lost it or gave one away,' she suggests, shrugging.

'Yeah, maybe,' I agree. I move my chair so that it's in front of her computer and take control of the mouse. Cleo reacts by standing. 'I've got to leave early.'

'Where are you going?'

'It's my birthday, I told you. I'm having a party. You should come. Get out of here for a bit?' She's annoyed. I look at

Melissa and Jamal, and realise they are quite dressed up for a normal working day. 'Is everyone going?' They nod. I've not been paying attention at all.

'You ignored my invitation,' Cleo says, briskly. Putting the strap of her bag over her shoulder. 'Come if you want. Or whatever.'

'I'll see how I get on here,' I stammer.

She shrugs and turns to the others. 'See you in a bit.' I watch as she marches towards the reception area, where Mo is waiting, wearing a smart shirt buttoned to the collar.

'She's upset,' Melissa says, not bothering to turn around and address me properly.

'Why?' I ask, perplexed.

'She had to cancel her first holiday with Mo for the shoot in Thailand. And you've been pretty horrible to her,' she explains, matter of fact. I blink – a moment of sympathy passes quickly. Does she know everything I've missed, everything I've sacrificed for this job? I'm irritated by her attitude. Annoyed that she doesn't understand what a privileged position she's in. Does she know how many people would want to be working on this?

Jamal peers over at me. I catch his eye and he quickly busies himself again. Melissa is the only one who dares to speak. 'She looks up to you, you know. We all know you're under a lot of pressure, but she's nervous, she's never done an overseas shoot before, and you're being very short with her.'

'Tell it like it is, Melissa,' I mutter back. But she's right. I've been so caught up by the film, by my own perceived

133

inadequacies, the fear that we are never going to find a conclusion to any of this. The pressure on my shoulders to deliver is unbearable.

What happened to you, Mari? Is it anything to do with what Alice said on the phone? Or your secret email address? Where the hell are you in all of this?

23

150922_THE JUNGLE_LUKE SPEED_MASTER I/V

'So, Luke. The jungle.'

He rubs his chin. Then he leans forward, his head down, as if winded. I wait, checking the shot in the monitor, watching as the seconds clock upwards, capturing this intimate, uncomfortable prelude before his voyage into the darkness.

'Why don't we start with the journey up to Chiang Mai?' I suggest softly, guiding him to it.

He repositions himself and looks directly into the camera lens. He's ready. 'We booked the trek through a travel agent on Koh Phangan. The train journey took for ever. We didn't want to spend the extra cash and get on a plane. Mari was still feeling terrible and slept most of the way, her head on my shoulder.' He touches his collarbone at the memory. 'Once we got to Chiang Mai she started to feel better. The first day was fine. Disorientating. But there was tentative laughing again. We met up with the group we'd be trekking with – there were about ten other travellers. All young westerners like us. I withered a bit when I saw them all.'

'Some of them told the police your relationship was strained,' I say, trying not to sound like I'm accusing him of anything.

He grimaces, irritated. 'We weren't in the best place. Mari wasn't herself. It was like the full moon party had left some sort of mark on her. People, again, exaggerating, making assumptions. Without knowing what was really going on with us. We weren't in the mood to make new friends.'

'So, you started the trek . . .'

Out of nowhere he stands up.

I stand too, clutching my notes. 'Luke? Luke, are you okay?' He turns away from me.

'I can't do this,' he says, pulling at the little mic clipped onto his neckline.

'You can . . . you are . . . you're doing so well,' I plead, wondering what has brought this on. I had high hopes for this interview, the last we are to have before the trip.

'I'm not ready, Cassidy.' He looks at me, deeply pained.

'What do you mean?' I ask, breathless. This is the most important interview to date. I need to know how he reflects on what happened, before we get out there, where I'm hoping there'll be a big revelation. Then we could then cut back to this, where he's still in denial . . . It's important for the film, I need to try and save it.

'I can't do it here. I'm not ready,' he says, pacing.

'Luke, listen—'

'I'll do it when we get there. I'll tell you what happened in the jungle, in the jungle.'

'But Luke—'

'Cassidy, I'll do it out there. Okay?' he practically shouts. 'Do you want me to walk out that door?' He points a shaking finger towards it.

And I shrink. 'Okay – okay. Please, Luke, sit down. Let's . . . let's do some general questions. I swear, nothing about the jungle, okay?' He relents. Walking back over to the chair, he drags it back, and settles into it. Duncan hurries forward and refits the mic.

Once Duncan's back behind the camera and the atmosphere has calmed, I ask, 'Luke, can you tell the viewer exactly what it's been like for you, over the last twenty years.' I sit forward in my seat. 'What do you want to say to everyone who thinks they know this story?'

He takes the question in, looking at his hands sadly. Then he readjusts so he's staring directly down the barrel. 'I want people to know that Mari is the only person I ever loved. Since that horrifying episode when I was eighteen, I've not been able to get close to anyone. Partly because I'm scared of what they'll think of me when they find out. Partly because . . . because . . . I'm scared of losing someone I love again. That year, my dad died.' He looks away for a moment, his chin wobbling. 'And then I found myself in the jungle searching day after day for Mari. Calling her name. Praying that one day I'd find her, and we'd go home. I dreamt about all the things we used to do. School, playing footy, or messing around in the

137

common room. I realised I never really appreciated how much we had ... and how stupid we were to try and find anything better. We had everything. Absolutely everything.'

He coughs, stifling a sob. He swallows and manages to continue. 'Then I did get home. But it was nothing like I remembered. People spat at me in the street. Friends wouldn't talk to me. My mum wouldn't even look me in the eye. I was still lost, you see, and I'm still lost today.' He looks like misery personified. 'But I swear – I did not hurt Mari. I've always told the truth about what happened out there.' He looks over at me, his face crumpling. 'There was a man. Cassidy, it's the truth, I swear it.' He begins to cry, his shoulders shaking, and I must fight the urge to go over and comfort him.

'There was someone else out there,' he whimpers, sniffing back tears. Dread washes through me as I picture the deranged man from my dreams. And for the first time, I really do believe him.

24

On the way home I start to cry. I can't help it. I duck into the
doorway of a closed shop as tears rattle down my cheeks. Why
am I crying? Is it over the film? Over Luke? Or my own past? I
force myself into some slow and steady breaths. 'Stop it,' I tell
myself, reflecting in the glass. I feel so out of sorts, my walls
in danger of crumbling, leaving me exposed.

My phone rings, and I take it out my pocket, sniffing as
I note Raef's name on the screen. I wipe my nose using my
sleeve and cough my throat clear, deciding to answer.

'Well?' he asks, excited.

'Raef, he didn't want to talk about the jungle today.' Silence.

'Okay,' Raef says. The word drags out, long and full of
disappointment.

I sigh. 'I don't want to rock the boat before we get there.
Look, it might end up working in our favour. Maybe it's good
if we interrogate it fully when we're in that environment.'

'Yes . . .' I can picture him scratching his chin, thinking
about how it could play out in the edit. 'How much master
interview have you shot?'

'We've done over ten hours across three interviews. We've got all the background stuff. Everything . . . except for the jungle and what happened the other side of the trip. But I'm thinking we do it out there, and again as a master interview once we're back. Then we'll be able to cut between the two.'

He sounds relieved. 'Okay – sounds good. Are you ready? When are you going, tomorrow?'

'Yes.'

'Good luck, Cass. Call me anytime you want. It will be great.'

'I will,' I say. I can't believe we're actually going.

'Don't panic if it gets overwhelming – just cover all bases and we can work it out in the edit,' he advises kindly. 'This is going to be a great film, I can feel it. It's a real character-led piece. Luke is great. I watched some more interview the other day, he's very likeable. Handsome. Vulnerable. You feel very conflicted. They'll love that.'

'Thanks, Raef,' I say softly. I don't like how he's describing Luke as if he's a character. Not a person. But that's what he'll turn into after we do this. It's my job to make sure that character is made up of true attributes. And not a lie.

I get home and begin to work out which clothes to pack. I send Rebecca a photo of my level-four mosquito repellent, as she told me about five times when I was in Deal not to forget it. And she sends me a laughing face emoji as a reply. Even though I know she's overly worried about the shoot and kept asking me if I'd be safe. I had to remind her I've filmed in war zones, although that did little to placate her.

As I chuck items on the bed, I pause intermittently. Luke. I've spent hours, days, with him now. Staring at his face. Listening to him talk. His expressions. The way he pleaded with me, the camera, the audience – to listen. There is this overwhelming vulnerability about him, behind those puffed-up muscles and bravado. He's scared of the jungle. But what is he scared of? Confronting the memories of this man, or himself?

I receive an email from Jamal:

The Thai police are sending a rep to talk to us on camera in Chiang Mai province.

Okay, well, that is some good news. We need someone in a position of authority to talk about that side of things. I feel a hopeful pang.

I look through my wardrobe and grab my new camouflage trousers, vests, and various cotton shirts that will help ward off insect bites. I'm going to look very glamorous on this shoot. I allow myself a wry smile as I chuck a red bandana towards my empty case. After it's full, I zip it closed and sit on the edge of my bed, my face in my hands.

I don't want to go. The thought drops like molten hot wax on skin, surprising me. Something bad is going to happen. I just know it.

My mobile rings and I walk over to my phone on the dresser. Luke. I clear my voice. 'Hey. How's the packing going?' I try to sound jolly.

'I can't do it, Cassidy.' His voice scratchy.

141

'What?'

'I can't go out there. I thought I could. But I can't go back.'

I can't breathe. Pressure swings through my shoulders and presses down, hurting my chest.

'You wanted to make this film, Luke,' I whisper, reminding him. 'We've all worked so hard . . .' I take a deep breath and will myself to take control of this. 'Luke. You have your whole life ahead of you. This film – it's your love letter to Mari. It's you, your story. Your truth. We can finally set the record straight about what happened to her.'

'Cassidy . . . please . . .'

I think of anything I can say that will turn him. 'No one will give you another chance to make this again if you stop halfway. They won't risk it if you do this to us. This is your one chance. Won't you regret it if you let it go?'

'Do you think I should do this, Cassidy?' His voice low and throaty. 'Are you sure?'

'You called me, Luke.' Even though I'm alone, my finger stabs into my chest. 'You have things you wanted to say. I'm here to listen. To collect those things. Put them in an order so people understand. You said you trusted me.'

'Do we have to go away?' His voice tiny – begging.

'Luke, the channel paid for this. They want scale. They want the big drone shots and action. They want this to be a top billing next year. That's how much they believe in you, and this film. Can you see that? You're telling your story after all; what's the point if no one sees it? Don't you want to reach the biggest audience possible if you're going to all this trouble?'

'If you were me . . .'

'Luke, I'm not you,' I snap. 'I haven't experienced what you experienced. I don't know what happened. Not in the jungle. Not really. Tell me. Help me show them. Help me make them understand what you went through.'

A long pause. 'Okay. I'll pack. And Cassidy . . . I do trust you.' His voice small. My heart tugs.

We say goodbye and with adrenalin pumping I put down the phone. My hands are shaking. I wonder what his motivation was for that call; if he is, in fact, a sociopath.

It would be to enjoy me begging. That's it, right? To hear a woman on the end of the phone begging him to do it. That's the reason. I grit my teeth together. The idea of it makes me feel dirty and I shudder.

THE ROMANCE

25

'Sorry, miss, what was that?' the taxi driver asks.

I freeze. I must have been muttering to myself. 'Nothing,' I reply. *Get a grip.* Another sleepless night; another nightmare. I almost long for my childhood visions; these are far worse. Now when I close my eyes and dare to fall, all I see is the man in the jungle. He waits for me in my dreams, ready to jump.

Last night, my nightmare morphed into something surreal, and most distressing. *He* got close enough for me to see his face, and wiped back the layers of putrid mud, clawing at the greasy sludge, and all I saw was Luke's face. I'd woken in a cold sweat and lay there, wondering if I was crazy going back into the heart of the jungle with him. And if Luke is telling the truth, could the stalker still be there, waiting for a new cohort of victims? I tut and berate myself at the silly thought.

And now here I am, on the way to the airport. I wish more than anything I could ask the driver to turn around and take me home. But that would be like single-handedly turning a freight ship. It's like I'm standing at a precipice, with a finger at my back, slowly applying pressure. Holding Luke's hand.

Part of me wishes I could turn back the clock. Never have taken this on. I was so cocky at the beginning of this. Is my ego my downfall?

I stare out at the late summer sky. Below it, the grey tarmac of the motorway sprints past. It occurs to me then: what I'm most scared of. It's not the jungle at all but the proximity to Luke for two whole weeks. No apartment to run home to at the end of each day, no space to deflate the intense time spent together.

How close is too close? How close do I want to be?

We arrive and the driver holds the door open for me and removes my bag from the boot. I look up at the shiny terminal building and swallow thickly. Nowhere to hide. I squeeze my thumb into my palm. Being this tired is like walking through thick sludge. Finding words for the simplest conversation is like trying to answer quick-fire questions on a game show. I pause at the automatic doors; they open with a swish. I stand there a moment. The doors begin to close in defeat, but I step into them with renewed strength. *I can do this.*

I check the digital board for the area relating to our flight's bag drop. As I walk over, I see them already huddled, caps on and rucksacks on backs. The group laughs, full of pre-shoot exhilaration. Cleo's wary eyes land on me. I need to do some work to repair the damage there. She's fed up. I need her on side and mustn't take my frustrations about the shoot, and my own limitations, out on her.

'Sorry I'm a bit late. Traffic. This is so exciting!'

I smile at Cleo, and gently squeeze her arm in comradery, and she softens. 'We're already checked in – go for it,' she says, pointing at the desk.

I glance at Luke. He looks tired. 'You okay?' I think of our conversation last night. He nods, cautiously. And I feel a rush of guilt for bringing him here. I try to shake away the feeling that this isn't right.

But it lingers.

I'm confused as Luke's ushered to a seat in first class. 'How did he swing that with Melissa?' I ask Cleo. This isn't some big budget entertainment show with money to send contributors flying around the world first class.

'He's afraid of flying. They worked something out. I think he paid for part of his ticket or something,' she whispers over her shoulder as we head into economy.

I look behind as he tries to get comfortable in his seat, shifting about restlessly, fiddling with the various extras in his luxurious box of space. 'See you on the other side,' I call over to him. And he looks up, in this longing way.

'Have a good flight, Cassidy,' he calls, as I walk away. I feel like I've left something important behind.

I follow the queue of people neck stretching, looking for their seats. Waiting impatiently for those in front to deposit belongings in overhead compartments and to finally sidestep into their allotted space.

We come to our row. My seat is in the aisle, next to Cleo. After sitting, I lean into the walkway and peer down towards

149

first class. I can see the edge of Luke's arm on the rest. Then the stewardess pulls the curtain across with a curt look in my direction. I roll my eyes and sit back with a huff. Cleo gets out her laptop and begins tapping away.

I pull my cardigan around myself. Exhausted. 'I might have a sleep; I didn't get much last night.'

'Okay, Cass,' is her reply.

I lean back on my headrest and close my eyes.

Next time I open them, I turn to look out the window, squinting at the bright sky and fuzzy white clouds. Licking my lips, I reach forward to look at the time on my phone. A pathetic half hour. Not enough. Cleo is still tapping away on her laptop, and I can hear the drinks trolley shaking somewhere not too far away.

Someone touches my arm and I look up, surprised. A stewardess leans towards me. 'Your husband has explained the mix-up. The seat next to him is free, so we'd love you to join him. I'm so sorry for any confusion.' I look down the aisle. Luke's face is turned towards me with a knowing smile, and a twinkle in his eye. I can't help but grin. *Oh, I see.* I don't really have a choice other than to go along with it. Besides, it's a good opportunity to put that tension behind us and get into the right mode for this trip. And, well, I've never sat in first class before.

'Oh, right, thank you.' I pull my bag out from above. Cleo looks at me questioningly, but I shake my head and purse my lips into a silent shush.

150

I go to him, walking through the half-closed curtain. 'Thank you, *husband*.'

'Congratulations from all of us here at British Airways.' The stewardess hands me a glass of champagne. 'We hope you have an incredible honeymoon.'

I raise my eyebrows and accept the drink. 'Thank you.' I take my seat. It is exponentially more comfortable than my previous encounter. 'What did you do?' I whisper, making sure none of them can hear.

'This seat was empty. It was a shame for it to go to waste. Besides, I barely made it up without having a panic attack. I'm not sure all this Valium I've got is enough to get me down again. You need to be my therapy dog,' he quips.

I snort. 'That's lovely. Great. A therapy dog.' I laugh. It feels good.

I hear a giggle and look over at the stewardesses who've obviously been talking about Luke. I think of him through their eyes. Handsome, and charming. 'So, I guess we just got married,' he says. Sitting back in his reclined seat, crossing his ankles out in front of him. I mimic his position. Turning my head, so we face each other. It is a little too intimate. But if I move back, it will seem like I've noticed. And cared. Or something. 'Are you married? Is there going to be some tricky situation to navigate when we get back, *wife*?' he asks, a teasing quality in his voice.

I let out a short laugh. I'm so far away from it. 'No. Never. I seem to get so immersed in what I'm working on I don't really have the head space for it. I barely see my family, let

151

alone have time to meet anyone. What about you? Has there been anyone special?' He frowns slightly, and I add, 'After Mari, I mean . . .'

He shakes his head. 'I've had a few . . . things, but whenever they got serious, I couldn't commit, or I'd tell them about Mari – I don't know. I think I'm pretty screwed up about relationships.'

'I'm sorry.'

'Once a girlfriend murderer, always a girlfriend murderer.' He looks ahead. Sadness permeates through the bitter jibe. I take another sip of my champagne. 'Maybe, after this,' he says quietly. 'Maybe once the film comes out and everyone believes me . . .' And I feel a stab of sympathy and swallow. 'Maybe then it'll be different.'

'Want to know something?' I say, feeling like I owe him a part of me, after everything he's given of himself. He nods. I pause dramatically. 'I've never been in love.'

He sits up, scoffing. 'What?'

I suddenly feel very vulnerable to have told him such a silly thing. He looks incredulously at me. As though he sees a completely different version of what he thought I was.

'But you're . . . you're . . .'

'What?'

'You're beautiful,' he laments and my cheeks heat up. He recovers. 'I mean . . . you should have been in love a dozen times.' He looks at me with a pained expression, scratching his head. 'Man, that makes me sad.'

'I make you sad?'

'I just think you should have been in love. Madly in love,' he says gruffly, as though the idea of it has made him cross.

'I've just been quite dedicated to my career, I guess. It's never been a priority.'

'What about when you were younger?'

'My mum was, er . . . ill. As a teenager I had to care for her a lot. And she didn't like me out late, because of what happened when I was a little girl. I have a younger sister too, so I was mainly in, watching her.' His impassioned expression softens. 'But you have . . . ?' He looks at me but can't finish the sentence.

I realise what he means. 'Oh god, yes!' I blush. 'I've just never pursued anything to a relationship. I've always been away working, they've got bored waiting, or I just never cared enough to let something really gain momentum.'

'Cassidy. I think the only onion that needs peeling around here is you.' He sits up in the seat and waves at the stewardess.

'What are you doing?' I whisper, startled.

She bustles over, grinning at her favourite customer. 'Can we have some more champagne, please? Maybe you could wing us a bottle?' He takes my hand and squeezes it, looks at me lovingly.

'I'm not meant to . . .' she starts. But then changes her mind as Luke peers up at her with those sparkling eyes of his. 'Okay,' she says conspiratorially and saunters back to the galley.

'Luke . . .'

'If this flight is the only time either of us are ever going to be married, we may as well celebrate.' I laugh. Yeah, why the hell not. Maybe everything doesn't have to be such hard work all the time. My shoulders fall, and I realise I'm relieved to be flying away from all the darkness back home. Maybe this will be okay, after all.

I wake with a start. The plane is silent. The lights are off. I have the blanket loosely tossed over me. Something is on my hand. I shift to look down at Luke's fingers gently resting on it. I delicately remove it from under them.

26

Suvarnabhumi Airport, Bangkok. We exit the plane in a daze and walk through the air gate. We are a weary pack, tarnished by the long journey and the time difference. This side of arrivals is quiet. We must have been the only plane to have landed. Elevator music plays tinnily as we stand on horizontal moving walkways. The innards of the building are made of slabs of exposed concrete, and it feels austere and dystopian. Like we have landed on a future Mars.

When we come out into the main terminal, the atmosphere shifts. A hectic buzz. People rushing in every direction. The sight of a young couple with large backpacks deep in conversation stops me in my tracks and I stare. Thinking of Mari and Luke. So young. So far from home. And I realise I haven't thought about her the whole journey.

'This way!' calls Cleo, leading the charge.

We load into the pre-booked van and begin to film our arrival into the city. Bangkok marches at us like an army. People, chaos. Noise and colours. I love it immediately. Duncan films Luke pensively looking out the window. He grumbles about not being able to get a still shot with the jerky movements of the vehicle as it weaves through traffic. I tell him not to worry. I want it to feel erratic, just like the city. I think of the possibility of using a filter in post-production over these shots, so it looks self-shot and aged by twenty years. I'll use this grainy, unpolished footage between the big sweeping drone shots and the high-resolution wides. I want it to feel like an attack on the senses, just how I feel right now. A frenzy of excitement to land in this vibrant, sleepless city. An explosion of all of it.

Luke wears an indescribable expression. Somewhere between crushed, hopeful – and sad. What is it? He probably couldn't explain it even if he tried.

Melissa booked us into a large chain hotel in Sukhumvit. I get out the vehicle and stare up at the towering glossy building. Far removed from the backpacking district and the Khaosan Road. The air outside is deliciously warm after the refrigerator bite of the air-conditioned van.

I leave Duncan with the cases fretting with the hotel staff and follow Cleo into the foyer. All glass and marble, high ceilings and elaborate flower arrangements. Cleo goes to reception and checks our group in. I turn to look for Luke. But he's not here. Cleo points back to the main doors. 'Looks like he needed a minute.' I follow her gesture and see the back of Luke's head the other side of the door, a plume of smoke rising around him.

'I'll speak to him,' I say, going back outside.

He's sitting on the steps, and I take the spot next to him, hugging my knees. 'I didn't know you smoked.'

He looks up. 'I don't really.' He offers me one and I take it.

'Holidays and special occasions?' I ask knowingly, taking a stick out the packet.

He shakes his head and peers at me. 'When I'm having to deeply excavate years of trauma and relive the worst thing that ever happened to me,' he replies dryly.

I light my own. 'Yep. Sounds like a good reason.' I blow out the smoke, and sigh, enjoying the nicotine hit. 'How are you doing, Luke?'

He sniffs, and looks back at me from his position, leant forward. 'I'm scared of the jungle,' he says, his throat tight. He points around. 'All this. This is fine.'

I look out at the sleek cars and taxis, mingling with the odd tuk-tuk. 'You won't be alone. We'll be with you,' I say, softly.

'You've never been to a jungle before, have you?'

I shake my head. 'Nope,' I admit.

'Being lost in the jungle is the closest there is to hell.' The intensity in his voice grates into me. Smoke catches the back of my throat and I cough.

'I can't imagine what it must have been like. But Luke, this time, you won't be lost. We'll be there two days – in and out. We'll have our fixer with us, he's incredibly experienced, one of the best. It won't be anything like last time, I swear.'

'Does the channel think I'm going to freak out? Is that what they want?' He looks at me, checking my reaction. 'Do they want me to explode – suddenly admit that I killed her?

Right? Is that what they're hoping? Because I didn't hurt her. I've told you – I told them—'

Cleo comes out and interrupts. 'Cass, the receptionist . . .' she begins.

'Cleo, just deal with whatever it is, okay?' I look over at her, annoyed she hasn't read the situation better.

'Fine,' she says, thrusting some key cards at me. 'I'm heading in. See you in the morning.' She marches off. I watch her grab her case and head to the lifts. It's late and we haven't eaten. I know she's desperate to get some room service and call Mo.

I turn back to Luke. He's fidgety and tugging on his cigarette. His large frame brittle and stressed. 'You believe me, don't you?' His eyes are moist. 'Because I don't think I can go further with this unless you do. You think . . . Cassidy . . . now you've got to know me . . . you think I'm innocent, right?'

I have to say it, there is no other way. 'Of course I do.' I'm not lying. I do. Maybe something happened out there, and he had to deal with it the best he could. Like Dr Ackerman said. How would any of us react in that situation? How could any of us say?

But I believe he is good.

I believe that much.

'Okay.' He nods his head as if firming up his confidence. 'Okay.' He smiles then, relieved. He flicks his cigarette out to the pavement and stands up. I join him. Then he embraces me. A big bear hug. I feel tiny inside his arms. I can't help turning my cheek onto his chest and closing my eyes for a bliss-filled moment. Then I force myself to break free from it and gently push him away. Even though it's the most peaceful place I've been for a long time. And I wish I could have stayed.

my back onto the chest and then turns to lift him, offering
drama. Then Luke comes in. He is the man in the jungle
but now always less dangerous is the need to escape plot I've
been once long ago. We all knew I could have stayed.

27

Getting into my starch-sheeted bed, I lie there waiting. Hours
pass. I finally drift off but open the door straight into darkness.
The dream. The deranged man in the jungle. I freeze and he
dances around my statue, terrifyingly close. But this time he
doesn't wipe the mask away, but corners me, a rock in one
hand, raised, about to smash down onto my skull. I cower in
anticipation of pain. But then *bam!* Luke rushes at him, pulling
him away. And I'm saved.

I wake panting. The room spins. My hand falls on my
heaving chest.

Finally, I sit up, trembling. I rest back on the headboard
thinking of Luke. And the ridiculous fantasy of him saving
me that's formed in my mind as I slept. I knock my head
back on the headboard in frustration, and wince in pain.
Why can't I stop thinking about him? What is happening
to me?

I touch my lips. I don't often think about my appearance.
Even with dark circles under my eyes he called me *beautiful*. I
exhale sharply at the memory of Luke's tender words. I can't

remember anyone calling me that before. Not like that. I've never let anyone close enough.

What am I doing? What am I entertaining here? I just need one good night's sleep. Just one. Then I'll be able to think all this through clearly.

Halfway through the first day of filming I'm irritated. It's like we're shooting an ITV travelogue, rather than a dark and brooding true crime series. I watch Luke wander the Khaosan Road through the wireless monitor in my hands. He points at stuff, saying things like, 'I think I remember something about that.' 'Maybe we ate there.' I sigh. Am I expecting too much? Will the good stuff come along later? Are these just pretty pictures to hang his interview off? I yank at my headphones, wiping off the sweat around my ears, compounding my unease.

'It's different,' Luke says, searching for something to say.

'What's different about it?' I call from a few metres away, so I don't get in shot.

'I just remember it being a lot more chaotic. These bollards here' – he points to the metal pillars stopping traffic entry and street vendors – 'none of this was here,' he says, gesturing to the clean, neat new pavements and modern drainage system. He paces slowly. 'I mean, it all feels very sanitised, even with all these people. It had this energy twenty years ago. Like anything could happen. Like you were on the verge of something exhilarating . . . dangerous . . . no rules.' He looks around. Disappointment radiates. 'It's like it's a different place,' I hear him mutter through my headphones.

Then recognition. He points up to a bar. 'That's it. That's where we went that first night. I can't believe it's still here.' We follow behind as he walks up the narrow steps and onto the large wide balcony cluttered with white plastic garden chairs and low bamboo tables. Young travellers are dotted around, drinking beers, looking hungover. They stare at our camera in disbelief.

Luke puts his hands on his hips, catching his breath. 'Wow. It's basically the same.' A stout man gets up from his place in one corner, a wad of bills in his hands. He's pointing angrily at the camera and shouting something in Thai. Duncan lowers the camera and Cleo and our fixer, Reggie, take their cue to run over with our filming licence and a location release form. Charming smiles all around. I let them deal with the issue and turn to see Luke standing by the edge of the balcony. Right where Mari was dancing, on the recovered CCTV footage. I look up to one corner and see there is still a camera. Watching.

Luke stares down at the throng of people milling below. His hands resting on the lip of the barrier. His huge silhouette. I try not to think of how it felt being wrapped up by his arms.

'All good!' Cleo comes up behind me grinning and waves a signed location release form in my face. The placated owner is back behind his desk counting bank notes. I motion to Duncan, and he films Luke in quiet contemplation. Looking down on the western travellers below. This will work well in the edit. I hate to burst the moment, but I do.

'What are you thinking about, Luke?' I call.

He turns, and notices the camera filming, and gives a little

162

nod of understanding. 'I'm thinking how much I wish I could turn back time. How I wish that I could be here, right now, with Mari and have done things so completely differently. I wish I'd kept her safe.' His voice breaks and I hold my breath as a tear falls down his cheek. It is a beautiful shot. That handsome, devastated face.

He wipes his cheek and sniffs, composing himself, and then looks directly at the camera. 'Is that what you wanted, Cassidy?'

Gone is his gentle tone. I look up from the monitor and into his eyes. Is there something sinister there I've not seen before?

We take a break from filming and grab some lunch from one of the vendors on the strip. I roll my shoulders back and contemplate ordering a cold beer, but that would not set a good example for the others. After I've eaten, I wander around some of the stalls.

Coming to a table of penknives, I run my fingers over the cool metal neatly lined up. Reggie, our fixer, joins me and picks one up. Melissa said he came highly recommended to help us circumnavigate both the urban and rural elements of the shoot. He certainly looks the part, with a leather cowboy hat, deep lines ingrained in his face, and long hair tied in a bun at the base of his neck.

'You should get this one,' he says, handing it to me. On the handle is a little carved elephant, made from an iridescent shell.

'I wasn't going to . . .' I've never owned a knife before.

'The elephant represents strength and longevity. A special animal here in Thailand. You should get it, it may be helpful in the jungle,' he says knowingly. He has a slight American accent. I overheard him telling Cleo he learnt English as a young man, when he lived in the States for a period. Reggie haggles in Thai, and once a price is agreed, I slip it into my pocket.

'Thank you, Reggie.'

My phone vibrates and I retrieve it. Raef: **How is it going? Call me when you get a moment. Good luck first day etc.** Brief and to the point.

'Just have to make a call,' I say, moving into a café with a *Free WiFi* sign. I phone Raef, picking at some old Blu Tack on the wall as I wait for him to answer.

'Cass – my little ninja.' I wince. 'How's Thailand? How's Luke doing out there?' I think of him in his safe office, thousands of miles away.

'He's okay. It's obviously tough being back here after twenty years and it was a long journey, and we're all pretty tired. Luke . . . he cried earlier. He seems really . . . vulnerable. He's spooked about going back to the jungle . . .'

'Nice,' Raef says. I imagine him flicking his pen against a notepad. 'Where are you going after this?'

'We've got one more day in Bangkok tomorrow, then we're taking the train down to the islands for the full moon, before we head up to the jungle, like they did.'

'Okay, nice. Don't let him off lightly, Cass,' he says, thoughtfully. 'I know it's hard to keep that barrier up with contributors when you are working closely like that. And you might get a weird sense of loyalty towards him. But remember, he could have killed his girlfriend. And you're there for her – for her family.'

I blink. How on point that is.

'Yes, of course. But Luke too – he could be a victim as well,' I point out.

A pregnant pause. 'Yes. There is that,' he says stiffly.

He doesn't know Luke like I do.

'But of course, Mari is always at the front of my mind in all this,' I add quickly. My cheeks burning as I feel the effects of the lie. Because it's not true, is it? I'm losing her, and myself, in this.

He moves on. Talking about how he thinks stylistically we should get this and that, and I nod and umm and ahh until he's distracted by something else and hangs up the phone.

I look back through the jumbled crowd to the others. Cleo is talking; she's stood up and gesticulating wildly, as if telling an anecdote. The men are laughing at the show. Luke's face creases up as he joins them. And I feel myself sinking inside a wad of confusion and confliction that I have no idea how to control.

28

That evening, I lie back in the bath. The adrenalin of the day rides through my shoulders and up into the moist air. I hear my phone beep and shake the excess water from my fingers and pick it up, scanning Jamal's reply to my earlier email.

Haven't heard anything yet re Mari's emails – will chase again.

How disappointing. Maybe they'll never surface. I reply, asking Jamal to get his friend to send them directly to me if he has any success. I want to be the first to see whatever is on there.

I flick down to another email he's sent.

Subject: Astrid. Hey, Cass – I think I've found her! Managed to get an email address, have sent an approach. Will let you know as soon as she gets back to me. Fingers crossed.

I grin. A glimmer of light.
Another email catches my eye.

This time that horrible feeling snakes through me. An anonymous message:

How was the market, Cassidy? Did you find what you were looking for?

Fingers shaking, I open the attached jpeg. In the photograph, Duncan is filming on the Khaosan Road, and Cleo is gripping the boom pole over her head capturing the sound. Luke is standing, hands on hips with a triangle of sweat down the back of his T-shirt.

My breath catches. The water sloshes as I sit up and take in the shift in gear. The mental image of a lonely troll behind a keyboard dissolves, and something far more sinister replaces it. Are we being followed?

I decide then. I'm going to call Raef. There are protocols and procedures for this sort of thing going on behind the scenes of a production. The channel will want to know, and possibly get their lawyers and the police involved. This is stalking now, and I shouldn't have this stress on my shoulders only.

Then I come to my senses and type in *Khaosan Road* to the Twitter search bar. And sure enough, earlier today, someone has posted a series of photographs of us filming Luke on the busy tourist street with the hashtag #LukeSpeedBackinThailand. I'm hardly surprised. We stuck out like a sore thumb. The troll must have swiped it from here. I wonder if the press will pick it up – that's the last thing we need. I'm just relieved I'm not being followed by a nasty piece of work, who's been bashing

167

me mentally with these nefarious emails. I force them back behind their dirty desk, where the horrid troll belongs.

But I'm still going to speak to Raef when we get back. I'm being warded off a story and it needs mitigating against. Someone out there doesn't want this film to happen. They've found out about my background and are using it against me. But why? It just doesn't make any sense.

No longer in the mood to relax, I get out the bath and pull on the thick white robe hanging on the back of the door. I walk up to the large window and stare down at the twinkling lights of the city. That fidgety adrenalin is pumping which I know won't let me sleep. I decide to go downstairs and sit in the bar and have a drink. Try to unwind before the horrific tossing and turning starts.

I walk down the carpeted hallway and push the lift button. *Ding!* It opens immediately and I step inside. The silent muffle of the journey, before doors open onto the busy foyer. People mill around wearing smart eveningwear. Laughter bounces and hushed conversations linger.

I enter the main bar. Grecian vases hold huge floral displays. Candles illuminate faces at tables. I feel a bit underdressed entering a such a formal space, wearing jeans and a vest. I think there is a more relaxed bar further into the building and decide to wander over, picturing a kind barman willing to pour me a few drinks in understanding silence.

Down the corridor are unused event spaces and conference rooms. I come to a stop next to one, hearing someone tinkling on a piano. My eyes move into the crack in the double doors. I see Luke sitting behind a large black grand piano. Practising the odd chord. Lost in his own world. The large room is completely empty, covered in rich red carpet and some gold-sprayed chairs are stacked in one corner. The door I'm leaning on moves, and a creak rebounds. He looks up. I'm forced to show myself. His confused face melts into a dimpled smile when he realises it's me. 'Hello, Cassidy. What are you doing loitering over there?'

'I couldn't sleep,' I explain.

He nods. 'Me neither.'

I walk inside, like there's an invisible piece of string pulling me towards him. I have barely any control over it. 'Did you keep up the piano after . . . ?'

He shakes his head. 'Not really. I found it difficult to do anything I used to love. I've only recently begun playing again. I'm a bit rusty.' Another lovely piece of dialogue which would have worked well in the film. I tell myself to make a note of it for our next block of interviews when we get back. My hand slides over the sleek body of the piano. 'Have you ever played?' he asks.

'Gosh, no. Well . . . I can play a very mediocre "Chopsticks".'

He laughs. 'Come on then.' He nudges over on the seat, allowing space for me.

'No! It's terrible. Honestly.'

'Come on, Cassidy. I'm waiting.' He pats the empty spot.

I look at the space he's made and decide to take it. As I sit down our sides touch. It is like there is a reverberating tingle of magic fizzing on my skin. I lift my hands and place

169

my fingers on the keys. 'Don't laugh at me,' I tell him and he shakes his head.

'I would never,' he says with feigned sincerity.

I begin the jolly tune and make a terrible crashing sound. He laughs at me.

'Oi!' I look over, pausing. 'You said you wouldn't.'

He coughs. 'Sorry.'

To my surprise, he gently takes my hands off the keys and repositions my fingers. 'Here,' he says. 'You need to pretend you're holding a tennis ball, with your fingers loose and thumb straight,' he says as he shows me. I swallow.

'Okay, go on,' he demands. I take a breath and begin to play. He was right. It does help. He gently lays his fingers alongside mine, and begins to play along, faster and faster. The charging sound runs ahead of us. And I laugh as I attempt to keep up. He expertly glides, forcing me to speed up. It takes all my effort and concentration.

Finally, when the song ends, we descend into laughter. Then silence. We look at each other. Red cheeks. His face inches from mine. His lips. Touching distance. I stand quickly. Back away, almost tripping.

'I need to get back. Get some sleep,' I stammer.

'Stay. We could get a drink?'

The thudding of my chest beats into my ears. I want to. I just want to be near him. So much it hurts. I back away. This thing we're doing. An open secret between us we can't speak of.

'See you in the morning,' I say, as I leave the room.

*

I lie back in bed. Thinking about Luke. About Mari. About the photo with the red bikini, and the man in the jungle. All the reasons I've come here, and how overshadowed they feel compared to these unexpected feelings for Luke.

29

We spend the next day filming around the various tourist hotspots in the city, all of which Mari and Luke visited twenty years ago. First, Wat Pho, the vast Buddhist complex, where the giant reclining Buddha resides. It is one of the most celebrated attractions in Bangkok. I fan my face with my hand as we film Luke. He lays some flowers for Mari and stands, head down, quietly reflecting. Men with shaved heads wearing orange robes step around him peacefully, nodding their faces into the prayer position of their hands as they pass.

I inhale a gulp of hot moist air. Closing my eyes for a moment, I zone out as though asleep for the splittest of seconds, and jolt. It is too still here – a break from the relentless pace of the city, but I'm drifting, unable to concentrate. 'Cass? Cass?' Duncan calls over. 'You got any AA batteries over there?' Cleo is fiddling with Luke's mic pack, and I nod, reaching for some spares in my bum bag.

Next, we head to the floating market. Long boats clutter the sides of the inner-city river. Shouts holler from every direction. Multicoloured produce gleams against the murky water.

Debris bobs. I stare down at a dead bird, its wings clutched together, like a sleeping dove. 'Cass, Cass?' I look up. Cleo is watching me curiously. 'You think we've got enough?'

I nod. 'Yeah, let's head back.'

She shifts closer. 'Are you okay? You just . . . don't seem yourself.' I don't like the way she's trying to look through me. The reason she's so good at her job is that she has great instincts. But I don't appreciate that now – when I'm trying my best to fly under the radar with all this stuff whirring around my mess of a head.

'I'm fine. My sleep. It's terrible. I might get something from the chemist to help,' I tell her, and she nods.

'That sounds like a good idea. I can run out for you, if you want?'

I shake my head. 'Don't worry.' And I notice her grimace, as if she's at a loss with how to handle me now. 'Cleo, I've been meaning to say what a brilliant job you're doing. I honestly can't imagine being out here with anyone else assisting. Thank you.' She looks at me in disbelief.

'Really?' she breathes.

'You're excellent. This film is yours too. Don't forget that.'

I can tell she is thrilled. 'Thank you, Cass. I really appreciate that. And this opportunity.'

'Let's get back,' I say, and she calls over to Reggie to find out about our ride.

I feel eyes on me and turn to see Luke searching my face with a troubled look. I look away quickly.

*

173

We pack up the kit and add the equipment to our cases which are already in the back of the van. Our night train down to Surat Thani is tonight. From there we'll have a short drive to the ferry and then a few hours by sea to the infamous Koh Phangan. The location of the party, and where Mari had that horrific comedown which seems to mark the point the trip turned on its head.

The full moon party is an important element of the film. We've carefully scheduled the shoot around it, as the event only happens once a month. It sets the scene – the pilgrimage of western kids heading to this one island to get off their heads. It was the last place Luke and Mari were truly happy and I want to get a sense of that. And of Luke now, almost middle-aged, still tarnished by his trip decades previously, walking through the throngs of kids having the time of their lives, at a turning point in his. I want to get some shots of him standing very still, as the crowds of youths mingle and dance around him. Flame throwers tossing balls of light in the air, and girls screaming with delight all doused in neon paint. I have a very clear image of it in my head.

We stand on the platform waiting for the train to roll in.

My phone vibrates. Jamal's emailed. Subject: Astrid. I quickly open it.

She got back to me – wants to speak to you. Apparently something happened in Bangkok she's never told anyone. She's on her way to a yoga retreat with terrible reception so will call you once she's back in a few days.

I'm disappointed he didn't insist on a quick call before she went off radar, but this is good news. I wonder what it is she has to tell. I feel inflated at the thought of something fresh and new that hasn't come to light before. Raef will be thrilled. My mind runs away with the possibility of interviewing her on camera. I wonder what she has to say about Luke. I look across at him and he catches my eye, smiling in a friendly, absent-minded way.

The train arrives, and I grimace as I heave my bag up the steps to the carriage, refusing help. The chairs are organised in pairs that face each other. I slide into one and pull out my laptop ready to work.

'Mind if I sit here?' Luke asks, pointing to the chair opposite mine.

My heart sinks. With him so close, I'll be hyperaware of every movement. 'Sure.' I shrug. Heat runs up my neck. My eyes flick back to my screen. I want to transcribe some of the cards we've shot over the last few days. I could get Cleo to do it, or even Jamal back at the office, but I want to familiarise myself with the material as I'm going straight into the edit to put some sequences together for the channel to look over when we get back. Having a clear idea of which scenes and shots I want to use beforehand will save me a lot of time.

Besides, I'm glad for the distraction. Once in the flow, I find myself forgetting Luke is even there. Tapping a last line, I look up momentarily. Luke has his headphones on. He's staring out at the scenery; the vibrant golden light of the closing sun settles across his concentrating face. I try not to stare. I try not to feed it. I quickly tap open the next file and begin to click through the footage making notes.

A pat on my shoulder. Cleo holds a menu up, indicating back to a man taking orders. I lift a headphone ear so I can hear what she's saying.

'I'm getting the pad thai – what do you want?'

I scan the options. 'I'll get the same.' I hand it back and refocus on my task.

A table between us is pulled out the side of the carriage as the food arrives, and I continue watching, writing notes and transcribing, as I scoop noodles into my mouth, occasionally looking up to see Luke, with a hand on an open book. His other elbow is on the table, chopsticks in hand. Then pensively looking outside, thinking. He catches me, and I blush, quickly averting my eyes.

Cleo, Duncan and Reggie are chatting away, drinking some beers. I should probably be social and join in. But I can't bring myself to make small talk with Luke in front of the others. It becomes intense so quickly. Cleo will be able to tell.

After dinner the train worker walks back through, turning all the seats into bunk beds. I stand hugging my laptop to my chest as I watch him perform the miraculous switch. I hadn't realised that because Luke and I were sitting opposite each other, we would be sharing a bunk.

'Top or bottom?' Luke asks, leaning on the mattress of the top rung.

I swallow thickly. 'Bottom.' My voice cracks. I chuck my laptop on the mattress and scuttle inside. Cleo and Duncan are sharing the bunk opposite, and Reggie is a bit further back. We could be on a tour bus. Clutching my toothbrush and a bottle of water, I go through to the toilet and take my make-up off and wash up. I yank my sticky vest off; using a wetted tissue, I mop away the moisture collected under my pits. Then put on the biggest, baggiest T-shirt I have with me.

I'm tilted from side to side as I walk back through the moving train to my bed. I leap inside, giving the black silhouetted scenery one last look before shutting the curtain.

I double the flimsy pillow over on itself and lie back, staring up at the bowed mattress above. The train rocks me, and the sound of its gallop causes my lids to close. And somehow, I manage to sleep.

My eyes flutter open as I feel someone slide in behind me. I gasp silently. He nuzzles into the scoop of my neck, and I close my eyes. His smell is overpowering. His arms skate around me, pulling me close. I feel his lips skim the soft skin below the back of my hairline, not quite kissing the most tender part of my neck.

'I'll go if you want me to,' he whispers.

I don't move, I just give a tiny shake of my head. 'Don't go,' I murmur.

My whole body aches. We lie there, paralysed.

It feels more real and raw than any encounter of my life.

30

When I wake, buttery morning light escapes through the curtains, the fabric swaying in motion with the train. There is the chugging noise, and the odd hoot of the horn. The narrow space behind me is empty, but I turn anyway, and stare at the creases in the sheet made by him. I tentatively touch my lips, and my nostrils flare at the thought of his breath on my bare skin. I sit up, raising my knees to my chest, holding myself tight. Laying a cheek on the top of my knees, trying not to let go of the magical feeling. Even though I feel an internal thrust to banish it away.

I yank the curtain back and watch hazy light fall on paddy fields. A huge blue mountain looms in the distance. I stare out at it, thinking about the film, and all the people who've put their trust in me. And how I am failing all of them. All at once that magical feeling I had wrapped around me like a cloak disappears and is replaced with revulsion and shame.

About half an hour later, I hear train staff coming through the carriage, waking people up and turning bunks back into seats.

178

I think then of Mari and Luke, twenty years ago. The intoxicating flutter of the next part of their adventure beckoning. Journeying far from the international airport and cosmopolitan capital city straight into the rural depths of this land. Coming out at coastlines, and palm trees, and horizons with foily ripped red and orange sunsets.

Mari's face flashes in my mind. I've barely given her a second thought since we touched down. I feel dirty, like I'm cheating on her, with him.

By the time I'm sat opposite Luke again, I feel his brooding eyes trying to connect with mine, but I refuse. I look at his balled-up fist on the arm of his chair. He gets up and brushes past me with such force, I feel like I've been kicked in the stomach.

It is funny how much can be said without saying a word.

'Did you sleep okay?' Cleo asks, as she crouches next to me, looking up kindly.

I nod at her. 'Yes – much better. The train rocking helped, I think.'

'There, you've found a solution!' She laughs. I smile at her. She's so sweet.

'What's the plan for when we get there?' I ask. 'Have we got someone picking us up?'

She pulls up the call sheet on her phone and replies. 'Yes, a minivan is taking us to the port and then a short wait until we get on the ferry.'

Luke sits back down, a few drops of water still on his neck from splashing water on his face.

I kick into director mode, forcing myself to shed the skin of all that other stuff and play the part. 'Great. Luke, if it's okay with you, we'll shoot you disembarking the train and the journey onto the ferry. We'll hang back. I might ask you a few questions. You know the drill by now.'

He looks away, grimaces slightly. 'Sure.'

Panic flutters in my chest as Cleo mics him up. Whatever this thing between us is, it needs to stop. I'm putting my career – and my precious film – in jeopardy. *It's okay, I can regain control. We haven't done anything wrong. Yet.*

Once at the port, we follow Luke onto the ferry. 'Again, it's different. New boats, I guess,' he muses, scratching the back of his head. His voice deflated and unenthusiastic. He gives the camera a side glance. We're not going to get much out of him today, I can tell. Once we've got onto the island, we'll call it a day. He can rest and get himself together for the next chunk of filming. I'll have a talk with him, sort all this out. And we'll move on.

We film Luke entering the hold and taking a seat and get a few shots of him as we set off. 'I think, let's stop there. Have a break. We'll go again on the approach,' I tell Cleo, handing her the monitor, collecting my headphones, and handing them over too. She nods, and I head to the bathroom. The door knocks back on itself, and I put my hands around the small metal sink for balance. I look at my reflection in the dirty mirror. *Get a grip.* I need to get a handle on this. I feel depleted in his presence.

A vibration and I check my phone. Raef: **Are you on the island yet? Good luck. Don't take any roofies and get lost in a rave 😄. How's Luke? Has he said anything that has surprised you yet?**

I sit down on the toilet bowl, and start a reply: **I feel like I'm losing control of this** . . . but then quickly delete it. I know he wants the money shot. The charming psychopath who finally reveals himself. But that isn't happening. There is no way Luke is that person.

I'd never feel like this if he was.

Once I've been gone longer than I should, I unlock the door and find the others. They're sat together on a cluster of seats. I take the one next to Cleo and get involved in the chat. Luke tells a story about an ill-fated ferry ride they took where everyone got seasick, and the journey became a chorus of vomiting noises. I mimic the others' laughter, unsure how to behave any more around them all, now.

I wake to whoops and squeals of excitement from young travellers on the ferry. I look out the window, covered in spots of saltwater, at the view of land ahead.

A rock in the ocean.

I glance at Luke. His seat is empty, his mic pack and wire discarded. I look around but can't see him anywhere. I head out to the deck. There he is, leant forward staring at the island.

'Are you okay?' I call above the sound of the motor. He doesn't reply, or even turn around. 'Luke?'

He stays very still, and I can only just make out what he's saying. 'I just feel . . .'

181

I take a few steps closer. 'What?'

He turns swiftly. 'Sad, Cassidy. I feel sad.' The force in his voice makes me nervous to continue.

'That's understandable . . .' I say, gesturing to the island, beginning the line I run to every time, that seems to quell his fears. But before I can continue, he bites back.

'No. It isn't *that*, Cassidy.' My lips move, but he jumps in first. 'No, it's not whatever you're about to say either,' he dismisses. 'You think you can talk anyone around anything, don't you?'

I look behind me to check no one can see this heated discussion. Cleo is deep in conversation with Duncan. He's pointing to some of the bags, looking upset.

Luke walks towards me. 'Because that isn't it. Whatever you are about to say.' His eyes are red and swollen. 'Of course I'm sad because something happened to the girl I loved and coming here started that in motion. I wish her life wasn't ruined, I wish her parents' lives weren't ruined, and my mum's too. I know it's selfish and I'm still alive and I should be grateful. But my life was ruined too. I thought I couldn't ever feel worse than I did, but I was wrong . . . this . . . this is worse.'

My mouth gapes, mind racing – how to solve this? All I can think of is Mari's cheeky crinkled nose juxtaposed against her dark bloody drawings. 'Luke. If there is anything about Mari you haven't told me . . . if there is something that will help your case, you have to—'

'Mari? Mari? For once this isn't all about Mari.' He pauses.

182

'Every time I like someone, I think they'll never like me back. In the back of their minds, they're always going to suspect me of this thing. Always.' He looks directly at me then. 'I can never just be me. Tell a girl I like her, that I want her. And that I want her to want me.' Our eyes lock. 'And you know exactly what I'm talking about, Cassidy.'

My lips part. Agony. Trying to find the right words, but I have none for this. My shoulders fall. Duncan rushes outside, the camera on his shoulder. Cleo darts ahead to put the mic pack back on Luke. They look at me nervously, worried they've missed an important piece of filming. But I'm just relieved they didn't catch anything he said.

Luke leans against the bar, staring out onto the island. I let the others film him, and I sink behind them feeling sick. I need to resolve this before we leave the island. I can't go to the jungle with him like this.

183

31

The minivan pulls up outside our resort, and we jump out onto the dirt road. I stand with Luke as Reggie and Duncan grab the kit from the boot. Cleo is talking to the concierge. Everyone is preoccupied.

'Luke, we need to talk,' I tell him, quietly.

He nods. 'We should,' he replies.

This is my fault, I've let it spiral. We're dealing with big emotions making this. None of them should be mine. Luke is in a vulnerable state – I should never have let it get this far. This is on me.

I hear a sob and look across the road – a young girl crying into her friend's shoulder. She must be about eighteen; wiping tears, talking to her friend. 'But someone stole all my stuff. My bag had my passport in.' Mascara runs down her face, and she's holding a solitary flip-flop in her hand. Her knee is grazed. Completely bedraggled after a night out. I watch the two girls hug and then walk away, the crying girl laying her head on her friend's shoulder as they wander slowly down the track, through an arch of palm leaves, back towards the beach.

'Cass,' Cleo calls, 'our rooms are ready.'

My phone vibrates. 'Okay, coming,' I reply, looking down at the email that's just come through. It's from Alice. She's asking me to call her, saying she's got something she wants to discuss. I tap a reply quickly, telling her to name a time.

Our resort is a complex of huts the other side of Haad Rin, the party beach, where the more exclusive hotels are. Tucked away from the booming music and excited drunk kids, all high, and snogging, I assume, feeling very old indeed.

I like my 'hut'. It's got a large bedroom with a little sofa area, and an outdoor shower at the back. After the long journey I'm glad to be outside, water falling on me, with the stars above. It feels very restorative.

I've sent Cleo out with Duncan to get some evening shots of the revellers. Travellers partying, flame throwers and dancing. The wasteful hedonism of middle-class youth. Basically, establishing shots of the atmosphere to capture the essence of the place and lay out this point of their story in the film.

Duncan was thrilled as he wanted to get his drone out and film some evening aeriel shots of the beach. Tomorrow is the full moon party; I'll feel a sense of relief when that's in the bag and ticked off our list. I've spent the run-up with a tendril of worry we'd miss a train, or something would happen, and we wouldn't get here in time and Raef would be furious.

I pull the light cotton robe around me and check the time; Alice should call any minute. I keep my phone in my hand as I pad around the room, organising my things. Finally, five minutes late, it rings.

'Hi,' I say, trying to sound relaxed. 'Alice.'

'Cassidy. Sorry, my meeting went over.'

'No problem. Thanks for getting back in touch.' I wait.

'I haven't been able to stop thinking about our conversation. I'd managed, over the years, to compartmentalise what happened to Mari and Luke. We all have, I think.' This sounds interesting. 'There was so much media attention around what happened.' She sighs. 'We were all complicit in a lie. Mari . . . Mari wasn't the girl they made her out to be in the press after they went missing. But none of us felt like we could say anything. Who wants to shit on a girl who's missing in the jungle? And Mr and Mrs Castle were so devastated. So, we all just sort of kept our mouths shut. And the papers were all filled with this trash about Mari being this perfect angel head girl. And we all thought, let them have that. You know? Their daughter is missing, probably dead, let them live in denial about who she really was, if that makes it easier.' She keeps going, as if now she's started, she can barely stop to take a breath. 'We all liked Mr Castle, a lot. He was like this eccentric professor who knew how to have a joke even when you'd been dragged up to his office for some reason or another. He was fair, and wanted us all to do well, we could tell that was genuine. But with Mari – he just fell apart. If she was anyone else, she'd have been expelled years before. But she was the apple of his eye, and we knew if we touched her, even a misunderstanding, she wouldn't think twice about making something up about

186

us. He'd do anything for her, quite protective really. She was his Achilles heel, I guess. So, it sounds bad, but we gave her a wide berth. We'd seen her turn on people before and didn't want that to happen to any of us. She even got a teacher fired once, inflating an accusation that she'd pushed her over. All because the teacher wouldn't bend the rules for her.'

'What about Luke?' I ask, transfixed.

She sounds sad now. 'Luke was a great guy. Worked hard, was friends with everyone from the alphas to the nerdier kids. He balanced us all out. Everyone had time for him. Which is why we all felt uneasy when Mari set her sights on him. He wasn't stupid, but just sometimes was too nice, you know? Wouldn't see the bad energy, wanted everyone to be what they projected. Even if it wasn't true.

'When Luke's dad died, we all went to the funeral. I remember thinking how weird Mari was, like she wanted to own the grief. Luke had to be the one comforting her. As if she couldn't stand the attention being on him or something.

'When . . . when they went missing and Mr and Mrs Castle put all this stuff out in the media about her – the perfect daughter, the head girl – we felt so terrible for them. We all went along with the fantasy. We felt as though it was the least we could do. As the weeks went on, we realised they were most probably dead. And thought if this is the spiel her parents need to put out there to get through it, then fine. You can't exactly go to a reporter and say, yeah, this girl was a spiteful and malicious bitch, can you? Why would we? We just went along with it whenever anyone asked about her.'

I'm reminded of the wary looks Mari's parents gave each other when discussing their daughter. 'But she was the head girl?'

'The teachers voted. Not us,' she replies simply.

'You think Mr Castle rigged that?' I ask, dumbfounded.

'As I told you. He was wrapped around her little finger. Another man under her spell. He adored her.'

I frown. This is so at odds with everything Luke has told me in his interviews. He's never described Mari as anything close to this. Why would he still be perpetuating a lie? Is he still under this spell, twenty years later?

'What was she like to Luke?' I ask quietly.

She sighs. 'He levelled her out a little and she became a lot easier to be around. But those last few years . . . I don't know. I got the impression he would do anything she asked. He got thin; he was less outgoing. But his dad was dying, and it was a tough time for him. Who really knows what went on behind closed doors in that relationship.'

'Alice, would you talk about this on camera?'

An awkward pause, a sharp intake of breath. 'I need to think about it. I'm nervous about . . . putting myself out there. Telling people things they don't want to hear. They'll think I was jealous of her or something. Especially as everything we said at the time contradicts all this.'

'Thank you, Alice, for talking to me. Do think about it. I think the more of the truth we can get out there, the more likely people will see Luke for who he really is. You want that, don't you? He's had so much of the blame thrown his way.

People assuming he was some sort of aggressor. But this may make people question that.'

'I'll think about it,' she replies quietly. We say our goodbyes and hang up the phone. I stand there thinking about all the interview I've shot with Luke. How nothing he's said even questions Mari's character. In it she is perfect. He has stuck to the script – like everyone else.

Why?

A few minutes later, there is a quiet knock on my door. 'Hello?' I call, walking towards it. Maybe they're back from filming already. I look at the time, annoyed as they've not been out long.

'Cassidy?' Oh. It's Luke.

I tug at the straps of my robe, bringing it around me and tying with a forceful yank. I open the door. He stands there, looking refreshed, wearing beige shorts and a white T-shirt.

'Hi, Luke. What can I do for you?'

'Can we talk?' he asks, gesturing into my room. I look back into my private space. 'Let me get dressed, and I'll meet you in the bar?' I reply, edging the door closed.

'Cassidy, please. Just a minute?' I relent and let him in.

'I don't know why I wanted to do this,' he says, once the door is closed. 'Come back here. Make this film.' He paces, hands cupped together.

'Luke . . .' I begin.

'I thought . . . I thought telling my story would somehow make people see that I would never hurt her. That I loved her.' He looks at me. Has he been . . . crying?

'Luke,' I say, thinking of my call with Alice. 'Was Mari . . . was she really . . . ?'

He looks at me sharply. 'What?'

I wonder why he is still protecting her after all these years. After everything that's happened. What did she do to him? What did he do to her? The question lingers in my mind. 'Was Mari ever . . . was she ever nasty to you?' I ask.

He shifts on the spot. 'What do you mean?'

'You've always said how well you got on. But was there a power dynamic?' I step forward. 'Did you ever feel manipulated by her?' I try.

He looks at me intensely, mulling it over. 'Cassidy. I don't know what you're getting at.' He shakes his head. 'No. Never. Why?'

I study his face, looking for anything that contradicts what he is saying.

It begins to rain. The flimsy curtain hanging over the open window shivers.

'I couldn't do this without you,' he whispers. 'If the best thing to come out of this is meeting you, I guess that is good enough.'

I shake my head. 'Luke, we must focus on making the film. Anything we think we are feeling, it's just the intensity around this journey we are on. We . . . we need to leave it behind now. Okay? It will jeopardise this film. Do you understand?'

He looks away, his jaw clenched. But he nods. 'Yes. I know you're right.' He pauses, as if he's going to say something else, but decides against it. We hear laughter and shouting from those outside who've been caught in the rain. 'I should go.'

I nod. 'Yes.'

He looks at me sadly. Then walks to the door, pulling it open, stepping out into the deluge. The heavy rainfall bashes out a greenhouse mist that rises from the ground. His shoulders are quickly sodden, his T-shirt turns opaque. He begins to walk and then stops, turning back around. 'Cassidy, you think I'm doing the right thing?' he calls over the sound of the storm.

'I do … But only if you're telling your truth, Luke. Otherwise – what's the point? Whatever happened, and your reasons for it – you need to be honest.' He nods sadly and backs further into the monsoon then begins a light jog to shelter.

I stand watching him disappear out of view. Struck by sadness or dread, maybe both. I close my eyes briefly and shiver, remembering the feeling of his breath on the back of my neck, and the new version of Mari I now have whispering in my head.

32

The night of the full moon we're out en masse, filming. Music pumps from every angle and cackles reverberate as revellers dance down the strip holding hands. I had low expectations that this would be some sort of spiritual mecca like the name 'full moon' suggests. And now I'm here they've sunk further. This is high consumerism. Sell, sell, sell. Giant Coca Cola signs, 7Elevens, leaflets being handed out for various after-party raves. This tropical paradise is now overbuilt and overused. A theme park version of what was here before. Young travellers are cash cows being wrung dry, and I don't blame them for it.

The hut complex where Mari and Luke stayed in 2002 is no longer here. Instead, there is an unappealing concrete building with a dirty hotel sign. We film Luke standing outside, telling us such.

Next, we walk out onto the beach, filming the screams and laughter. A *Full Moon Koh Phangan* sign is lit up in flames that reflect into the dark shallow waters. Shirtless teenagers covered in luminous paint gyrate hungrily onto one another.

We try to get the shot I wanted, of Luke in the middle of

the crowd with the party going crazy around him. I'm not sure it's going to work, after all. They moon their naked bums at the camera, shouting, 'Hi, Mum!' as they pass, being idiots. But maybe that's the point.

'Let's just go down to the spot on the beach where you asked Mari to marry you,' I suggest to Luke. We walk to the quieter end of the cove and Luke points and shifts around. Swallowing as he stares out at the breaking waves, as stars twinkle impossibly bright against the blotted navy sky. He recounts the story. His words are stilted, hard to get out. He isn't enjoying this. He must feel on show with a camera crew following him surrounded by these hyena-like youths.

We walk over to the bar the couple used to frequent, and where a photo was taken on the night of the full moon in 2002. I have a copy of it on my phone and get Duncan to set up a shot at the exact distance and angle. Then we film Luke having a solitary drink in the same spot.

'You want to get anything else?' Cleo asks, shaking her arms out from the exertion of reaching over heads with the boom. I look around. I think we've captured enough of this. The whole thing is making me feel quite depressed. Maybe you need to be eighteen to appreciate it. Although I'm not sure I would have. But I was different to other teenagers. I never really understood socialising, or boys, growing up. When I did make it to a gathering or house party, I never knew how to act, and always ended up with regrets.

'I think we've got enough,' I say, turning to Cleo. 'I'm afraid it would be good to get some of the party as the sun comes up.

The morning after, walks of shame, that sort of thing, so we can get a sense of how terrible Mari felt the morning after.'

Cleo nods, enthusiastic as always. She likes filming when I'm not around as she can play at director and is the sort to grab an opportunity. 'Sure, I can do that with Duncan.'

'Great.' I smile.

Luke comes over to us as we pack up. I take a cursory look back at the table in the bar, thinking. 'Did you lose the other disposable camera?' I ask, remembering the receipt.

'Sorry?'

'There were two cameras – Mari bought a twin pack. I found the receipt for it in her bedroom.' Cleo gives me a funny look. Like she can't understand why I'm so stuck on it.

'You went into Mari's room?' he says, stunned.

'They haven't touched it since she went missing.'

I observe him as he thinks back. He must have so many memories of being there. Making out on her bed, or Mari drawing his portrait as a playlist he put together played softly in the background.

He looks out at the water. 'I have no idea about the camera. It was twenty years ago, Cassidy,' he says, shutting down.

I frown, a new frustration building. *I know you're holding back.* I think of my conversation with Alice. I know he's hiding something about Mari, unless . . . was he so blinded by who his girlfriend really was?

We pack up. Tomorrow we're heading to the mainland and catching the train for the even longer journey up to the jungle, which is way past Bangkok in the other direction. Raef was explicit he wanted us to take the exact route they did, to keep this trip as authentic to Luke's maiden voyage as possible. Luke and I begin to walk back to the hotel. Our shoulders knock together as we walk down the dirt track. I take a faster stride, to gain some space.

It feels relatively calm when we enter the foyer of the reception building. Everyone is at the party. Even the residents staying in this more exclusive resort wouldn't have come to the island, over full moon, if they hadn't wanted to partake. We walk silently through the main building, leaving Cleo chatting to Duncan as he rolls a cigarette out front, discussing a meeting point for a few hours' time when they'll shoot the early morning GVs.

Luke and I walk silently out the other side of the reception area, past the dark rippling swimming pool, to the complex of huts on the other side. I try to walk slightly ahead, so I can take the turning to my room, and wave him goodbye from a distance.

'Cassidy.' I turn. A few metres, but a chasm between us. 'Can I come with you?' he asks.

I should say no. That would put us in a dangerous space.

'Luke . . .'

'I don't want to be on my own . . .' he says, swallowing.

'Luke, I'm really tired.'

'Just for a bit, just to decompress before I go to bed. I won't stay long.'

'Luke.' I say his name begrudgingly, hoping it will deter him.

'Cassidy,' he repeats in the same tone, with a cheeky lean, and I smile.

I sigh. 'One quick beer,' I relent.

He looks pleased, grins, and then joins me walking towards my hut. I glance behind, to make sure none of the others noticed.

My hand shakes as I unlock the door. I turn on the light and begin sorting messy piles of things. Luke opens the minibar, grabs a couple of bottles and it knocks closed with a muted thud. He cracks them open and takes a long sip, as he hands me the other. 'I think you've got a nicer room than mine. I'll have to nudge Melissa,' he says, a cheeky glint in his eye.

I take a glug of beer. 'I wasn't expecting you to go all diva on me, Luke,' I shoot back.

An awkward pause, as he turns around the room, looking at my things. 'How do you think the filming's going?'

I take another long sip, enjoying the cool popping liquid, licking my top lip before answering. 'I think it's going well, Luke. I think the viewers will find it gripping. Lots of jeopardy,' I explain.

'Jeopardy,' he repeats, slowly, considering the word. 'You use that word a lot.'

I laugh. 'Do I?' He nods. 'I suppose I do. It's very "TV". Well, we've talked a lot about wanting lots of bums on seats for this. And a device used to keep people invested and gripped in a story is ramping up the jeopardy.'

'And what's the jeopardy here?'

I think for a moment, careful with what I want him to

196

know. 'I suppose the fact we still don't have a lot of the story at this point.'

'The jungle,' he muses. 'Will Luke Speed dish the dirt?' He takes another swig of beer. 'I get it.' He nods. 'A ticking clock.'

I purse my lips. I don't really want him to know what I'm thinking, as it may break the fourth wall for him, and it's important, as the contributor, that he reacts naturally to whatever is ahead, so it doesn't come off contrived.

We're standing at either end of the room. Fireworks go off in the distance. He takes a step towards me. I put my beer down. The fireworks keep going, *pop, pop, pop*. Then the main lights to the room flicker, threatening to go off. I move a hair from my face and look over at him. We stare. Fixated. From opposite sides of the room. 'Luke,' I start. A pathetic attempt to ward him off. He steps forward. *Pop, pop*. Flicker. It's as though a magic spell is being cast.

Now there is but inches between us. A deep thudding in my chest. He's taller than me, by nearly a foot. The flickering lights finally die, and we are bathed in darkness. It feels like a sign. As if we've been covered, hidden. Like we are no longer here at all. He delicately places a hand on my cheek, and I can't help but raise my chin. Anticipation builds as he lowers his face towards mine. I close my eyes.

Finally, our lips connect, and I let out this tiny involuntary moan. I think I've secretly wanted this from the very first time I saw him. No, maybe earlier. Since I heard his voice on the phone. He takes my hand; our fingers dance as they intertwine. And we go to the bed. Sitting on the edge kissing, becoming hungry and urgent, as though this is more important than breathing. He pulls at the straps of my white vest, and I flap away his hands, so I can quickly pull it off, over my head. Removing my bra, I watch his eyes fall on my breasts for the first time. 'Are you sure you want this?' he asks.

I can't think about that now, all I can think about is him. Wanting all of him. I don't answer, I just dive towards him. Throwing my arms around his shoulders and kissing his lips. Our tongues twist around each other. Enjoying every second of this sensory overload. I pull at the fabric of his T-shirt, and he lifts it over his back. I gasp as our skin meets for the first time. I can feel him straining from inside his shorts and my fingers shake as I undo them. Holding him in my fist for the first time. I feel drenched in longing for him. I can't think of anything else. All the other times, I've had to fake it. Force myself into it because I thought that's what I should want. Always feeling disappointed afterwards that it didn't leave me wanting more or turn that part of me on. This is different. It is how I've always wanted to feel but I've never even had a taste of it.

The moment when he is about to enter me, our eyes lock. And he asks me again, 'Are you sure?' And I grab him, pulling his lips towards mine.

33

The next day it rains. Not showering thundery monsoon rain, I don't think I would have minded that. This is more akin to grey London drizzle. The others are exhausted, having been up since four a.m. filming. But this suits me fine. I couldn't cope with enthusiastic chatting, not today. I just want to silently stare into the abyss. I'm spiralling in panic – electrified by the impulse to run towards what is lethal and all-consuming. I've never wanted to self-destruct before; I've never understood why you'd want to give up the comfort of control. I get it now.

We pile onto the ferry back to the mainland. The undulating movement makes me feel sick. I ask Cleo if she wants to direct the transition, and she nods, pleased, as I hang back sipping watery coffee from a polystyrene cup. Completely closed off. Hot flashbacks. Catastrophising consequences. But what my mind seems stuck on is that phone call with Alice, and what she told me about how Mari bewitched Luke and clung on to him like driftwood. I dare a look over at him. He's desperately uncomfortable being filmed today. He is trying to be polite and nice to Cleo, I can tell. What could Mari possibly still have on him that he can't be honest about her, twenty years later? Can I . . . am I . . . the one that will finally break that spell?

I avoid him on the train, and make sure I'm sat with Cleo this time around, so we share a bunk. I can feel him trying to catch my eye, but I refuse. How can two people be so very close, and then so very far apart in such a short space of time? I see a fluttering movement in front of my face and realise Cleo is waving to get my attention. I hope she doesn't start asking about the film. I'm can't think clearly about it now, I'm muddled by all this other stuff. Last night – and Alice. What does it mean? What have I done?

'Cassidy,' she says, leaning forward, lowering her tone. 'All good? You still seem distracted.' Her eyes interrogate mine, and I wish we weren't stuck in this carriage so I could walk away.

'I'm fine,' I deflect quickly.

She shakes her head, and her voice lowers to a whisper. She leans forward. 'There's this thing about Luke I can't put my finger on. He's hiding something.'

I swallow. She's right. He is. But it's not what she thinks.

'We need to be careful, in the jungle, Cass – we don't know what he's capable of and—'

'Cleo, it's okay,' I say swiftly.

Her neck jumps back, as though I've smacked her. 'What if it isn't? Cass – you must see it too. He's . . . he's . . .' She tries to find the words. 'We're about to go into the jungle with him. The last place his girlfriend was seen alive. Aren't you scared?'

I look at her. She has no idea what's been going on behind her back. She's got this all wrong.

'Cleo. I'll do the big thinking around here. You stick to your job, okay?'

She blinks. A nod. 'Okay. Whatever you want, Cass,' she stammers, pausing before getting up and charging to the toilets. I hear a sob. *Urg.* I wipe a layer of sweat off my brow. Feeling terrible.

The next morning, we change trains in Bangkok, and everyone gets involved in their own methods of passing time. Books, films and work. Aside from filming en route, I do everything I can to avoid Luke and his brooding eyes. By the time we make it up north I am exhausted by it. I wish I could run away from this. But how can I run from myself?

It is the next day, and we are at a police station in Chiang Mai province. I've left Luke at the guest house with Cleo. Duncan and Reggie are far easier to be around right now. Cleo felt relegated, I could tell, but I told her that spending some time with Luke, calming him before we hit the jungle, is an incredibly important task.

The Deputy Commander-in-Chief of Provincial Police Region 5, who has been given permission to speak to us, sits behind his desk. A pile of papers in front of him in an old-fashioned wire tray. He is a large man; his tight khaki shirt bulges. Medals adorn his chest. Sweat runs off his face and he wipes it away with a handkerchief.

'You know how often foreigners disappear on treks? Never!

Very rare for this to happen. They didn't stick to the rules. They went off on their own without telling the guide. The money that we spent trying to find them. Stupid,' he spits. 'We want everyone to be safe. They put themselves in danger. Hundreds of thousands of dollars spent. We had helicopters,' he blasts as we set up. I look at Duncan pointedly and he understands we need to hurry up, we're missing out on a lot of good stuff here. Finally, we're ready, and I hop onto a chair by the camera. Duncan gives me a thumbs up.

'Okay, are you comfortable?' I double check the red dot is alight. The police chief's scowl disappears, and he smiles for the first time since we entered the room. My heart sinks. 'Great, can you tell us the usual protocol when this sort of thing happens?'

'Tourism is very important to this part of the country. We do all we can to safeguard from anything like this happening. As soon as they were reported missing, a huge rescue team launched the search. We liaised with the British embassy. The family. It was a . . . cohesive effort. We were pleased when Luke was found. A breakthrough! We did our best. But we soon understood the story we'd been told wasn't the truth. We'd been misguided. We concluded that the most likely outcome, the real reason for this very unusual situation, was the boy. Couldn't charge him. No body!' He shifts about, his smile forced out further, trying to stop a full on-camera rant. 'We want anyone thinking of coming to visit us to know it is safe here. There are no strange men hiding in the jungle.' He laughs at the idea of it. 'That is an impossibility.'

'But there are nearly five hundred square kilometres of jungle out there. Isn't it possible that something was missed?'

'We never found any evidence of anyone living up there, following them,' he states flatly. 'We have specialist trackers. Best in the world! We spent most of our annual budget trying to find that girl. Nothing. He buried her. Most likely outcome.'

'But you couldn't find any evidence that Luke did something to Mari,' I say pointedly.

'Miss Cassidy, you know as well as anyone that homicide is usually committed by the person who is closest to the victim. Very, very low possibility that it is some stranger with no motive.'

'The evidence, though? Couldn't she have just got lost, died . . . naturally?'

He sighs. 'Then why did he say there was a man?' he asks, cocking his head to one side. 'It doesn't make any sense, does it?' His eyes narrow at me.

'But there is no evidence of any wrongdoing,' I say, standing firm. 'What if he had some sort of mental breakdown . . . ?'

He gives me a look. 'They walked into that jungle together, and only one person came out.' He huffs, looking at the camera. 'Enough. Enough of this. We're very busy.'

'But Deputy Commander Chen, a lot of people may think it is better for you if Luke is the guilty party. You tried your best, I'm sure, but all eyes were on your small team to pull off this investigation . . . You never thoroughly sought out this man, did you?'

I've taken it too far and he's cross. He stands up and pulls his mic off his shirt. I gesture to Duncan to keep filming. 'Are you suggesting that we didn't do our job?' He gives me a furious look. Duncan glances over. 'We may be a small town, Miss Cassidy, but we sent a first-class team.' There is something about the way his eyes shift that makes me think there is more. 'The most likely explanation is the one in your face, Miss Cassidy. That man. We don't want him here. You understand? Don't cause any trouble, do your filming, and then get out.' He slams his hand down on the desk. 'The ending of your film is that he is guilty. Get him to talk, or you are just wasting everyone's time.' He shouts something in Thai to one of his colleagues. I nod at Duncan, signalling to cut.

The truth of it is, the most convenient outcome for them is that Luke is guilty. It will be hard to open them to other possibilities, the narrative has served them well so far. We are no further along in instigating a new search in the area after this interview. Unless we find something out there, or . . . Luke remembers.

34

It's the next day, first light. I'm standing on the porch of the guest house drinking coffee, looking out at the twitching jungle. All we've talked about the last few months is coming here. This place where civilisation ends, and nature takes over. Where Mari was swallowed whole, never to be seen again.

My heart beats a little faster when I think of Luke. *Bang!* A flashback to his hand gripping mine. Moans of pleasure. I shake my head. Needing a physical action to banish it. If anyone ever found out, or we took it further, the film would be dismissed, and there would be a scandal. My subjective view horribly influenced by these overwhelming feelings. If Raef ever found out, all the trust we've built up and his notion of my ability would be wiped out in a second. There would be a black mark against my name – no one would touch me. Even worse, it's not just my career I've put in jeopardy, but Raef's company and his reputation too.

But Luke. If he is innocent, is there even the smallest possibility this could be something? I let the idea of it play in my imagination for a moment. Him coming to mine, stroking

Herzog before falling into bed. Waking early – croissants and coffee in paper cups from the café around the corner. Laughing as we strolled down Brick Lane. Would he move into my flat? Or would we start afresh somewhere completely new?

'Cass, we're all packed up,' Cleo tells me, pulling me out of my contemplation. I jolt in surprise as her hand touches my elbow. I place my cup down on the breakfast table and follow her around the porch to the front of the house. The van boot is open, and our kit all packed up inside.

'Where's Duncan?' I ask, looking around. Reggie is studying the map. Luke is sat on the steps of the porch looking dazed. Our eyes catch for a second. We both look away. I have kept my distance since we arrived. I need to speak to him and bridge some sort of truce to get through the next few days. Focus on the purpose of this, which is for Luke to finally tell his side of what happened in the jungle between him and Mari, like he's promised.

'He's having an issue with the drone. He'll be back in a minute.' Cleo makes sure Luke is out of earshot. 'How did the police interview go yesterday?' She steps closer.

'He's completely biased, of course. All he cared about was saving the name of the tourist industry around here. Having some nutter in the woods, waiting to jump out and hurt people, isn't the best advert, is it? Maybe they're worried they didn't do all they could to find this man.'

She nods, looking concerned. 'So, you think . . . there could be?' She swallows thickly. 'Someone out there?' She glances over to the thick bush.

I sigh. 'Cleo, it was twenty years ago. We've got nothing to worry about.' I think about Dr Ackerman's theory. 'Besides, it may be something else. Something more nuanced that the police wouldn't have considered. Like the psychiatrist said,' I remind her, squeezing her arm. 'We'll be perfectly safe, we're with Reggie. No one knows this jungle better than him.'

She nods, eyes wide, scratching her bottom lip with her teeth. 'Okay, Cass.' I give another cursory look into the dense jungle and then at Luke. What is this going to do to him? Will he crack? And what will happen if he does?

Duncan storms out the main doors. 'Cass?'

'Yep?' I walk towards him.

'Bad news, I'm afraid.'

'What's up?' He sounds very alarmed, but he often gets het up about things easily rectified.

'The drone is broken,' he says with a pained look.

'Broken?' I say, exasperated. Melissa is going to kill me. 'How the hell did that happen?' He gives me a piercing look and I soften. He'll be just as devastated about this as me. The kit is his thing. He takes a lot of pride in keeping it in top condition.

'What's the footage saying?' I ask, walking over to him, looking down at the screen on his phone.

'It's not very clear. I was testing it this morning.' The footage is a bird's eye view of the nearby jungle. But then it totally collapses. Hurtling to the ground. And then goes black.

'Shit,' I whisper. I look over at Cleo and Reggie. 'Are we

getting a replacement?' Reggie is on the phone. Cleo nods over at him, as if to say, that's what we're doing.

'Because we need it for the next few days. It's important. If we don't, we won't get the main establishing shots of the series: Luke standing on the vantage point.' I can't help the panic bursting through. I almost feel teary with it. Cleo looks taken aback by the strength of my emotion. Up to this shoot, she's always seen me as unflappable.

'Cass. Don't you think I know that?' she replies flatly.

'They seem like they're doing their best,' Luke interjects. I look over at him, open-mouthed at his involvement. And then I feel shamed at his disappointment with how I'm reacting by taking it out on the team.

'Sorry. I know you're doing all you can to get it sorted.'

Reggie gets off the phone and walks over. 'So, we can get a replacement, but it won't arrive until the day after tomorrow.' I rub my lips together, thinking. I need to call Raef. This would mean moving the whole schedule back. New flights. More nights on the ground with all our day rates. Extending expensive kit hire. He won't be happy. I get out my phone and walk away from the group, giving Cleo a flick of a look, so she'll know who I'm calling, and she sends a sympathetic nod in my direction.

It rings out and I begin to leave a voicemail, but he calls back as I'm mid-flow. 'Cass. What's up? You got a confession yet?' He laughs. I don't join him.

'Raef, our drone is broken. It will take two days to get a

replacement. We either wait for it to be delivered – which means an extra two days here and pushing everything back . . .'

'Jeez, Cass.' His jovial tone is gone, and he sounds strained.

I search for a solution. 'Maybe a few of us can go over and wrap the trek and Cleo could bring the drone across—'

He cuts in. 'Melissa wouldn't like Cleo doing that trip alone. I think the risk assessment says crew needs to be doubled up outside of main tourist areas.'

That's the thing about Raef, he comes across as big picture, but he knows exactly where the red lines are, mainly so he can find loopholes to get around them.

'You shoot, don't you?' he asks.

'What?' My shoulders tighten. 'You think I can shoot the most important part of this on my own, whilst trying to get the interview out of Luke, and trekking through a jungle?'

'You've self-shot before.'

'Raef, not for years. Besides, never in an environment like this . . .'

My mind races, thinking of another way to solve this problem. The thought of shooting on my own is giving me heart palpitations. 'What if Duncan came on the shoot and I went with Cleo?' As soon as I utter the words, I know it won't work. Duncan is very talented at making things look pretty, but he could never do the interview with Luke, as he has no idea about the editorial side of things. Besides, Luke won't step one foot in there without me.

'Cass? Are you crazy? No. You and the fixer can go with Luke. And then the others will be able to get close enough with the new drone for the mountain shot by the time you get there on day two. It will be easy. Up and down. Get him to tell you what happened. Drone shoot on the last day. *Boom* – out the jungle and straight back to Bangkok without having to change any flights or add any shoot days. I'm happy, the channel will be happy. You'll be happy. And we'll get this new series commissioned off the back of that.' I hear in his voice it's a done deal.

'Raef . . .' But he's not here. He doesn't understand what a mammoth undertaking this is. But there is part of me that wants to appease him. Wants to prove I can do what he's suggesting – get back to London with the interview in the bag and all the prestige that will go with doing it all on my own. 'Okay. Okay, Raef, I think that will work.' We chat a bit more about logistics before I say goodbye and turn back to the group.

'Okay. We have a plan.' Everyone gathers. Luke hangs back. 'I can shoot, Cleo, you can't. I don't think it's a good idea anyone going into the jungle on their own. We only have three shooting days left – including today. So, Cleo, Duncan, you will stay back and wait for the kit. I'll go ahead with Reggie and Luke.' Eyes blink at me in shock. 'By the time we hit the vantage point you'll be up the river at base camp with the new kit, close enough to film us on the drone.' It only has twenty minutes of battery life before it needs changing over, so has a limited distance it can cover. If they can get it downriver to base camp one, they'll be able to get close enough in range.

Duncan, worried, steps forward. 'Are you sure you can

handle that, Cass? It will be hard work shooting in those conditions.'

I give him a look. 'I'll be fine. I've shot my own films before. Alone,' I say pointedly. He shrugs. But he's right. I've never shot on my own like this.

'Reggie, you know the jungle better than anyone, right?'

'Yes – I've taken many groups out. Not this exact location, but I know the terrain well,' he says with ease which makes me feel like we'll be more than safe in his capable hands.

'Great. Fine. Sorted.' I smile at them to shelve any concerns. 'Problem solved.'

Luke steps forward. 'Wouldn't . . . it be better . . . if there were more of us?' he asks, voice quivering. And I realise he's scared. The more feet on the ground, the thicker the safety buffer will feel, I'm sure.

'We'll be fine, Luke. It's a few days. Reggie is a pro.'

'Okay. If you . . . if you think it's for the best.' He grabs his backpack from the stoop.

Cleo grabs my arm. 'Can I have a quick word?'

'Sure.'

She pulls me over to one side. 'Cass, are you sure? I don't think it's a good idea you're alone with Luke like that.'

'Why? And we won't be alone, we'll be with Reggie.'

'It's *Luke Speed*, Cass. And you're going into the jungle where his girlfriend disappeared under *suspicious circumstances*.'

'Cleo, come on.' I shake my head. 'Has any part of his behaviour worried you since we've got here? Honestly, it's ridiculous.'

'You're going back *there*. Who knows how he'll react? Besides, you'll have to be thinking of all the filming, all the editorial stuff, while trekking in the jungle – possibly with a contributor in meltdown. It's just not fair . . . Raef should never have suggested putting all this on you . . .'

'It's for the film. We need to get this. This is the whole reason we came out here. Besides, I'm one hundred per cent positive that Luke didn't do anything wrong, and he'll be fine. I know how to deal with him.'

'Okay. Well, it's your film. If you think this is for the best.'

She's thinks I'm not taking her seriously. But she has no idea what has been going on behind the scenes.

'Yes, it's the best thing for the film,' I reply, turning swiftly back to the group and clapping my hands together. 'Great. Let's get set up and do this thing.'

35

The van takes us through winding dirt roads, with looming jungle either side. We pull up at a clearing and I look out at the still, olive-green river with an ancient wooden jetty jutting out. This body of water snakes into the centre of the impenetrable jungle where we'll spend the first night at base camp, before beginning the trek the next morning. The burden of what is ahead has settled an apprehensive stillness over the group. I've tried to lift the mood, but my stilted bravado does nothing to hide my nervous interior and in the end, I lean into the subdued atmosphere. Only two days until all of this is over, and I can focus on making the film from the comfort of Soho with one giant piece of the puzzle ticked off.

Over the course of the next forty-eight hours Luke will finally divulge what happened out here between him and Mari in the run-up to her disappearance. I can go back to Herzog, and my flat, and my normal life – and I'll lock away what happened between us for ever. I can pretend that none of this ever happened. Make my film and move on to the next.

A wave of dread. Who am I kidding? How can anything ever be normal again?

I wish I could close my eyes and open them again and be on the other side of this.

A long wooden boat with faded pink and blue paint is tied to the end of the jetty. It looks like it's seen better days, and my heart sinks. There is a dirt-smeared motor at the back with a cheerful Thai flag sticking unwittingly from it. I help yank some of the kit out of the boot and trudge down the short path. Reggie hops inside and Duncan hands him bags which he anchors into the centre using elasticated rope. I watch as he lines up the two machetes, securing them tightly. The sun reflects off the blades, and I feel a wave of fearful sickness.

This all feels very real. I look at the van longingly, wishing I could run back. Refuse to do it. But we've come too far, and I have no choice but to press ahead.

The rest of the camping equipment and camera kit are loaded, and I stare at the mound of responsibility there. It's going to be tough thinking about the mechanics of filming, whilst also staying on top of the editorial, not to mention the physically draining walk. Hopefully I'll be so distracted and involved in the minutiae of that, I won't have time to think of what happened between me and Luke on the island.

Luke steps into the boat and winces as he looks into the jungle on the other side of the water. He's not said much all day. No wonder. How will hindsight judge this? I almost laugh then. I'm building this up to be something far bigger than it needs to be! A short trek in the jungle – thousands of people do this across the world every year and are completely fine.

Cleo steps towards me. The planks of wood below her feet creak. 'Check in with me every evening, okay?' She presses the satellite phone hard case into my hands. Our mobile phones won't work once we get a few miles from here. And I'll need to find a clearing between the canopy to get this one to connect.

'I'll see you on the dock at the base camp in two days,' I tell her. Her eyes are filled with worry. 'Stop looking so stressed! It's going to be fine.' I grin at her. 'Just don't get too drunk on those buckets,' I say, and she allows a laugh to escape. 'And I want my tapes transcribed,' I remind her. 'I don't want to find all you've achieved is a great tan,' I tease, but I'm not worried, Cleo is a hard worker and I feel terrible I've short-changed her during this production. I'll make sure she gets her dues – I'm even considering giving her the first producer credit I know she's desperate for.

Reggie holds out a hand and helps me into the boat. The skin on his fingers and palm rough like sandpaper. Reassuringly worn, like every challenge and lived experience has left a mark. I smile at him in his leather cowboy hat, feeling comfortable going into the unknown with him. This whole trip he's quietly got on with what's needed doing. Never causing a fuss. Ironing everything over wherever we've gone. I trust him completely and would never have agreed to this if it weren't for him.

The boat rocks underfoot, messing with my balance, and I

sit down quickly to avoid falling. Luke goes to sit behind me. 'You go up front,' I order. I'll be filming our ascent into the jungle, and I want him at the bow. We shuffle around each other awkwardly. His hand touches my arm and I stare at the spot as though it's left a burn.

We set off. The motor makes a little *puh-puh-puh* noise as we slice through the stagnant water. I watch Cleo and Duncan get smaller and smaller. Something brushes my leg and I blink in surprise and look down to see Luke's finger gently stroking my ankle. I pull my foot away; my eyes narrow and I shake my head at him roughly. He turns back, wounded. How is he ever going to feel comfortable exposing what really happened to them out here with our relationship so strained? I need to talk to him once we get to base, discuss how we need to maintain some sort of professionality to get through this shoot. Then I'll deal with it properly once we're back.

I film our slow expedition into the depths of this wilderness. The sun shines onto the snaking river spliced between the thick canopies. Birds fly across, dipping low, causing delicate ripples. Monkeys jump from branch to branch in an attempt to follow this exciting new development in their environment. I ask Luke to turn around, so his back is facing the bow, and film the intricacies of his face as he takes it all in. I imagine this shot in the film. Viewers watching him haunted by a veil of loss as memories flicker.

Every inch we motor through, I feel the disconnect from 'real' life.

'How come tourists don't come up here any more?' I call

to Reggie. Refocusing the camera on him at the back of the vessel, with one hand directing the motor. His eyes ahead as he steers us along.

He touches the peak of his hat as he thinks. 'They used to, even after the failed rescue. I heard that the tourists requesting this hike were those who'd heard of the story and wanted to show off to their friends they'd been here. More recently reports started to come back about strange things in the forest. Stuff was going missing from backpacks. Guides refused to take anyone up this way after a while.'

My smile freezes. 'What?' My arms feel weak. Luke stares at Reggie in disbelief, a look of horror plastered. 'Do you think there could still be someone up there?' I ask.

Reggie shakes his head, smirking. 'Nah. People love a story, don't they? Kids exaggerating – feeding the legend most probably.'

I smile and nod. Yes, that must be it.

After a while, I put the camera on my lap. I can't continuously film. We have three spare batteries. So, four in total that can record about five hours of footage each. That's twenty hours across three days. Should be plenty. Memory cards, another thing I'm going to have to keep an eye on. As usual, I'm incredibly paranoid that I'll lose the tiny plastic squares so have a waterproof Ziploc bag I'll keep around my neck.

Losing them would be the worst thing imaginable. We are insured, but the consequences of having to re-shoot all this makes me shudder.

Sound. Another thing to worry about and ensure is switched

217

on and running. It all sounds simple in practice, but when you're lost in the adrenalin of action, stuff can get forgotten quickly, and I don't have anyone around to nudge me a reminder. I bite my thumbnail, head reeling from everything to remember to fully cover this. The last thing I want is to arrive at the edit without a vital piece of audio or with a shot completely out of focus that I'm desperate to use. Then, out of nowhere, a bigger, darker thought swells.

What if we don't get out?

I almost laugh out loud. That's ridiculous.

I notice Luke watching me and try a reconciliatory smile. We need to park all this and focus on the next few days. I haven't been well. Not sleeping, all those memories from my past haunting me. The emails twisting the knife in. I've dealt with everything terribly and let my personal life erode my professional one. *Stop it*, I demand.

I need to remember who I am, and why I am doing this. Mari. I'm here to find the truth about what happened to her, in the very place that bore witness to it. Luke is finally going to be honest about what happened. And I'm going to capture it.

I check my phone. It hasn't gone offline quite yet, and a few dwindling bars hang on. I flick through the notifications. I fall on a new email from Jamal, and I sit up in surprise at the subject.

Hey, Cass. My mate came through. He said he'd send the file directly to you, like you asked.

218

My breath quickens as my eyes dart across the screen, looking for the email in between all the guff I've been cc'd into. I find it and click. A file attached. 'Mari Castle emails'. In the body of the email:

They are only 'notes to self'. No other traffic to or from.

Another bar of signal is lost. My fingers shake as I quickly download the file onto my phone so that it won't matter later when we're completely off grid.

Licking my lips, I give Luke a cursory look, before I open the first one:

Mari.Castle1984@infinitymail.com
03.07.2002 19:30:21

Hi Mari,

What do you think dying is like? Do you just get turned off, like a switch? Or is there something magical waiting for us? That feels kind of egotistical to me. Out of all the animals and bugs and sea creatures WE have a heaven. And they don't. It just doesn't seem very well thought out. Like, how come only chimps managed the evolutionary path to humans? Why the hell aren't there some sort of ancestors of dolphins trying to sell my dad a car, or a meercat cousin on the board at Microsoft? Why haven't any of them even bridged the gap of intelligence even slightly? Isn't that just a bit weird? Maybe we are aliens. Or maybe there was some truth to that Matrix film.

I've never kept a diary before. But it's been a crazy year, and I'm about to embark on an adventure. So, I thought it was time. I don't want Luke to find it in my bag or catch me writing and ask what it is. So, thought I'd get me a brand-new email addy – how cool is that? A secret CYBER diary. How very new millennium of me.

Poor Luke. I think we both know our relationship has fizzled out. We just don't know how to be without each other yet. We need to learn that bit. Just like how we learnt to be together.

This will be our last adventure together, one last hurrah. Our final resting place. How tragic. But everything must end. Including us. He's all I've known. But no relationship could survive what we went through this year. We've never even talked about it. But it's there the whole time, like a silent ghost trailing us wherever we go.

The thought of him with anyone else makes my insides shrivel and squeeze together. But I need to find the strength to do it. Not just for me. But for both of us.

There is no way we can be together by the time we touch back down in Heathrow. I need to be free.

He doesn't know that, of course.

I think he'd die if he knew.

I promised I'd never leave.

I promised him so much.

But sometimes you need to hurt the ones you love.

Brb! Packing to do.

Breathless, I look up. Luke notes the strange look that must have formed on my face. 'Cassidy, are you okay?'

I swallow thickly. 'Yes.'

Mari. I hold the phone close to my chest. She's come back to tell me her side of the story. Part of me wants to drop my phone in the river and never find out. I know there are secrets waiting to be discovered. My eyes track Luke, wondering what she'll say about him, because I know there's something he's been keeping from me. A whoosh of nausea. I feel it travel up my throat, but I gulp it back down.

'Cassidy,' Luke says, 'are you sure?' He reaches over and places a hand on my knee.

I close my eyes and think of her. *Mari, Mari, Mari. Where did you go?*

What did you do?

Because I feel more than ever that this has far more to do with her than it ever had to do with Luke.

THE HORROR

36

With every pump of the engine, my insides constrict, rendering me stiff with dread. The murky green water pools around the front of the rig. Trepidation lingers. I chug at my water bottle as the persistent noise of the jungle ebbs and flows. I wipe my face with the saggy hem of my T-shirt and proceed to pick the camera out of my lap. If I hold the bulky weight for too long in one position, my arms begin to ache, so I hike it onto my shoulder to alleviate the pressure. My phone burns in my pocket. But I don't dare read on. Luke is so close we are practically touching, and I don't trust my face to stay neutral.

I risk a glance above the monitor at his pensive face. Mari was going to break up with Luke. What if he found out? What if she told him in the jungle and it brought on a rage he'd never encountered before? Could he have seen red and switched?

No. Luke isn't capable of that. Unless . . . Maybe Cleo is right. Maybe he is more dangerous than I have let myself believe. Because of lust. Shame runs through me once more.

Do I even have the ability to have a objective view any more? Another thought kicks in: have I been manipulated? I look at his benevolent face in the monitor as he scans the mangroves and feeding birds. His grey T-shirt, splatted damp, flaps lightly in the breeze. He notices me filming and presses his lips together in a bittersweet smile.

I cough, and ask, 'What's it like being back, Luke?'

He blinks a few times, ruminating. 'I never thought I would be here again,' he croaks, scratching the side of his head; a tic I've come to understand means he's about to say something revealing. 'I remember lying on the boat, going in the other direction, once I'd been found. Realising I really was going home.' He points back the way we've come. 'It was like being carried by angels. Something I dreamt of happening every second I was stuck out there.' He shakes his head sadly. 'I had no idea of the nightmare waiting for me. It wasn't over. It never was.' He looks down at the deck of the boat. Pulling his arms around himself, in a hug. 'I promised myself I'd never come back here.' I zoom in to get a tight shot of his face etched with sorrow. He looks directly at the camera. 'But I have to. For Mari – and her parents. I'm doing this for them. Not for me.'

'We're here,' Reggie calls from the back and the noisy motor is shut off as we drift towards the dock. We fall into an apprehensive silence. The boat knocks into dark damp wood, startling us into action. I look up from the camera screen and over to the cluster of mangroves with roots like witch's fingers dipping into the water. The odd bird squawk rises above the irrepressible hum. The jungle itching with movement from invisible tenants.

The boat sways, and Reggie jumps out and ties it up. Then he reaches his hand to me, and I make the awkward hop across, almost slipping on the waterlogged slimy wood, but he grips me firmly and I find my balance. It takes a minute for the rest of me to catch up and my vision rides in front of my eyes, the jungle dangling.

Reggie begins moving our things from the boat over to the jetty. Luke helps, I film. We only have the basics, and we'll streamline again before the trek, leaving any extras down here, at base camp.

We're setting off at first light tomorrow. Then we have a whole day trekking to reach the second camp where we'll spend the night. Then, on the final day of the jungle shoot, we'll walk up to the vantage point by which time, hopefully, the others will have sorted the drone, and made it up the river to get close enough to fly it up to where Luke will be standing at the top. It is one of the most important sequences of the whole shoot. Raef wants to use it in the opening titles as it will show the scale of the whole series. The endless imposing jungle and how small Luke is compared to it. The perfect set-up to establish what is to come. One man against this vast snake-infested jungle.

The muggy atmosphere licks my body like a slug leaving a trail. The air is oppressively thick, and I need a break. Once I've captured enough of the arrival I sit down on the bank of the river and take off my comfortable well-worn Birkenstocks, replacing them with thick socks and the walking boots production bought me for the hike. Flies buzz feverishly around my head, compounding my claustrophobia.

'Cassidy?' Luke says.

I realise his mic has fallen from its place. 'Hang on.' I hop up and walk over to him, threading my hand up his T-shirt. I can feel the curve of his muscles as my hand reaches up to the neckline. My cheeks flush.

'Are you okay?' he whispers. His face is inches from mine. I nod, unable to speak. Clipping it back on, I take a few steps back, checking its position. 'Cassidy, please – can you even look at me?'

I check Reggie is still busy getting the last of our things out the boat. My pupils slowly make their way up to his. 'Are you ready?' I ask. 'To tell your story? To finally tell me what happened here?'

His voice is hoarse. 'Yes. I told you. I'll tell you everything.' He takes a few steps towards me. 'Cassidy, I . . . I can't stop thinking about you,' he whispers. 'I need to know . . . do you feel the same way about me?'

I shake my head. 'Luke, let's just get through the next few days, and then we'll talk, okay?' He looks frustrated, and I reach my hand out to his and squeeze reassuringly.

Reggie begins walking towards the treeline laden with bags, and I put out a hand to stop him. 'I'll film you guys discovering the path and walking into base camp. Luke, once we get there, if you could talk about the differences now to then, how you feel. All that good stuff. All right?' I raise the camera up, looking at the integrated monitor on the device. Checking it's in focus and it's not overexposed. It's so green everywhere – it's messing with my head. Have I got the colour temperature right? I blink at the screen, blinded by the uniformity of the shade, worried that it's making their faces look a sickly jade.

I lied to Duncan. I haven't shot on my own for ages, and I've never filmed on this particular model before. On the shoot for *Missing*, I had a crew so I could concentrate on the editorial. I'm having to wear at least four hats now: I'm the cameraman, the soundie, the AP and the director. I don't want Luke or Reggie to notice I'm out of my comfort zone. I must keep any insecurities I have around my ability hidden.

I put the headphones on, and my senses dull. All I can hear is Luke's breath and the light patter of his chat with Reggie. The camera dents into my shoulder, the monitor flipped towards me so that I can see the shot. Leaves and branches whip at my legs and arms as I brush past them, and I occasionally glance ahead to ensure the path is clear. I'm realising my main danger will be tripping as it's difficult to check my footing while so focused on what I'm capturing. Two whole days of shooting like this. *Argh*. A wave of heat and I draw a sharp intake of breath to stop myself getting overwhelmed. If Luke can survive out here on his own for months, I can do a few days.

I hang back as I listen to Reggie and Luke navigate through the bush chatting. Luke is talking about the chickens. 'I never managed to catch one. Even when I was half crazed with hunger and would have torn their legs off and bitten straight in, given half the chance.'

I smile as I listen to them talk. That will be a nice line to use. Luke comes across how he usually does, sharp, funny, good-natured. Easy to talk to. Mari's email lingers in my mind, and I press my teeth into the fleshy part of my lip.

A loud squawk and I turn my head up to see a large multi-coloured bird on a branch ahead. It is beautiful, the sound is not. It rattles my head, causing it to throb. The men have stopped talking and I watch as they leave the shadowy path and step into a sharp stream of light. I drop the camera to my side and walk towards them to see what has caught their attention. Base camp. We all stand there staring at the three bamboo huts on stilts with long narrow ladders leading up.

I readjust and take a static shot. 'Reggie, sorry, can you move?' I ask so I can get Luke on his own, rediscovering this place he left behind long ago. One good thing about doing this myself is that I'm not constantly worrying whether Duncan is getting what I want. I'll know exactly what's been shot when I'm looking through footage in the edit.

'Would you mind going back on the path and walking out again?' I ask Luke. 'Just so I can film you coming into the space, from this angle?'

Luke gives me that uneasy look – the one he does when things are slightly produced for the film. 'Sure, Cassidy.' He walks past me and back up the path, humming. I realise it is that Red Hot Chili Peppers song he played on the piano at the school. I lick the sweat off my lip, and I look up at the towering trees. A monkey laughs at me from across the way. A mean, sinister cackle, as if about to play a prank. This place is so beautiful, but also utterly threatening.

Luke walks back into the clearing, and with hands on hips he slowly wanders between the rickety structures. I've only ever seen photographs of the camp which are plastered all over the internet. 'Which one did you sleep in with Mari?' I ask, knowing the answer. He walks over to the central hut and places a hand on one of the stilts. 'See, here?' He points and I walk over. *M&L 4EVA* is cut into the bamboo. I get a close-up.

'And when did you realise you were being followed?' I ask.

He pulls an involuntary grimace. 'Not here. Later, once we were lost.' He swallows like he has a bad taste in his mouth and looks out into the bush. 'The first night I heard him, I just thought it was coconuts dropping, or animals shuffling about.' He coughs. 'But then . . . I heard the laughing.'

I remember reading about this. It cooled my blood and muffled my ears in an instant. Most of the translated report you can tell the detectives think he is lying. The language they use. They're mocking him. He leans on one of the spindly legs of the huts, and I take a few steps backwards to film a wide angle. Then I hit the record button and let the camera fall by my side.

'Right. This is home for the night then,' I say cheerfully, masking my unease.

'I'll get some wood for the fire,' Reggie says.

Luke stands there staring at me. I quickly look down at the camera and pretend to be engrossed in checking the playback. Once I hear Luke walk away, calling, 'I'll help,' I dare to look up.

232

37

Mari.Castle1984@Infinitymail.com
18.07.2002 18:02:32

Hi Mari,

I'm all packed! Spent a small country's GDP in Boots. Got everything on the list I found on that backpacking forum. Mum and Daddy are acting all jittery. They are so uptight. I know they'd prefer me to stay here FOR EVER. There is no way they'd ever let me do anything like this without Luke. He's perfect in their eyes. Daddy keeps muttering, at least you'll be with Luke. Like he doesn't trust my judgement one bit.

Luke is the captain of the football team. Luke wins prizes at the science fair. Luke plays the piano like Chopin. You could literally give him anything and he'd master it. Plus, he is just a nice guy. And it's hard to come by a nice guy at my school. You'd never catch him snogging the drunkest girl at a party. Not like the other boys in my year.

I knew if I got him, Daddy would leave me alone a bit. It took me until the third year of school for him to even look at me. Patience is something I'm good at. I can wait.

Luke has always brought out my good side. I agree, I've mellowed. But Luke's different with me now. It's like he's noticed that, maybe, I don't have a good side. My mask has slipped. Since what happened. I did it for him. Why can't he understand that?

I'm not sure I can even type it here . . . I've never even said it out loud. Sometimes I surprise even myself with what I am capable of.

'Cassidy!' I stuff my phone in my pocket. Luke is standing behind me, holding some freshly cut wood, a small axe in his other hand. My eyes linger on the blade. 'You look like you've seen a ghost,' he says, chuckling.

I grin. 'Sorry, just saw an email Raef sent earlier. You know what he can be like.' I walk over to the fire pit: a blackened ditch in the ground between the huts. Reggie is bent over, with a lighter, gently blowing into the cluster of wood. A delicate stream of smoke now flows from it.

Afternoon is melting into evening. The inescapable drill of crickets clicking follows us around. I watch Luke, thinking about Mari's words, wondering what secret he shared with her. What did she do to him? Could it be why he's still lying about her now?

Protecting her – or maybe himself?

I take out a hard-boiled sweet I swiped from the hotel

reception counter and untwist the plastic slowly before sliding it between my lips. As the sugary bullet sweats in my mouth a plan appears. I know what I'll do. During the interview, once he begins to open up about what happened here, I'm going to ask him what this big secret Mari was hiding is.

Surprise him with it.

He has no idea I know anything about it. He'll be so startled, he'll give himself away. And I'll be right there, with the camera focused tightly on his face. Shock and awe.

He looks up at me and smiles, and I feel cruel for plotting. It passes quickly. This is for his own good. He needs someone, me, to unlock the gate of the cage he's been sealed within for twenty years. Whatever Mari did, whatever happened here, he needs to stop protecting her and tell the truth. It is the thing that will finally free him. It has to be.

'Right. Shall we go over the next few days?' I say.

Reggie pulls out the map. It was hard to procure; we had to apply for it at the local district office. It has ground elevations marked and everything. Reggie's finger drags up a long red line. 'This is the official track, where you must have got lost.'

Luke nods, following his finger. 'Right.'

'Think you'll remember where it happened?' I ask.

He shrugs. 'It was near the next camp. Everything looks the same out there, I doubt I'll find it.'

I nod. The story in his police statement is that they were at the back when they set off on the second day. Mari had a funny turn and needed to vomit. Luke called out to the group to wait as he followed her behind a bush. A brown snake slithered

235

out; they'd been told about these during their safety talk. A Malayan pit viper. Deadly. Gripped by fear, Mari ran into the jungle and Luke followed. Finally, deeming it safe to rejoin the path, they'd searched and searched, but couldn't find it.

I've read the guide's statement. He said it would have been a near impossibility they could have got lost so easily – they went back and searched the area extensively. He'd said it was as if they were trying to shake off the group. Which is an extraordinary claim. Since getting to know Luke, I've thought there was a possibility the guide could have been covering for himself.

'So, we'll head up to the next camp, the last place you were with the group. Then the next day we'll reach the summit.' I look at Reggie, checking, and he nods. 'How many hours do you think it will take to get here?' I ask, pointing at the red triangle on the map which marks the next base; it actually doesn't look that far. I feel geed up by this.

'Eight hours, minimum.' He gestures to the camera. 'Usually, it would take five. But not with all this equipment. It doesn't look far, but there is elevation, and difficult terrain.'

'I won't be filming the whole way. I'll pause occasionally to ask questions, and get a bit of the trek, but it will all feel very samey in the edit. Pointless to film the whole thing.' I turn to Luke. He is staring at the map with a grimace. His lightly tanned face has paled. I squeeze his arm. 'You all right, Luke?' He nods unconvincingly. 'Not long now,' I whisper.

My phone makes a shrill noise. My alarm. Time to check in with Cleo. I walk over to the bags of equipment and crack open the hard case containing the satellite phone. Pressing down on the power button, I walk away for privacy. After trying to get through a few times with no luck, I finally trudge back to the river, away from the trees, so the satellite has a better chance of connecting.

'Cass? Cass?'

'I'm here!' I shout. It feels like days since we left them on the riverbank, not hours.

'Oh, good.' She sounds relieved. 'All okay over there?'

'Yes, all going to plan. We're at base camp. Leaving at first light.'

'Brilliant. How are you all?' she enquires.

'Fine. In good spirits,' I say, pausing, wondering – should I tell her about the emails?

'Did you hear from Jamal? He said—' Her words trip out excitedly. She knows.

'Yes. I got them. I didn't get a chance to download them before my service shut down.'

'Oh,' she replies, deflated. 'I could get him to send them over to me?' Her voice rises with the idea.

'No. Don't. It's fine, they can wait a few days,' I tell her. Why am I lying to her when we're a team? I should be sharing this information. But I want it for myself. I want to be in on the secret before anyone else.

She coughs, deflated, and changes the subject. 'Hey, listen, it sounds as if there might be a big storm in the early hours of tomorrow night, or the morning after. The guy I spoke to about it seems to think it's fifty-fifty whether it will pass over you guys. So, make sure you pack all the waterproofs as it might not stay like this.'

'Thanks, Cleo.' I scan the spotless sky. The light blue is becoming blotted and dark.

'Okay, well. I hope it all goes well. Nearly there, Cass,' she says, relieved. 'I wish I was with you so I could help.'

'I . . . I wish you were here too, Cleo,' I admit. 'It does feel quite overwhelming doing all this alone.'

'What?' she cries, humour ringing from her voice. 'Cassidy Chambers. You are going to smash this and everyone will think you're even more badass than they already do.'

I laugh. 'You're too much.'

She always knows the right thing to say. We say our good-byes. I let the phone fall to my side and stare out to the water. The slow current pulling the dark liquid along in oily swirls. I step down to the end of the little jetty. The wood creaks and water pools through the gaps as it takes my weight. Pausing, I look up at the stars breaking through the docile fading light.

When I get back to the clearing, night has fallen. The others are illuminated by the orange glow of the fire. Reggie passes Luke a bottle of some sort of alcohol, and Luke laughs at something Reggie says. 'Any of that left for me?' I ask, stepping forward. Luke nods, raising the flat bottle of whisky in my direction. I take a long hard sip. It burns, shuttling through my insides and settling in my belly.

Luke jerks up, standing, and looks out intensely into the bush. 'Did you hear that?' he whispers.

I shake my head and walk to the edge of the clearing. I can't see anything. Moonlight doesn't reach down here. I turn on the torch on my phone and point it out at the dark green flopping leaves. But the light doesn't stretch very far. All I can hear is the omnipresent background noise, and the fire as it fizzes, pops and crackles. 'I can't hear anything, Luke,' I reply softly, looking up at his troubled face. He shakes his head. Our first night out here was never going to be easy.

I hear something then. A rustle. The shock of it scurries through me and I scream.

Luke's head swivels. Reggie stands, dropping the stick he's been prodding the fire with, and grabs the machete out from where he struck it, in the trunk of a tree. He joins me, staring into the darkness. 'Most likely a chicken,' he explains. I swallow. Of course. A chicken. My heart hammers and I try to steady my voice.

'It's fine, Luke. Just a chicken.' Luke's hands are trembling. I should be filming this.

I walk over to the camera, which is languishing on the tripod, and snap it off. I'm about to press record, but Reggie and Luke begin to talk about something else, and the moment is lost. I feel a bite of frustration as I put the camera down. My heart pounds at the memory of my scream, and I swallow thickly as the thuds reverberate through me, filling me with dread.

38

I look across the bamboo floor to where Luke is lying beneath the haze of mosquito net. He's inside his sleeping bag, facing the wall. I take out my phone from where it is nestled below and hold the glowing screen up to my face. My fingers itch for the next instalment of Mari's diary. I open it. But then, the sound of movement.

'Cassidy,' Luke whispers. 'Can't you sleep?' His finger pulls back the net, his head pokes out the curtain edge.

I put my phone away and do the same. Looking at those striking blue eyes, my mind can't help but run towards that intense night we shared. 'No . . . I'm not sure I can.' A loud squawk pierces through. 'Strange how noisy it is out here, isn't it?'

He nods. 'You'd think you'd get used to it. But I'm not sure I ever did.'

'I suppose I've always been quite gung-ho about coming here. But I never realised how . . . how . . .' I was all prepared to deal with Luke's fear. I never thought I would need to manage mine, too.

'It's okay, Cassidy. No one can prepare you for this. I think there is something about being completely isolated, away from phone masts and civilisation, that makes you feel like you've lost all the rules that make you feel safe.'

'Yes . . . yes . . .' He's right. That's what it is. No police a 999 call away. No stranger to run out to on the street and beg for help. No network of family and friends to call.

'It makes you feel unhinged,' he mutters.

Unhinged. I consider that choice of words. 'Unhinged.' I can't help but whisper it back.

'You know – crazy. Like anything could happen to you out here and no one would ever know.' His eyes gleam. Is it excitement? Or fear? I pull the bag up higher around me and swallow.

'Luke, will you tell me tomorrow, about what you remember?' His frame shifts. 'You're not just putting it off, are you? You will . . . you will tell me?'

His voice is coarse. 'Yes. I said I was going to.'

'The truth,' I state, staring over at him. 'Whatever it is you came to me wanting to say?'

'Of course. That's all I've ever wanted to do. The whole point of all of this. The truth.'

'Okay, great.'

Silence. He looks away and scoops himself back behind the mosquito net. I am left cold. Am I just being manipulated into telling the story he wants? Am I kidding myself that I have control over any of this? I press my lips together at the memory of the kiss. That can't have been anything but real.

Maybe he's still lost in the plot he has propagated because he has never been able to face what he did. Like Dr Ackerman said. *Unhinged.* The word runs around my head, playing. Maybe there wasn't anyone following him. It was just Luke and Mari, slowly going mad from terror and lack of food and water. Out here, maybe they couldn't keep up the pretence about what they'd done.

Footsteps up the ladder, the hut creaks with every step. For a moment I stiffen, and torchlight beams into my eyes. I put a hand out to cover it. 'Sorry.' I relax at the sound of Reggie's voice, and he pulls off his headtorch and shines the glare onto a wall. 'Fire's out,' he says. 'You guys okay up here?' We nod. Reggie is sleeping in the next hut over. He isn't scared like us, and is happy to be alone. 'Night then.' He gives a cursory look at the next rung behind before disappearing.

'Night,' we reply.

'Night, Cassidy,' Luke says tenderly.

'Night, Luke,' I whisper back.

I turn to face the wall and pull out my phone, lowering the screen light to as dull as it will go.

Hi Mari,

We are getting on the plane tomorrow! I can't wait. I had to sit through the most irritating family meal last night. Luke came over and did his usual perfect routine and Daddy lapped it up. How is it that people can be so naturally themselves, so comfortable in their own skin, and people just like them, while others must pretend to be someone else to be accepted?

242

All those bullies suddenly changed their tune once I'd partnered up with Luke. So fickle. They hated me one day for being the headmaster's daughter. And then the next they loved me because I was Luke Speed's girlfriend. And neither of these things had anything to do with me. All I had to do to be accepted was change who I was associated with. Life is just a game; it just took me a while to work out how to move the pieces around.

Am I only defined by who I am to other people? Who is Mari Castle, anyway? I'm not sure I even know. I just know it's easier being me if Luke is on my arm. I wonder what shape I will take when he isn't there any more. I find that thought quite thrilling. It is true what they say about love being close to hate. Everyone thinks I should be thankful. Like he is some sort of charity worker. And I'm lucky to have him. That's what annoys me more than anything, I think.

I would never have upset any of those idiots at school if they hadn't made me an outcast. And then when I wasn't one any more, they couldn't take a dose of their own medicine.

Daddy has always been just a tiny bit scared of me. Nervous. Like he's frustrated he can't contain me. But he understands someone like Luke. Straightforward, perfect Luke. I bet he wishes Luke was his child, not me.

I hear something below. I freeze. There it is again. Something beneath the stilts of the hut.

I sit up. Using the torch, I look over at Luke. His shoulders

243

rise and fall – fast asleep. 'Luke,' I hiss but he doesn't stir. There it is again. Fear like ice on a lake cracks through me. I open my mouth to call Luke again but think better of it. It's probably nothing and I don't want to scare him.

I wrestle my bag off and flap the net away. My bare feet rest gently on the knotted planks of bamboo. I close my eyes briefly. *You can do it.* I refuse to be afraid. Once at the entrance I peer down, using the phone torch. I can't see much. The fire is still smoking. I lie on my front, so I can get a visual underneath the stilts. Empty darkness. I must have imagined it. A chicken? No. Maybe a larger animal. A boar possibly? I've heard they can be quite dangerous and one of the reasons these shelters were built on stilts. I flick the light over to Reggie's hut; it is swathed in darkness.

Shaken, I go back to my makeshift bed. I must sleep. We have a long, exhausting day tomorrow. I shuffle into my bag. To calm myself I pretend I'm at home in my flat. The ghastly honking call of an unknown animal breaks my meditation. No, I mustn't let my mind wander. I'm in London behind the service station and the drive-thru McDonald's. There are police sirens and drunk people shouting. The low beat of music pumps from the bar across the way. I'm there. Not here – in the middle of this haphazard maze of trees and cliffs and mangroves and caves. *I'm not here . . . I'm not here.*

My eyes spark open when I feel his body slot in behind mine. The heat of his breath on the back of my neck makes me shudder. I close my eyes as his arms encase me. I should tell

244

him to get off. To leave me alone. But I don't. He holds me. I'm dreaming. That's all this is. I don't speak. I just allow the only person I've ever loved to hold me. Because I don't know if I'll ever get another chance to feel like this.

39

Birds singing aggressively high-pitched morning songs wake me. Thin strips of dull light stripe my face through gaps in the roof. I hear the soft undulation of Luke's breath as he sleeps, back at his spot on the other side of the hut. A sharp whistle from below. 'You guys up?' Reggie shouts.

Luke stirs and stretches.

'Yes,' I call. 'Down in a minute.'

Luke stands and begins to pack away the net, then tightly rolls up his sleeping bag. I sit up, watching. The silence between us is weighted. 'Big day,' I murmur. He stops what he's doing and looks at me. His shoulders slump.

'Cassidy. I . . . I need to tell you something.'

'What?' I hold my breath. Is this it? A confession?

'I love you,' he states simply. 'I really love you.'

I frown. A pain in my chest. 'Don't.' I get up and busy myself.

'Listen to me.' Desperation swims in his voice. I thrust my shirt on over my vest. 'I've not felt like this since—'

Exasperated, I turn and step towards him. 'Don't say it,' I demand. 'Luke. We're here to work. To make a film that will reshape your future. That is what you should be focusing on. Not this. Not us.' My finger flicks between us both. 'Please. Let's be professional. Get through this. Let's do what we came here to do. Please don't . . . don't . . .'

'What?'

'Please don't come to me in the night. I can't . . . I can't . . .' I try to find the words.

'I know you feel it too,' he pleads.

'Please, Luke. Let's get through this. I can't get through the next few days, making this on my own, and deal with the mess we've created. If you care about me at all . . . please can we forget all about it while we're here.' He grabs my arm and I stare at the tight, desperate grip. 'Maybe . . . maybe once we've proved you had nothing to do with this, then maybe we can explore this. Just not here, not now.' I give him a last despairing look, before swiftly walking to the edge of the hut, turning and stepping backwards down the ladder. Away from the conversation.

'We're up,' I call down to Reggie, as I jump onto the ground. He's standing, staring at something by the fire. I stop next to him and peer down, to see what has transfixed him. 'What is it?'

'I thought it looked like footprints,' he says, prodding at something in the dirt. I look down. There are shapes of impacted mud, half brushed away, in a pattern of ovals which could be interpreted as bare feet.

'Did you guys come down last night?' Reggie asks.

'No,' I reply. I stare at the marks. It could be . . . but it might not. Hard to tell. I hear Luke manoeuvring to the ground. 'Let's not tell him about this,' I whisper. 'It's nothing.' I quickly move my boot over the patch, destroying it. Reggie gives me a stunned look but doesn't say a thing.

'What are you two doing?' Luke asks, walking over. 'Staring so intently at the ground?' An amused tinge to his voice.

'Oh, nothing. Let's get some coffee on the go!' I say, changing the subject. It wasn't footprints and there's no point spooking Luke at the beginning of a very hard couple of days. I'm just on high alert because of what Reggie said on the boat, about the urban legend of someone out here feeding a frenzy of stories. There is nothing to be afraid of, it's just talk.

The only thing to fear is the jungle itself.

'No coffee,' Reggie says quickly. 'We need to ration the water we take up, so you can't drink anything dehydrating until we're safely down the other side.'

'Fine. No coffee. Can I swim in the river? I could do with a wash before we make a move.' I feel so utterly disgusting after the hot sweaty night, I can't start the hike like this lugging around a camera.

'Yes. It's clean. No crocodiles around here,' he says with a side smile.

'Great. I'll just go for a quick dip. I won't be long. We have time, right?' And he nods.

I walk back down the path to the river. Once on the bank I pull off my top, my bra, my cotton trousers, leaving my knickers on. I walk into the water further along, away from the jetty. It's less murky here. Almost clear. Tiny little see-through

248

fish rush away as I wade out. I pull my arms in front of me and let out a sigh as the water runs off the slimy glaze of sweat. I flip onto my back and stare at the clear sky. A moment of calm before the strenuous hike.

Once washed, I pad back over to my things and search for my phone in the pocket of my trousers, heaped in a pile. I glance up at the path, to check I am alone. Just one more diary entry, and then I'll go back. Shaking off the water from my fingers, I unlock it and continue.

We've arrived in Bangkok. Mum and Daddy paid for a nice hotel for the first night. While we 'get our bearings'. Luke wanted to stay in and enjoy the hotel. Watch movies and have bubble baths and cuddle. How could he have wanted that when he'd seen what's outside our window? He sulked as we left. He'll always do what I want in the end. He doesn't want to cause an argument. Because if he does, we might say things we don't mean. Or things we mean. And neither of us are ready to do that.

We got to this bar overlooking the Khaosan Road. I'd never felt so alive. I wanted to jump off and dive into it. Music pumped and I danced along the front. Luke looked over at me, embarrassed. He used to think everything I did was wonderful. Not any more. I ignored him. I'd never felt so free. I wished I could turn into a bird and fly off into it all. Being human is so limiting.

I heard some clapping and turned around. There was this couple who look like they'd been travelling for a while. They were sat relaxed, lounging around. With deep tans and sun-kissed hair. We ended up joining them. They're Dutch – Astrid and Sander. They told stories of islands, and trekking and night trains and magic mushrooms. They were showing off a little, as though they could tell we'd just arrived, and they belonged.

We got drunk. Someone had the idea of going to Patpong. I'd heard some of the year above talking about it. It's the red-light district where all the sex shows are. I wanted to go. Luke obviously didn't. He's always putting the brakes on whenever there is something that isn't in his plan. Or is slightly 'edgy'. Then Astrid put her hand on Luke's knee: Come on, British boy. Don't be such a bore. And just like that he was up for it.

How will I ever break up with him knowing there will be so many willing to take my place? How will I ever let him go? Could my stupid human jealousy take it? Why do I want to keep something mine, even though it's run its course?

He's coming back – gtg. See you later!

'Cassidy!' Luke appears from the treeline. He stops. 'Oh.' He stares at my nakedness before blinking. 'Sorry.' He scratches his head and turns around. I hurry on my clothes, the material clinging to my wet skin. 'Reggie says we need to get going,' he explains.

'I'm coming,' I reply, slipping my phone back into my pocket – Mari will have to wait.

We unpack and repack with our trek in mind. Anything we don't need will be left here. I have a lightweight backpack I'm going to wear on my front to hold the camera during the trek. Then I'll be able to easily access it if I need to whip it out en route. The mic is a problem. Best thing to do is keep it on him twenty-four/seven, or it'll kill any spontaneity of moment if I have to hurry over and reattach it. The top mic on my camera won't pick up the sound very well if I'm more than a few feet away as the incredibly noisy jungle will drown out his voice. I count the AA batteries, and we have enough to keep it running. I just really need to keep on top of it, and make sure I change them over. And make sure he remembers to turn it back on after going to the toilet.

We pack our sleeping bags and a couple of tarpaulin sheets. One for ground cover, the other to tie above us if it rains. I look up at the sky. Still no sign of this storm Cleo warned of. We ration out our clothing, food and water to tide us over. Water is going to be our heaviest weight. Reggie carefully works out how much we'll each need, putting three large plastic bottles in his bag, after filling up our smaller bottles to carry on us. 'Drink often but sparingly,' he tells us. 'There are a few water sources out there if we get desperate.'

'How did you get so adept at surviving out here?' I ask him, impressed with his extensive knowledge.

He looks distant for a moment. 'Guiding tourists mainly. When I was a young man, it was a good earner. And the village where I grew up edges onto this national park, so it's always been second nature.'

'How did you find water, Luke?' I turn to him.

'By collecting rainwater, mostly,' he replies softly, closing his mouth quickly, without elaborating.

I film the silent movements of preparation. Close-ups on Luke's frown and contemplative face. 'Tell me, how are you feeling, Luke?' I ask.

'Good. A bit nervous.' The sound of his voice wobbles into my headphones. I would have preferred wireless earphones, not least for the heat, but again, battery life is a problem when outside of a central charging point. And I only have one external charging pack which I'm saving for my phone. These are thick and padded and weigh down on my hot, damp head. 'I feel like she knows we're here. I feel like she wants us to find her,' he adds, looking up at the lofty trees.

I want to keep Luke as free from carrying kit and camping equipment as possible. So, Reggie and I are laden. As well as the bag on my front, I have a full pack on my back.

'Cassidy, are you sure you're okay with all of that?' Luke asks, sceptically.

'I'm fine. Let's just get going.' I take a few steps, finding my balance.

Reggie heads up the front. A blue chipped post marks the path. These are dotted up to the next base camp. 'Day one in the jungle . . .' Luke says in a Geordie accent to puncture the unease. I laugh. It catches in the back of my throat, and I swallow. Here we go.

40

I film as Reggie hacks at overgrown foliage on the underused dirt track. The swishing thwacks add to the eerie mood beneath the trembling canopy. Patches of light escape from above and litter the cluttered floor. Roots poke out from the ground in humps, waiting to trip me up. It's tough filming conditions and after ten minutes I stop the recording and tuck the camera away.

I think of Mari's emails as we walk. What she said about Luke being different to the other boys in her year, it lingers in my thoughts. Forcing me to recollect my own experiences at school. How, as an outsider, I desperately tried to fit in. My obliviousness and eagerness to please made me a target, I suppose. I wonder if boys feel shame like we do, its sickly grip the night after we've been taken advantage of. Or if they feel proud, that they got what they wanted.

Blood gushes to my cheeks as I blink back the remnants of the other night. The feeling as I held him. Gasping at the pleasure of that deep connection that I'd never let myself try for. Together. Beautiful, consented, wanted joy. I wanted him.

Badly. Unless . . . unless . . . he's guilty of this crime. And he's been playing a part and lied to me. Because if something is built on dishonesty, that isn't consent. Is it? That's something far more sinister.

A bird calls, and I feel Mari whispering to me. She's trying to tell me something. Asking me to listen, a warning. But my body. My whole body is desperate for him again.

We stop for a rest about two hours into the hike. I watch on, conflicted, as Reggie hands Luke the spare machete. I chew my nail as Reggie teaches him how to use it. Luke's muscular arm forcing the metal blade down, whipping it against the air, as he practises. I take a breath, reminding myself Luke is not someone I need to fear.

Inside the canopy the air is listless. Fusty, with limited breeze. I glug down some water, and pour a little onto my hand to wipe my drenched face. I take out the camera and film Luke. His T-shirt with deep half-moons of sweat under his arms. He rubs his eye and blinks with a wince. Perspiration blisters out from his stubble and a tear of water makes its way down his neck.

'Gosh. That was a chaser,' I laugh, trying to loosen the atmosphere that hangs around us. I wish Cleo was here to tell some jokes. 'I can't believe how much further we have to go,' I say, trying to get him to talk. 'It must have been terrifying here, on your own,' I add quietly.

He looks over and notices I'm filming. He nods, deciding to play along. 'I think I always thought I was just going to die.'

He sighs. 'At one point I was ready to. I'd made peace with it. Anything was better than trying to survive out here for one more day on my own.' He talks to the camera. 'Back in the UK, I often wished I had died. It would have been easier. For everyone.' His words send a jolt through me. This is good. This is what I need. His guts. I need raw emotion. A reflection of that poor eighteen-year-old boy, stuck in the jungle. No way out. *Imagine if it was my son!* they will think as they watch. Empathy opening as they finally see him as human. The way I see him. Not the malicious killer they've all presumed.

'What do you think he did to her?' I ask with trepidation.

He looks up, quickly. 'What?' he whispers, unsure he heard me right.

'The man, following you. You said once, your imagination takes you places in your dreams. Can you tell us what happens in them?'

He shakes his head, giving me a pained look. I think of Dr Ackerman, and how he said Luke may have deflected his own actions onto an imagined character to deal with his own guilt.

He sighs, his voice laden. 'Everything. The worst a man can do to a woman.' He stares me down. 'Causing her more suffering than a human should ever experience. That haunts me. I hope it was quick. I hope he did it quickly.' I film him sitting there, looking down. Pondering that thought. 'I feel very close to her right now. Closer than I have for twenty years,' he whispers. 'I feel her presence all around.'

This moment could be the right one. And I ask. 'What happened the last time you saw her? Were you . . . on good terms?'

He frowns. The intimacy, gone. 'When I'm ready, Cassidy. When I'm ready.' *When?* I think. When will he be ready? What if he never is? All this build-up is good if it culminates in something actually happening. Otherwise, what is this all for? Why did he start this?

'Okay? We should keep going,' Reggie says, already up and raring to go. I press the button, stopping the recording, and slip the camera in my front, pulling off my headphones and mopping off the excess sweat with the sleeve of my shirt.

We fall silent as the ascent becomes tricky. The sound of swishing machetes and snapping twigs as we walk. As the ground steepens, and my thighs begin to burn, my vision blurs and I blink the excess moisture away.

When we get to the next plateau, Reggie bangs the machete into the trunk of a tree, pausing to take a gulp of water. I'm relieved he's finding this tough too, it's not just me.

But Luke continues, furiously swiping the knife left and right, a newfound strangle of aggression with each swing. 'Luke?' I call. He continues, and I call him again. 'Luke!' He pauses, staring upward, facing away. It takes me a moment to realise the sound I hear is crying. I whip out the camera and try and put the headphones back on. The wire is twisted and pulls at my neck like a noose.

I step forward, wanting a closer shot. The wide is in the bag. I'm constantly having to think about what I will need in the edit. I get close to one side, just as he wipes some tear residue away. His face appears on the screen. I look at his expression in the monitor. The anger residing there sends a shiver. 'Is this what you want?' he shouts, a gruff, angry quality to his voice. 'Is this what you wanted for your fucking film?!' I feel the rage rising off him, and I move the camera and open my mouth to placate him. 'Turn it off,' he whispers roughly. 'Turn it off!' he shouts, putting a hand over the lens. I lower the camera, holding the top handle, and let it hang by my side. I haven't pressed stop.

'Luke,' I say, exasperated. I appreciate he's upset, but he's got to understand that we need to film this whole experience – the highs and the lows. This is the problem with filming as well as dealing with a contributor, you become so engrossed in the mechanics of the film, you forget to deal with all the emotions, too.

'You know what the worst thing is?' he asks me through gritted teeth. He lowers his voice to a whisper, so only I will hear through his mic, and Reggie will not. 'I'm not crying over her. I'm crying over you.'

A punch of emotion in my stomach. My sweaty finger slips on the record button as I hastily attempt to turn it off, but it's too late, what he said has been recorded. *Shit*. 'Luke,' I mutter. 'Sorry – I . . .' I just desperately want this to be over. I squint up as large dark clouds infest the patch of idyllic blue sky.

'I'm sorry. We'll take it easy,' is all I can muster. Thinking of what I've done. How I can get to the other side of this without my career in tatters. I have betrayed the one person I had hoped to find in all this: Mari.

41

A few hours later the rain starts. At first, just tiny little pin-pricks I can barely tell if I'm imagining. Darker tumultuous clouds rumble in the gaps between leaves above. The rolling crash of thunder and then the unmistakable tapping starts. Large bulbous drops slap down, cascading from leaf to leaf to the floor. I raise my face to it; it feels good against the oily sweat layered on my skin. 'Wait!' I call ahead, taking off my backpack and finding the plastic cover for the camera. I case it carefully, Velcroing it in place. I put my phone and external battery pack in the waterproof Ziploc bag around my neck and fold the batteries and other electrical equipment into plastic bags and repack them. Just when I thought this trip was tough, something comes in and ups the ante. Taking a pack of condoms out of the filming bag, I walk over to Luke. He gives me a startled look as I rip one open. I turn him around forcefully and undo the battery pack attached to his waistline.

'What are you . . . ?' Luke asks, confused.

I take out the condom and force the pack inside the

rubber. 'It'll keep it dry, and hopefully stop it breaking.' I chew my lip, worrying at the thought, but then remind myself we do have a spare, just in case. I let him go, and we continue our trudge.

After an hour of heavy rain, the dirt ground begins to pulp and move with my feet, forcing me to yank on knotted brushwood to propel myself forward. My hands feel red raw from the effort.

A loud bang of thunder. I jump.

'You okay?' Luke shouts over the uproar.

'Yes,' I reply roughly, unwilling to admit I'm struggling. Just then, my foot slips and I find myself falling back. I bang to the ground. Something hard digs into my lower back, as if I've been hit by a wooden bat. I cry out in pain as I slide down the path, pressing my teeth together at the harsh throbbing pain.

I lie there a moment in shock. Splodges of water hurtle towards me, and my hand slips in the gritty mud as I try to prop myself up. Luke's face appears. 'Why say you're okay when you're clearly not?' he says roughly, clasping my hand tightly, helping me back to my feet. Our chests inches apart, we are both panting, soaking wet. A waft of his scent. I swallow.

'My back,' I moan, wincing.

He turns me around to look, and lifts my shirt, his fingers gently pressing on my skin. 'You'll have a bruise.' I yank my shirt down. 'Now give me some of your stuff to carry. This is insane, you carrying all this while I basically have nothing.'

I think of all the equipment I have on me. 'I'm fine. I just slipped.'

259

'You're infuriating,' he tells me, exasperated. 'Let me carry something for you. These conditions are brutal.' He begins to mutter to himself. 'This was insane. A crazy idea making you do all this.' He looks at me and says in a clear steady voice, 'Cassidy, let me help.'

Instinctively my hand clasps around the bag on my chest protectively, like a baby in a sling. On my back are all the spare batteries and extra filming equipment – all the integral elements I need to do my job. 'Cassidy,' he says firmly. Finally relenting, I yank off the straps, and let the bag drop onto the floor, and tug out the spare camera batteries, handing them over. He adds them to his backpack. Putting the bag back on, I feel much lighter. He's right. It is helping.

'How much further, Reggie?' he calls.

'Not long now. An hour, maybe two?'

'Come on, let's get this over with,' I say.

As I walk, I list what is ahead. One more night, up to the summit, drone shot, walk back down. With a revealing, emotional interview at some point along the way. We've done the hardest part of the trek – I keep this thought front and centre with each step.

'Are you okay?' Luke calls back.

'Yes,' I shout. My hand grazes the spot where I fell. I can feel the blood pulsating, rushing to it, and I'm sure there will be a hard purple bruise. I grimace as I walk. Luke watches me sternly. I walk more boldly, not wanting him to fuss.

Our expedition slows as the track becomes narrower, tangled and disorderly, and it becomes more time consuming for

Reggie to cut a path through. I curse. I've been so distracted by the toil, I've neglected to get any of this struggle on film. I bite my lip, holding my frustration in. I wish Duncan was here. I'm so focused on the trek I can't think straight about what I need to capture. I'm overwhelmed. I can't handle this. *Calm down. Think.* All I need to do is conscientiously get the building blocks to tell this story in the edit.

The added jeopardy of the storm could work well in the film. If I have enough of it covered. It may end up on the cutting room floor – after all, it isn't an integral element in Mari and Luke's story. But it does show how tough the conditions are out here and if Luke's journey back to the jungle becomes present tense, not past, this could be a vital part of it. 'Cover all bases,' I whisper to myself.

Rain slaps on the lens as I film Luke and Reggie struggling to make a route up the path. I stop, film, wipe the lens and catch up and then go again. I do this a few times. Exhausted, I slip the camera back.

Finally, after what feels far longer than a couple of hours, we make it to the next group of huts, and I begin filming again. The ones on stilts by the river look angelic compared to these all covered with dead leaves and moss. The bamboo is riddled with mould. Reggie yanks open a door, and it's like a bag of dust is thrown out.

'No one will have been up here for a while,' Reggie says.

'Did it look like this when you were last here?' I ask Luke, a leading question to get him talking. The camera is digging

261

into my shoulder, and I readjust it, but I can't find a more comfortable spot. I wince in pain but keep going.

'No. Obviously,' he says flatly. We're all depleted, but we're only out here twenty-four more hours and I need to make them count. I peer up from behind the camera and give him a look, and he softens. 'It didn't look like this.' He walks over to one of the huts and places a hand on the wood. 'They must have been quite new then.' He looks around, thinking. 'We spent our last night here with the tour group.' He looks uncomfortable.

Come on, Luke, I need more than this.

'Where did you sleep?' I mouth at him, pointing. Wanting him to show the camera the site without my voice getting in the way. He nods and stands back, looking at the three structures. Then he points to the one on the right. 'I think this was where Mari and I slept.' He goes to the door, but there is a rope tied between the door and the loose frame. He yanks the machete out of the tree and hacks at it. Finally, its taut binding falls loose. He threads it out and opens the door. I walk over, to cover what he discovers. Inside is nearly empty but for five makeshift bamboo bedframes and a few dry, curled-up leaves at the back, where part of the roof has collapsed.

'We shared with this group of Germans. One of the guys snored all night, Mari didn't sleep a wink. No wonder she felt so rough the next day.'

I get a few close-ups of the inside of the shed and we go back outside, and I film Luke wandering around the site. After a bit of that, I decide to take some static shots. We left the tripod down at base camp, it would have been impossible to carry. So, I can't get the perfect fixed shot. But I lock my elbows to do the best I can. I wander around getting tight shots of details. I stop at a tree. Long cords of thin rope hang from it, in different stages of plait. After filming, I let the camera hang loose, and take one in my hand, squeezing the water from it. 'Reggie, what's this?' I call.

He joins me and takes a look. 'Looks like handmade rope, made from bamboo.' He walks behind the tree and finds some discarded stripped branches; he kneels and picks one up. 'Doesn't seem very old. Maybe some locals came up here.' He doesn't sound very sure.

I frown. Locals. That must be it.

The rain has stopped. I crane my neck from side to side, relieved to have the toughest part of the trek over. Respite. Reggie hangs the tarpaulin and makes an area for the fire. 'We should try and find some dry wood,' he suggests, pointing towards the bush.

'I'll help,' Luke offers, grabbing his machete off the ground.

I look up at the sky. We have a few hours of light left, max. It is a good backdrop for the interview, with the huts in the background. And it is relatively bright, compared to the thick undergrowth of the path.

'Luke, why don't you stay behind? We could . . . we could have a chat, on camera. About . . . you know?' I turn my head to one side, suggestively. 'I could set up a nice shot with the huts in the background . . .'

He shakes his head quickly. 'Not here. I can't do it here.'

263

I grit my teeth into an exasperated smile. 'But why?'

'I'll do it at the top. That'll look good for your camera, right? Up there, with the jungle below.'

I chew the inside of my mouth, thinking. Yes, it would look good. I just hope he's being honest. 'Okey dokey,' I say, trying not to show my frustration. Pressure builds in my chest. How many more times is he going to say no?

As I watch Reggie lead Luke between the trees, I put the camera away. My shoulders smart from where the straps have cut into my skin as the damp fabric of my vest twisted into it. I kink my neck, trying to get a better look at the red and angry marks.

I get under the tarpaulin and yank off my boots with a relieved moan. I wiggle my toes and roll down my socks. My right heel has been pinching and I look behind to see a large blister. I should have done what Melissa suggested and worn them in. I touch it with a grimace, staring at it for a while. Are you meant to pop them? This is all starting to feel far more survivalist than I was expecting: a quick hike. A few simple shots and an interview. It was all so much simpler on paper.

Mari.

The thought of her has struck me out. As though her name was whispered in my ear. There is no sign of the others returning. So, I take out my phone and begin to read.

I was well and truly drunk by the time we got to the red-light district. I'd never seen anything like it. Certainly not in the leafy 'burbs back home. The strobing lights distorted my vision as we walked past bar

264

after bar with half-naked girls gyrating on poles, curling their fingers to gesture us inside, calling 'Farang! Farang!' as we passed.

I tripped in my sandals and Astrid asked, 'You okay?' I nodded and she grinned, holding my hand. I looked down at the confident clutch and smiled. Girls don't often take to me. I asked her how long she and Sander had been together. And she laughed.

And then she told me something that surprised me. They aren't together. They are friends. Sometimes with benefits. But mostly just friends. They are free to do what they want, whenever they want. I'd never heard of that before.

I remember feeling so sorry for those girls at school who never got kissed. Proud that I had someone who was mine. Ownership. The thought just never occurred to me that wasn't the point. It felt like a door opened to this whole new way of thinking.

We decided on a club and my heart started beating so fast. I'd never been anywhere like that before. It felt dangerous. And I am drawn to darkness.

I sat in the booth. Astrid on one side, Luke on the other.

And then the lights went down. My knee was touching Astrid's and I didn't look at the Thai girl on stage. I just looked at her. The way the light caught her blonde hair and her plump pink lips.

265

She noticed me staring. And grinned. And then I just leant
forward . . . and I kissed her.

I don't know where it came from. I just wanted to take her. I slipped
my tongue in her mouth and our smooth skin pressed against each
other. Our breasts touched. I put my hand on the side of her face
to pull her even closer. As we stopped a small trail of my saliva on
her top lip caught in the multicoloured lights. Her cheeks red. It was
so soft and urgent. I liked it. I really liked it. Luke yanked at my arm
and pulled me away, closer to him.

I sat back, dazed, and saw the look on Luke's face. Open-mouthed.
Furious and, I think, a little turned on.

The whole thing was so confusing. But also not.

I don't think it was kissing her, or a girl or anything. It was kissing
someone who wasn't Luke. I used to think he was the best kisser in
the world. I used to crave it, you know? Now it feels like something I
dread. Something I want to squirm away from.

Oh god. Then it really went sour. I got this surge of nausea. I ran
back up the stairs, past all these naked women, and threw up
against the wall outside. Luke followed me and stroked my back
silently as I heaved. He always comes and saves me. Even when
I've done something wrong.

I just kept repeating, sorry. Over and over. All he said was, it's okay.

266

Once I'd finished, I turned, wiping my mouth. I saw this old Thai lady staring at me, giving me a haunted rotten look, which made me curl up inside. It's like she saw it. She saw what I'd done.

I'm dirty and wrong. I'm not a person at all but just a piece of flesh walking between disasters.

I gasp. This must be what Astrid wanted to tell me. Why has she never told anyone before? I think of the intimidating Thai police officers, and Mari's elderly, religious parents. How did that kiss make Luke feel? I hear footsteps and stuff my phone back in my pocket. 'Hey.' I smile. They are holding small piles of chopped wood in their forearms. Luke looks at me apprehensively. I think of the Mari in the emails. How different she is to how he's described. Why didn't he tell me about this kiss? Was he embarrassed . . . or maybe because it's a motive? I swallow at the thought.

There aren't two sides to a person. There are many. The person they portray, the one they keep hidden. And the person other people desperately want them to be. We all hold back the darker version inside of us. Some are better at it than others. What is truth anyway? Even that is layered with miscommunication, assumption and resentment. It is just a puzzle of pieces handed in by different people. They never all fit together perfectly. We even lie about ourselves, and not always intentionally.

What did you do, Luke? I want to cry out, scratch his face and kick against him in frustration. *Tell me so I can love you how*

I want to. So I can give in to this thing that has followed me around since we met.

I would give it all up for him. I would. If he is the person I think he is and want him to be.

The thoughts play out as I watch Luke help Reggie with the fire. My arms hang loose in hopelessness, a river of thoughts and emotions running past.

Night falls on our little camp, and as Reggie boils the bag of rice, we sit in weary silence. Far from civilisation. Miles from anyone else.

42

The fire crackles as we process the strenuous day. Orange light bathes Luke's face as I steal glances at him watching the flames, deep in thought. Reggie pokes the fire with a stick and sparks hash in the listless air.

'You got what you needed today?' Reggie asks.

I press my lips together. 'Yes, it's been great.' Not wanting to air my concerns in front of Luke.

'Want to trek off the path a bit tomorrow – to see what it's like, further in?'

I shake my head. No part of me wants to veer off that path, even if we are in Reggie's safe hands. 'I don't think we have time,' I reply. I look down at the dregs of rice in my mess tin and spoon the last of it into my mouth. I don't feel hungry, even though I should be famished, and force it down my throat with water.

Reggie gets out the whisky and hands it to me. 'Medicinal,' he says with a wink. I'm glad of the burning liquid which momentarily tempers the sickly pump of adrenalin. I go to hand it back, but he replies, 'Feel free to have some more.' And I smile gratefully, before stealing another glug.

The alarm on my phone shrills. Cleo. I long to connect with the others and jump up. 'Where did I . . . ?' I mutter as I walk over to the bags.

'I think it's in mine,' Reggie says, pointing.

I unclip the straps and undo the tie. Rummaging around, I find it wrapped in a plastic bag. We didn't bring the hard case: too bulky.

Turning on the power, I check the service – none. I look up at the thick canopy. 'I just need to find some sky,' I tell them.

'I'll come with you.' Luke stands up.

No, I need privacy. 'It's fine – it's clearer over there.' I point further up.

Reggie hands me his headtorch. 'Don't go further than shouting distance,' he warns.

I walk quickly to a spot where I can see a clear ceiling of stars. My heel itches with pain and I wince. I can't wait to hear Cleo's voice and my hand shakes as I hold up the phone. Relief drills through me as I watch the bars grow. It crackles a few times, and then begins to ring. Cleo picks up quickly. But static trails around her voice.

'Cass! Are you . . . the storm . . . worried . . .'

'Cleo? Cleo, can you hear me?' I ask.

'Cass? Cass, you there?'

'Yes! Can you hear me?'

'Now I can.' Her voice is more solid, and I'm relieved. 'Are you okay? We couldn't believe it when they said the storm was a direct hit.'

'We're fine. The conditions are tough.'

'Has he . . . has he said anything?' More crackling and I try not to get frustrated as I make out her voice. '. . . interview . . .'

I look back towards camp. I can just make out the glow of the fire. 'Not yet. He's promised once we get to the top.'

'Oh.' She sounds disappointed. 'That's good,' she adds, unsure.

'I've decided it's the perfect spot for it. Will look great with the jungle below.' I make it sound like my idea. I'm not sure who I'm kidding.

'Please don't leave Reggie's side, okay?' More crackling. 'I have a bad feeling . . .' The phone cuts out. I remove it from my ear and stare, before trying the number again, but nothing happens. A sickly feeling washes over me, like a premonition.

I take out my phone, using the opportunity to read from Mari's diary.

Hi Mari,

It's been a few days since I've managed to get away long enough to write. Since Bangkok, Luke hasn't left my side. He's upset about what happened, I think. But too scared to bring it up. So am I. I feel like it will be the conversation where we both admit we shouldn't be together any more, and we're both too scared to start it. The beginning of the end. The crack that began last year extended further through us. I wonder if we'll just ignore it until the damage is

271

so apparent, there's no way we can close our eyes to it any more. I wonder what that damage will look like. I wonder what the final straw will be.

We've decided to spend the next few weeks island hopping. But it's like we've forgotten how to be with one another, so I have no idea how we'll get through them. We're bickering about everything. Where to eat. What to drink. Who to talk to. Where to stay. Money. He's made a stupid budget thing and is being incredibly petty about every baht I spend. It's infuriating.

And the pettier he gets, the more I want to poke him. I'll go do a shot at the bar when he says not to. I'll take my clothes off and run in the sea naked at midnight when he says there might be rocks. I'll do it. I'll do it all. Because then maybe, he'll leave. And I won't ever have to think about what I did any more.

'Cass! Cass!'

They're shouting for me, and I twist on the spot. 'Yes!' I call. 'Coming!' I trudge back to camp, thinking of what Mari has told me. This doesn't sound like a couple proposing to each other on a moonlit beach. The abrasive light of the headtorch darts around, landing on Luke's face and he winces. 'Sorry, she wanted a long chat,' I say, feebly. And he eyes me suspiciously, as though he knows I've been doing something behind his back. 'We should get some sleep,' I say, as I walk to the fire.

'You're limping,' Luke says accusatorily. 'What's up with you?'

'Just a blister, on my foot,' I explain.

'Let me look at it,' he demands.

I shake my head. 'No, no, seriously, it's fine.'

He shakes his head angrily. 'Cassidy. Come here and let me have a look.' He points at a spot by the fire, and I do as I'm told.

I take off my boot which was only loosely tied, and he puts my foot gently in his lap, pulling down my sock, using his pocket torch to inspect it. Reggie leans over to assess it as well.

'I'm surprised this hasn't popped already,' Luke murmurs. 'We should do it and get some antiseptic and wrap it up,' he says. Reggie nods, agreeing. 'Otherwise, it might burst on tomorrow's hike and get infected.' Reggie throws the first aid kit over and Luke catches it with one hand. 'Can I use your knife?' Luke asks and I nod, fishing it out my pocket. He leans the blade into the fire to sterilise it. The skin around the blister is thick and it takes a while. Liquid trickles out, and the taut skin flattens, like a popped balloon. Luke dabs some cream on it and carefully lays a surgical plaster over the top, firming it in place. 'Better?' he asks gently, looking at me with great care.

'Thank you,' I croak. 'Looks like I'm not as tough as I thought I was,' I quip.

'You don't need to be tough, Cassidy,' he says gently, still holding my foot. I look down at the carefully plastered area. I realise no one has ever looked after me. I've never let them. I remove my foot from his grasp. 'Let's get ready for bed,' he says, standing up and opening the door of one of the huts.

*

273

As we shut down the camp for the night it begins to rain, trees shake and loud strikes of thunder ricochet; lightning cracks, closer than it's ever been before. We pile up the kit in the hut we've decided is the sturdiest. We're all sleeping together tonight. There is enough room, and the other huts are badly damaged. Mari's emails will have to wait. We have some dry clothes in plastic bags and change into them to sleep. 'We can get back into the wet stuff in the morning,' Reggie says. 'Smart to keep one set dry.'

It's too hot in here. I lie on top of my bag and listen to the jungle festering. I call up the image of home, trying to remember every inch of it. The cosy sofa with a quilt thrown on the back. Herzog curled around himself as he sleeps. Then, I put my hand in my pocket, and realise my pocket knife isn't there. Luke didn't give it back. I want it – it makes me feel protected. I'm not sure from what. 'Luke, have you still got my knife?' I call into the darkness.

'What?' he hisses.

'My knife. Could I have it back? I don't want to lose it.'

'Oh. Right.'

I hear shuffling and raise my phone screen towards him as he searches. 'I think it's in my bag, it'll still be there in the morning,' he says, giving up and settling back down. 'Sorry, I must have packed it by accident.'

I scratch my lip with my top teeth before sighing and fighting out of my net. 'What are you doing?' he asks as I walk over to his bag.

'I just would prefer to have it now,' I tell him, undoing the straps and feeling around. Opening the various compartments.

'Wait, sorry. It's here,' he says. I turn as he pulls it out. 'Must have fallen into my sleeping bag.' The sound of metal slashing against the floor as he sends it my way. I fish it up and get back into bed, gripping it in my palm. Trying to ban the image of the man in the jungle from my thoughts, in case he populates my dreams.

43

My eyes spark open at the sound of Luke shouting. 'No!' he cries, his voice trembling with fear as the strangled wail permeates the sticky air.

I sit up. It's pitch black. I can't see a thing. Is he having a nightmare? 'What's going on?' I mumble. Grasping around for my torch or phone.

He's pacing, breathing heavily. 'There's someone out there,' he pants, panic streaked through every syllable.

Light jolts into the space, causing my pupils to dilate and my head to throb. Reggie is up, his torch on, the beam flinging around the tight space, and all I see is a muddle of limbs. The mosquito nets pinned to the ceiling like hanging ghosts.

'There's someone out there,' Luke repeats, his voice shaking, his hands gripping either side of his head.

'What?' My mind rushes. I get up and go to him. Pulling at his arms, trying to get his attention. He can't lock eyes with me, and there is a ghastly horror-struck look on his face. 'Luke? Luke?' I can't get through to him, it's like he's gone somewhere else.

'He's out there. He's coming to get me.'

'Luke. Luke!' I cry, trying to get him to calm down. 'Luke, it's okay. It's okay! I'm here.' I grip his chin, so he has no choice but to meet my eyes. His heaving peters out, and he blinks as he takes in my face. 'It's me, Cassidy.'

'Cassidy,' he whispers. Warmth floods back into his eyes. Then he tries to explain. 'I heard someone knocking. It woke me up.'

I turn around to see Reggie shifting on the spot, looking concerned.

'Luke, do you ... do you think you could have been dreaming?'

He frowns. 'Are you ... are you saying I made it up?' He points at the wall. 'They were knocking on the hut. You heard it, right?' He switches to Reggie, hands together, pleading. Reggie shakes his head apologetically. Luke looks so vulnerable, so taken in by this fear.

'It must be very hard for you to be back here, Luke. Dreams can feel very real ... almost like ... flashbacks?' I say carefully. The look he gives back is incredulous.

'Fuck you,' he spits. The venom in his voice makes me freeze.

'Sorry,' I whisper. 'I'm just saying it might not be what you think.'

'Why does no one ever believe me?' he cries, balling his hands into fists. 'There is someone out there. They are messing with us.' His voice wobbles. 'We should never have come here.'

The camera. Where is it? I walk to the back of the hut and

pick it up. Luke realises what I'm doing. 'You can't be serious?' he cries.

'This is important, Luke.'

'Someone is out there, probably on a mission to kill us, and you're thinking about filming? That's insane, Cassidy.'

I swallow that down. 'You want to tell your story? This is the story, Luke! You, scared. The possibility of someone out there.' I fling my hand in the direction of the door. 'This is the story!' He takes in what I've said, as he paces around the tight spot, the unstable structure shaking with his every step. Then he bangs his fist against a wall in frustration.

I calm my breathing. There can't be someone. Luke is over-whelmed, scared. He's coming to terms with what happened out here. This is all part of it. Like Dr Ackerman said. He could have deflected his own actions onto this imagined man, to deal with the guilt. The truth could be rising to the surface. There could be a big revelation on the other side of this frenzy.

I feel inside the backpack for the radio mic but think better of it. Asking him to put it on might send him over the edge. We're in a contained space, and the integrated camera-top mic will do. I press the power button and check the battery. My shoulders fall as I remember there isn't night vision on this model of camera. I left the smaller one that has it back at base deciding it was a luxury item we couldn't carry. Oh well. I just need to make do with what we've got, and it may be atmospheric – action mixed with the frenzy of torchlight.

Reggie puts on his boots and walks to the door. 'I'll go have a look,' he says stoically.

'Reggie, I don't think . . .' There really is no need.

'Be careful.' Luke steps forward, a worried look scraped across his handsome face.

I don't have the heart to belittle this whole thing in front of Luke. 'Yes, be careful.' Reggie takes his machete; he's taking this seriously. It's very sweet of him to placate Luke by checking the site.

'This was a stupid idea,' Luke mutters. 'Coming up here.' He's wringing his hands. 'It's happening again, just like last time. They didn't believe me and look what happened to Mari.' I step back into the wall so I can film him. He looks at me, dumbfounded. 'We're all going to die out here and all you can think of is the film!'

He shakes his head furiously at me, before bulking towards the door. 'Reggie, wait – I'm coming with you,' he says, wedging on his boots.

I look around for mine. 'Wait – I'll come too,' I say. My mind already whizzing with how I can cover this. Maybe hold my torch out ahead of the camera? Would that work?

Luke gives the camera a hate-filled look and strides at me with force. 'No. You stay here. Sit at the door so it's wedged closed. Do not open it for any reason unless it's us.' The gravity in his voice makes me nod.

He walks out. I film them leave, watching their silhouettes disappear into the black void. Then I close the door and sit with my back to it, like Luke ordered.

It's impossible there is a stalker out there. Luke is struggling being back. A slap of guilt across my face. It's my fault. As I

279

blink, images of the man, ready to attack, dangle hauntingly in my imagination. I hug my knees tightly, suddenly afraid to be on my own.

I look at the time. It's four a.m. Sunrise is imminent. I feel for my pocket knife and grip the handle. *Hurry up.* Finally, footsteps. I sit up, trying to work out whose they are. My senses are on high alert.

'Cassidy?' My name is hissed. It's Luke. I carefully move my weight from the door to let him in.

'Where's Reggie?' I ask, peering into the darkness for another figure to emerge.

'I don't know – he went into the bush to have a look and never came out,' he says, worried. 'I found this.' He throws Reggie's torch onto the floor with a clatter. I stare at it, perplexed.

'He'll be back in a minute,' I say, my voice strained.

Time moves slowly. 'Maybe it was the rain? The knocking you heard.' He replies with silence. 'Or a boar?' I mutter and he ignores me again.

I check the time. Reggie has been gone fifteen minutes. Far longer than needed to check the perimeter. 'He'll come back soon.' My voice comes out in a whimper.

'I'll go have a look,' Luke says, running his hand down his face.

'Don't leave me.' I grip his arm. I'd been so sure there was no way we couldn't be alone out here. But now . . . now I'm not so sure.

'I'll just have another quick look and come back. Lean

280

against the door, okay? Don't move,' he says roughly. 'Don't open it unless you're sure it's me or Reg,' he says, firing orders. Nodding, I grab my boots and scramble them on as I sit with my back to the door. I feel too vulnerable without the option of running. But the thought of dashing into the dark abyss makes me feel sick. All at once our remoteness feels incredibly rattling. I look out across the floor to the camera. The red light still on. I forgot to turn it off. I'll leave it running.

I close my eyes tightly. All I can hear is Luke shouting Reggie's name in the distance. Every little speck of noise causes me to grit my teeth in apprehension. 'There is no one out there, there is no one out there,' I whisper to myself. Then I hear a distant strangled scream. My body freezes and runs ice cold. I close my eyes tightly. Then the nursery rhyme begins to play its sickening tune. *Ring-a-ring o' roses . . . a pocket full of posies*. I try and eject it and replace it with something else, but it won't shift. And soon my lips are joining in, mouthing the hateful song. My hands over my ears.

Then. *Bang!* Something pushes against the door.

I force my body onto it and scream.

Bang!

No – it can't be. I can't die out here like this.

'Cassidy!' Relief – it's Luke. 'Cassidy, it's me, open the door.' I'm nearly crying I'm so relieved. I move away, and he pushes it open. He's panting, trying to catch his breath. 'I can't see anything. It's so fucking dark.' Terror trickles from every note. 'There's someone out there, Cassidy, I know it.'

No. This isn't happening. 'Where is Reggie? I thought I

281

heard a scream,' I whimper. I felt so safe out here with him. He can't be gone.

'I heard it too,' he croaks. 'I . . . I came back. Let's wait for first light and I'll have another look. I'm sure he's fine. He has his machete.' He can't be seriously thinking Reggie will need to defend himself? Luke leans back against the wall and slides down it, panting. He grabs my hand, squeezing it tight, and I wince at the strong grip he has on me. 'It's okay. I'm not going to let anything happen to you,' he says.

I want to believe him.

But did he say that to Mari?

44

At first light we gingerly open the door. The camping area is deserted. The charcoal languishing in the fire has turned a ghostly white. Reggie made that fire but hours ago. And now he's gone. I put my hand over my mouth and let out a sob, and a tear rolls down the bridge of my nose and onto the ground. Luke strides around shouting, 'Reggie!' I join him. The sounds of our screams echo into the undergrowth, unanswered. I look around for the satellite phone. It isn't where I thought I'd left it. We frantically search.

'Where did you last have it?' Luke asks.

'I thought I put it back in his bag. After the call.' I look up at the clearing and go back to search. All I can remember is reading Mari's email. Could I have dropped it? We look everywhere. Unpacking and laying everything out. Our actions become hurried and frustrated as we go. Finally, we stop and look around in a disappointed haze. Our things are everywhere as we haphazardly tore everything apart. With nothing to show for it. I can't believe I've lost it. Luke goes to check the clearing one more time, coming back empty-handed.

'What do we do?' he asks with a look of desperation.

'We should wait.'

'But for how long? What if he's not coming back? What if he's lost?' He swallows. 'Or something.'

'Reggie wouldn't have got lost,' I tell him.

He gives me a side glance. 'Cassidy, you heard it too.'

I refuse to acknowledge it. 'Maybe he's hurt?' I chew my nail. 'He could have fallen.'

'I've looked!' he says, exasperated. 'If we search further out, we'll most probably get lost which wouldn't help anyone.' He's right. 'We need to go back down and get help,' he concludes.

Think, Cassidy, think. Duncan and Cleo will be on the boat to base camp right now. From there they'll set up the drone and send it out to the vantage point where we're meant to rendezvous. If we go back down now, we'll miss it. We're so close to getting that pivotal shot – just an hour or so, I remember Reggie saying as he pointed to its location on the map. If we go down now, that's it. It's lost for good.

'We should go back down. Get help,' Luke repeats, checking my reaction.

'That will take the whole day.'

'So?' he spits. I chew my nail. I want that shot. 'We could go up and get the shot. And then go back down.' I shock myself as the words leave my mouth.

He looks at me hotly. 'Are you mad? Reggie needs help. And there's some lunatic out there!'

Now, in the cold light of day, could there really be a man

284

out there, or am I just buying into Luke's terror? He had a nightmare, and we heard a bird or a monkey or something – our brains were fixed in fear and turned it into something else. Reggie is a bit lost. He's adept at survival – I'm sure he'll be okay for a few extra hours. Besides, he'd feel terrible if a twisted ankle were to jeopardise the film.

But what if I'm just telling myself what I want to hear? 'I know, I know.' I rub my forehead. *Think, Cassidy, think.*

Then it comes to me, and my words trip out as an idea forms. 'If we get up to the summit, we can tell them we need help through the drone.' I turn to Luke with a flourish, having cracked it. 'And it will take *less* time!' I add excitedly. 'They can use their satellite phone and get help straight away, rather than take the whole day to go back down to them.' I'm pleased. 'There. That makes perfect sense.'

He nods, understanding. 'Do those things pick up sound?'

'No,' I admit. And he frowns. 'But they'll understand we need help – we can make them understand. They'll see us shouting and mouthing it to them. Cleo will understand.' Then another idea. I scramble in my bag and find a notepad; it's half waterlogged but there are dry pages. 'We can write them a note. They will see it!' I say triumphantly, holding up the pen and pad to show him.

He pauses, thinking. 'Okay.' He puts his hands on his hips and paces around in frustration. 'Fuck!' he shouts. 'This is so fucked up!' he cries, shocking a group of birds into flight. We stare as they soar into the canopy and out into a patch of blue.

Away.

285

Mari.

I blink.

We pack up. As there are only two of us now, we can carry even less. We don't need the camping equipment as we're due to head down today. We're leaving it. Melissa won't be too bothered about used camping equipment. It's the hired camera stuff we need to return she'll be having kittens about.

I look around the hut for the camera. It's at the back, where I left it last night. I should get a few shots of the campsite this morning before we leave. Maybe even do a piece to camera, or get Luke to, and talk about our missing guide. Just in case I need it later. It's wedged; Luke must have moved it in the chaos of the previous evening. I press the power button, but it doesn't turn on. Then I remember I didn't shut it down last night. The battery will be dead. No matter – we still have two charged. I grab one out the bag before lifting the camera up.

I move my hand away and look down at the water collected on my palm. It's wet. Heart beating, I quickly replace the battery and try the power button again. Purple and green fuzzy light hisses on the screen. I swallow down thick putrid saliva. *No.* I turn it off again. And try once more. A drop of water plonks onto the ground from the base. Panic twists through me, like a rusty saw eking its way through wood. *No,* my insides shriek. Nothing happens. Cursing, I flip off the battery and hunt around for the other spare. I know it's no use, but I clip it on and jab at the power button again. 'Oh god,' I moan. *No.* I put my head in my hands and cry.

'What's wrong?' Luke comes into the hut, hearing me.

'The camera is broken,' I whisper in disbelief.

He stares. 'What? How?'

'I . . . I don't know. There must have been a leak in the hut.'

'Hey, hey . . . don't cry.' He comes over, and puts his arms around me.

I push him away. 'Don't.' I point my finger. 'Don't you dare be nice to me. I've messed everything up. It's over, I've ruined it all.'

'Cassidy.' He sounds just as helpless and wretched as I feel.

I stand, the camera making a dull thudding noise as it falls from my lap and hits the floor. This has turned into a nightmare. All starting from when that sodding drone broke.

This shoot is cursed.

'Look, we're at a low point right now, there must be a way of doing this. What about your phone? You can film on that, right? We can still finish this thing. You see . . . you see . . .' I bat off his suggestion, annoyed.

'Reggie!' I scream to no one as I walk outside. 'Reggie!' I call again, my throat red raw from anguish. 'Where is he?' I ask no one in particular. Walking around, looking, screaming his name. The jungle still and silent in reaction to my outburst.

Luke grabs my arm and attempts to soothe my panic. 'Look, Cassidy. We need to stay calm. We have a good plan. Let's just get everything ready, get to the summit, and then by the time we pass back through here, Reggie will be waiting for us. I'm sure of it.'

'But the camera is broken! What is the point of us being

here if we can't even film it? We came to tell your story, which you apparently wanted to tell but you haven't told me a thing!' I'm heaving now, I can barely breathe I'm so full of exasperation. 'This is the worst – the most horrific . . . and then all this stuff with you. Are you messing with me? Are you enjoying this? Are you making me love you for some sick reason?' I bang on his chest. He pulls me in and holds me.

'Cassidy. No . . . no . . . I told you. You know how I feel about you. None of this matters. All that matters is us.'

'Is there really someone else out there? Have they . . . taken Reggie?' I whisper into his chest.

He just shushes and lets me cry. Gently brushing the back of my hair until my heaving subsides.

'It's okay, Cassidy. I'll protect you . . . I'm not going to let anyone hurt you.'

45

'I'm going to have one last quick look for Reggie before we go. Have a final hunt for the phone, okay?' Luke says. 'I'll be back in a minute.'

'Be . . . be careful,' I stammer.

'I won't be long,' he says. Our eyes lock. Then he cups his hands to his mouth and calls Reggie's name. I spend the time searching for the satellite phone. Thinking about Duncan and Cleo arriving at the jetty by base camp, completely clueless about our predicament. *Better not cause us any more trouble*, I remember the Deputy Commander saying. I think of the press attention. FILM CREW IN MARI JUNGLE RESCUE CRISIS. I can't bear to think about explaining this to Raef.

I stare at the broken camera, discarded on the ground. What if everyone's been wrong about the man in the jungle? Dr Ackerman, the police, the media . . . me. I heard something that first night, and those could have been footprints by the fire. What if the stalker is real, and he's hurt Reggie? He could have stolen the satellite phone from by the fire. I watch the handmade ropes in the tree sway. What if we've never been alone? Reggie . . . Oh god. Could he be dead?

I sit in a slump. Hanging on to every note of Luke's voice shouting in the distance. *Mari*. I get out my phone and continue reading:

We're on Koh Phangan for the full moon. I thought I'd be having the time of my life. But Luke and I are not getting on and we're both miserable. We bumped into Astrid and Sander again, luckily. We've been trying to hide our relationship woes. But I'm finding it hard watching how free and happy they are. When I feel so trapped.

We're going to do pills at the full moon. Maybe then I'll be able to turn my head off. I want to escape. And only now I'm here I realise that I can't escape myself just by getting on a plane. Oblivion is my only answer. I wanted to go on a trip. I thought this was the adventure. But it's not.

Maybe it will purge me. Maybe I'll be able to stop thinking about death. Maybe I'll come out the other side a new person. Maybe I'll be able to stop thinking about what we did.

I'm starting to think I might tell you. Maybe writing it down will actually help.

And no one else is ever going to read this, are they?

290

'Nothing,' Luke says, stalking back into the camp, his shoulders slumped forward in hopelessness. 'I hope he's okay.' He scratches his head. 'We need to get going, get some help up here as fast as possible. What time are we meant to meet the drone?'

'In almost two hours,' I reply, checking the time.

'Okay, let's get on with it.' He hikes the straps of his backpack.

I nod in agreement, before, 'Wait.' We need to document this. The story we were telling, in past tense. That doesn't matter right now. We need to tell *this* story.

I take out my phone and flip the screen to film myself. I look at my stricken face. My lips are swollen, my face oily and red with damp hair slapped onto mottled skin. 'Cassidy Chambers here. I'm making a documentary about Luke Speed.' I look over to him. 'Mari Castle's boyfriend. We're currently in the jungle at the second base. Near where they lost their group twenty years ago. I . . . I can't believe I'm saying this. But our guide has disappeared. And the camera has broken. And what was meant to be a simple shoot filming the locations from the story has taken on a life of its own. And . . . has become the story.' I hear something and stop. Luke spins around too. We pause and wait. But nothing emerges. 'The satellite phone has disappeared.' I purse my trembling lips together. 'We are going to head to the summit to try and tell the others what's happened so they can call in some help.' I take a deep breath. 'We think . . . we think someone could . . .' Luke catches my eye. 'There is the possibility someone could be out here with us.' I blink as the horror of the situation floods my system.

'Come on, Cassidy, we should go,' Luke says.

I flip the phone around to show Luke standing there dishevelled, his chest heaving. And then I turn it off and jam it back in my pocket.

We begin the hike. Following the worn blue posts up the path. I try not to think of anything but each step I take; watching Luke's broad back as he takes the lead, slashing the machete back and forth to rid the path of lingering branches and big heavy leaves. At least I'm with him. He's not the slim, defenceless eighteen-year-old who was here all those years ago. He could take on anyone that comes at us.

I take out my phone and film him for a while. God knows what this documentary is going to look like now. It's certainly not what we pitched to the channel. This added drama may be a huge selling point. I just have no idea where it's heading. Or how it will end.

I press stop and take a swig of water.

'I'm going for a pee,' I tell Luke as I walk into the bush to find a good place. As I undo my trousers, he meets me in the little area. He leans against a tree, facing away. I don't think he likes being alone out here.

'You done?' he asks.

'Yep,' I reply, standing and pulling up my trousers.

A crashing sound. The hoot of birds as they fly away.

'What was that?' His head whips towards the path, the way we came.

I heard that.

'Come on.' He grabs my hand. Pulling me into a run, bush blurs past and we finally hide behind a large shrub.

'Maybe it was Reggie,' I breathe hopefully. He looks at me dead in the eye, a shaking finger rising to his lips, his face glimmering with sweat and mud.

'I can't hear anything.' I listen again. 'We should keep going or we'll miss the rendezvous.' He slowly nods and we stand, clinging on to each other's hands.

'This way,' he whispers, still careful not to make too much noise.

We trudge further. 'We should have hit the path by now. Is this definitely the right way?' I ask him.

He nods, his jaw clenched. 'I thought so.' He keeps walking, I get the sinking feeling that none of this looks right.

'Wait!' I stop in my tracks and his hand leaves mine.

He turns. 'Come on, Cassidy! We're going to miss the drone.'

'No. Let's just get our bearings. We might be going in the wrong direction.' I pivot on the spot. It all looks the same! The thought of being lost in this dense jungle is making my insides squeeze. Can we rewind time? Just a few minutes?

'I'm sure it was this way,' he says, trying to get me to walk on.

'No, this doesn't feel right.' My eyes tracking every tree, every trunk, every twisting root. Looking for something, anything, that could be familiar. But there is nothing.

46

Panic – utter panic. Everything rotates on an axis as claustrophobia coils around me. The moist air clutters my throat and I can't breathe. 'Look, we just have to go up.' His words swim in my ears as I attempt to reengage with this reality.

Lost.

We're lost in the jungle.

The idea of it screams within. We can't be. This can't be happening.

'Cassidy?' Luke says, gripping my arm, getting me to focus, pointing to the terrain which climbs on an upward tilt. 'We just need to go that way – then we'll get to the summit.'

I shake my head. 'We need to find the path. Otherwise, who knows where we're going?' I fumble around looking for the map. My shaking finger tracks the path to the second base. And then the top of the hill to the summit. Maybe that *will* work. I look ahead at the ground we'd have to cover. It's dense with roots and branches – a chaotic mess far harder to get through than the path which, although quite overgrown, was easier to navigate than this. 'We don't have much choice,' I realise.

We twist through the tentacles of bush. Luke hacks at anything stopping our ascent. It takes an age to cover a few metres and with every step I feel full of fear we're going in entirely the wrong direction. At the next water stop, I look at my half-filled bottle. We left the bulk of our reserve at the last base, thinking we'd be shortly passing back through. I need to ration the rest. What if we run out? I'm sure Reggie said there were water sources out here. But how would we find them?

I try to calm my breathing to stop the panic taking over. Luke shifts around, rubbing his face anxiously, as he sits, slumped on a rock. He's lost in the very place he spent months on the edge of dying all those years ago. He spits on the ground. His face twisted, all the softness – gone. It doesn't feel right. *He* doesn't feel right. I think of the last time I spoke to Cleo, how she told me not to leave Reggie's side. How she said there was something about Luke she wasn't sure of.

A thought festers. He was with Reggie when he disappeared – what if . . . what if . . . ?

'Luke.' My voice trembles. 'How come you didn't follow Reggie into the bush?' My voice tiny. His neck snaps in my direction. A spark of recognition in his eye, or is it hurt? My fear has turned on me, making me think the worst of everything, everyone. The darkness is insidious here. The last thing I want us to do is turn on each other. But is that what the jungle does to people?

'What are you trying to say?' His voice strained, and he looks out at the dense bush, frowning. I take out my phone and press record. Hiding it by my leg, the end pointed towards him to pick up his voice. *It's time for some of those tough questions I promised, Luke.* 'Because . . . you were with Reggie. And now . . . he's gone.'

'Cassidy. Are you seriously suggesting I hurt Reggie? Why would I do that?' His bloodshot eyes wild as they stare me down. 'How could you think that? I . . . I . . .' He begins to form a sentence, but it shuffles away. Silence.

There is something going on here. I feel dread creeping through me. The camera was on his side of the hut. The knife he tried to pocket. The knocking he heard while we were sleeping. No one else heard them. Did they? Did he make them up?

And Mari. All the things she's told me. None of them match up to his version of events at all. He is capable of lying. Mari has shown me that.

'I know you and Mari had a secret. Will you tell me what it is?'

He frowns. 'I have no idea what you're talking about.'

'Something happened, in Cambridge before you came to Thailand. I know your relationship wasn't as rosy as you've made out.' I carefully look down at my phone, the little numbers tracking the recording. It's getting this. 'What happened? We're here. Just you and me. And who the hell knows if we'll ever get out? Don't you think it's time to talk?'

He shakes his head. 'I . . . I . . .' His mouth slams shut.

I shift closer – angry now. 'Come on, Luke. You called me. You said you were ready. You said you wanted to tell your story. If not now, Luke, when? When?'

296

'There was nothing. No secret. I don't know what you're talking about.' He stands up, brushing down his trousers. 'Can we please just get up to the summit? I swear, when you get your camera back and we're out, we can finish your film. But this is about survival, Cassidy. This is about getting out of here alive.' I try to read him, looking for signs of anything that might catch him out. He is lying. I know he's lying – Mari has told me the truth about their relationship, and it wasn't all puppy love. But why? Why would he spend all those hours filming those master interviews and not be honest?

It just doesn't make any sense. Is he still living in a world of denial, unable to face what truly happened between them?

I am silent as we crawl. Our bags get caught in low-hanging branches, forcing us to crouch. My fingernails are packed with mud, and my back is sore from ducking. Danger reverberates as birds call, signalling to watch this sad procession of lost souls struggling through their home.

We stop and carefully sip more precious water. I stare down at a mosquito on my arm, its needle beak sucking my blood. Smack! I move my hand away to see its legs twitching in the throes of death. A smudge of my blood next to its squashed head.

'Are you okay?' Luke asks, waiting for me to catch up. Even though his voice is laced with care I can't bring myself to look at him.

'We should have hit the top by now,' I moan. 'We've been on the move for hours. Even if we find it, we've missed the drone.'

I look around, feeling trapped. I don't understand this terrain at all, it doesn't seem logical. Where I thought we should have broken free at the top has just become a messy plateau of more of the same. Luke sits down next to me, exhausted. He puts an arm around my shoulder and pulls me close. His smell. I close my eyes for a moment to enjoy the warm feeling, but now it's laced with something sour and unnerving.

'You know what I can't wait for?' he asks me. I shake my head. 'To take you home and tell you all the things I've wanted to say. Do all the things I want to do to you.'

I push him off me. 'Don't.'

'Wait!' He looks up, registering something. But this time, he doesn't look afraid, he looks excited. 'Can you hear that?'

I listen. Water. I can hear water.

We rush. My limbs are scraped and slashed as we fight through. Finally, we burst out into a clearing. We run towards some rocks and peer over. A drop and then, below, a rushing river. 'If we follow it, it should take us down. That's what they always say, right? If you're lost in the jungle, follow water.'

'But where will it take us?' Luke asks, unsure.

I get out the map. There are various blue lines and I have no idea where we are. But they all seem to run down to the sizeable river we first came up. We're going to get out of here! I turn and hug him. But his arms don't circle me, as they usually do. I let go, realising he isn't going to return the embrace.

'I just want to go home,' I whisper. All thoughts about the film. About Mari. Gone. I just want the safety of my bed, my cat. Rebecca and the baby.

'That thing you said about the secret. How . . . how did you hear about it?' he asks.

I freeze. 'Just something someone said.'

He swallows and moves two steps away. Looking at me curiously, his eyes narrowed.

'Why didn't you tell me about the kiss?' I whisper.

'What kiss?' He peers at me.

'Mari – she kissed Astrid in Bangkok.' He flinches. 'Did that upset you?' I say cautiously, observing his reactions.

'Who told you that?' he asks, put out. 'Can we just . . . can we just change the subject?' he asks roughly.

Luke's lying. I can't make it right in my head.

He looks over, chewing the corner of his lip. A darkness has taken over his handsome face. His stubble thick, his eyes sore, blinking rapidly. He comes over, an arm around me so I can't move. It isn't a hug; it's a grip.

'Stop it, Luke. Please. You're hurting me.' Tears rush to my eyes.

'Come here,' he says roughly. Pulling me close. 'Why are you upset?' he asks, pushing the water off my cheeks with his palm forcibly. He imposes his lips onto mine and I try to push him away.

'Get off!' I shout and he releases me. I stumble back and trip. Falling awkwardly on my ankle. I scream and grab it. The pain like a rod of fire burning deep.

Luke crouches next to me. 'Let me see, let me see.' He flaps my hand away and unstrings my boot, rolling down my sock. He holds my ankle which is floppy and raw. Swelling up before

299

our eyes. The pain gushes up my leg to my stomach, a nauseous surge. Our eyes meet. 'You should film it,' he says simply.

'What?' I croak.

I look at him. His eyes glazed. Excited. He pats around in my pockets, looking for my phone. Finding it, he juts it in my face. 'Go on. You need to get this. All this extra . . . what do you call it? Jeopardy.' He smirks. 'You need it for *our* film.' His words slither out like a snake. 'Go on, open it.' On autopilot I type in the password and press record, shaking as I point it at his face.

I feel a cold surge then. The feeling of bile wanting to travel up, burning everything it touches. 'Our film?' I whisper. The way he said it makes me feel cold. He smiles grimly. It is a smile I've not seen him wear before. I watch it on the screen of my phone. There is a wild look in his eye. Then, before I can tighten my grip, he snatches it from my hand.

He looks down, smug. And begins to fiddle. Looking for something. 'What have you been creeping around looking at behind my back? What is it, Cassidy? It seems very engrossing; you've been desperate to get to it this whole time we've been here.' I try to get up to get it back but my ankle – I can't. 'Mmm . . . is it in your emails? No . . . somewhere else. Let's have a look, shall we?' Then he grins. 'Hi Mari.' He puts on a cutesy girl's voice. 'I can't wait to tell you all about it. Maybe I'll even tell you my secret . . .'

He starts laughing then. A dark, booming laugh. And I don't feel protected by him. I feel caught out. Trapped. I hop towards him. 'Give it back,' I plead.

300

'Do you think I give a shit about what Mari-fucking-Castle's secret is?' He laughs and throws the phone on the ground between us. The laugh continues. Bent double, hooting. His soft, willing personality has shifted.

'You know why I don't give two fucks, Cassidy?' He leans towards me, enjoying this. My eyes widen. 'Because I'm not Luke Speed.'

47

'What?' I peer up at him. 'What do you mean?' I lean forward and dare to touch the distinctive mole on his face. 'Luke?' His unkind expression only deepens, and I snatch my hand back, as if bitten. Has he gone mad? Is this some sort of psychotic episode?

'You wanted this film so badly, you were willing to ignore all the facts,' he states. I take a few steps back, in shock. 'Your ambition. You think you're above everything. You never even questioned it,' he says, pacing now, a haze of adrenalin rising off him. I try to move, but my ankle causes me to cry out in pain. My phone sits in the dirt between us, and my desire to have it safely in my pocket takes over. I grimace as I retrieve it.

'If . . . if you're not Luke, who are you?'

He laughs again and rubs at the beauty spot on his face. 'A tattoo. The bloke thought it was a bit weird. Girls usually ask for that sort of thing, he said.' He pulls at his eyes, taking something out of them. Contact lenses, I realise. When he looks back at me, the deep blue has been replaced with the darkest brown. He looks completely different, as if he's peeled off a mask. 'I've been wanting to take them out all *fucking day*,' he screams. The jungle shudders around us, and I realise his streaming eyes weren't red from the heat, after all.

'You called me,' I whisper in realisation. The last few months clutter my mind as I mentally retrace my steps.

He laughs. 'I knew you'd like that. To be chosen. Even before I met you, I knew exactly the type of person you were. Ambition over everything, and everyone else.'

'Who are you?' I ask again.

He shakes his head roughly.

It can't be true. I think of the grinning teenager in all the photographs, he looks just like him.

He paces around, the glee of finally being able to reveal himself unmistakable. 'I knew you'd fall for it. I just had to find the right story. The right suspect of a crime that I could replace.' He looks at me with satisfaction, and a cocky smile parades.

'You chose this story because you could pass for Luke? But why?' He shakes his head slowly, not ready to divulge the rest. Who is this imposter? 'But we checked your paperwork,' I say, unable to fathom how this happened.

He snorts. 'You checked Luke's paperwork. Not mine. Easy to get your hands on when you know the right people.' He grins. He's enjoying this. The control. My eyes trace his face. He looks just like an older Luke with that distinctive mole and deep-blue eyes. Twenty years changes a person's face, and build. I'm filled with humiliation; how could we have missed this?

'But your passport . . . we got on a plane . . .' I stammer.

'I'm so scared of flying, Cassidy,' he mocks, feigning fear. He pretends to make a phone call. 'Melissa – honestly, don't worry, you send me the amount for a standard ticket and the details, and I'll do the rest.' I think of Melissa at her desk, surrounded by paperwork and spreadsheets. She must have been relieved to tick something off her list.

'Tell me who you are,' I demand.

'And then I got lucky taking that punch!' He hoots. 'Would have paid someone handsomely if I'd thought of that. I had to hide my glee that whole train journey back and put on my saddest face.' He looks at me with an exaggerated downward frown.

'Is that why you didn't want Cleo to call the police?' How stupid I was to think it was to cover his humiliation, and some sort of humble fear of causing fuss.

'It's sick how obsessed people are with other people's pain. *Sick.* I read all the books, all the articles about those two privileged idiots. The police reports, which someone had very helpfully uploaded onto a cold-case amateur sleuth site. And then I just had to sit and throw it all up, with an embellishment or two, for your precious interviews. And you fell for it!' I think about what Raef said about my interviews. How I haven't been able to get any real new information out of Luke, just details. He's been stringing me along, saying there is some sort of huge revelation about the jungle, but there isn't one. Because he doesn't know. He was never here.

'Why have you done this?' I whisper, panic shooting through me. The danger I am in palpable. Lost in the heart of

304

the jungle, with a complete stranger.

'*You*. You think you can just take things from people, and they won't care? They won't wonder how someone could live such a successful life made of lies about other people? Without wanting to get some sort of comeuppance?' He pauses, looking at me. 'I never thought I could get under your skin like I did. I never thought in my wildest dreams you'd let me go where we went.' His eyes wander up to my chest and I feel light-headed and repulsed.

'Who are you?' I shout. 'If you aren't Luke . . . who are you?'

He spits on the ground. 'We were happy before you came along. He would never hurt anyone.' A pause for dramatic effect. 'He was the best father anyone could ever have.'

'Father?' I say, dazed. 'Who?'

'What does it feel like to be manipulated, Cassidy?' The words tear through me. 'What does it feel like to be totally out of control? In the palm of someone else's hand? Your life no longer yours.'

Sobs escape me. I begin to cry; I try and stop but my chin crumples.

'Stop crying,' he orders in frustration. 'You don't get to cry.' He marches towards me, grabs me, and pushes the tears off my face. Our eyes lock and my fear compounds. Who is this man? What is he capable of? Then he lets me go, and turns, wounded. 'I went to see him in prison. He said he'd rather top himself than stay in that place. That's pain. He'd never hurt anyone. Anyone! And you think he did that? You pinned something so disgusting and monstrous on *him*?'

'Prison,' I whisper. I look at him again. An old family photo I saw that was leaked to the press around the time *Missing* was released. An arm around the shoulders of a young teenage boy. Max Barber's son. The man found guilty of Molly-Ann's murder, after our own investigation. What was his name . . . ?

'I loved him. He was a good father. He would never – *never* – do what you said he did.' His face curled up, all grotesque with grief. 'You think he would do those things to a little girl? You told the world he was this animal – this monster.' I swallow.

'Connor,' I remember. He jolts at the sound of his real name.

With the DNA evidence there is no way his father is innocent. But how traumatising it must be to find out who a much-loved family member really is.

'Connor.' I stand, limping. The only way I'll get through this is by building some sort of bridge. He's a big man and I can't run. 'I believe you. I believe you. Let's get out of here and we can set it right.'

He ignores me, pacing, ranting. 'All my meticulous planning paid off. It had to be the right story – long ago to the public, but something you'd be desperate to cover. A big scoop you wouldn't want to pass you by. And I had to be a good fit. I went through hundreds of cases. Until I found Luke. The same age. We look similar – I could pass with a few small tweaks. He hadn't been seen for years. It was perfect. The more I investigated it . . . the more I realised it would work. I had to do all my research and get up to speed on this story. All the little details I found on Facebook from students at that ridiculous

306

school, reminiscing about smoking corners and school plays – you loved it. I had to ruin you, Cassidy. You and your perfect little career. Just like you destroyed us.'

'You chose this case because you pass for Luke Speed. And no one has seen him for years.' I can't believe this is happening. I lower myself to the ground as I take on the weight of his story.

'He's probably dead in a crack den somewhere. Pain, you see, does things to people. And look! It worked. You lapped it up. All those pointless hours of interview. You fell for all of it.' He laughs out loud. 'All I had to do was learn one song on the piano. I was proud of myself for that one. I'm quite talented, don't you think?' He smirks. 'And look at us now. Out here, on our own. Just us.' He walks over to where I'm collapsed. 'Now, what do you think I should do?' Wild with excitement. He doesn't seem to care about our predicament, out here, lost. Alone. In fact, he seems to be revelling in it.

I try to stand. It hurts. I rest my hand on the rock, trying to anchor myself onto something real.

'There is no way you can make it out of here alive on your own,' he says. I stare at him in disbelief. He looks so different. *My* Luke. He never existed. I'm overcome with a sort of grief.

'That's sick,' I splutter.

He grimaces. 'I never meant to take it this far. But then your bosses got involved. Oh, a trip to Thailand! What a psychopathic idea. Take a poor man, who'd suffered a nervous breakdown, back to the place he lost her? Well, it sounds like poetic justice for you to suffer the same fate.' I shake my head.

Unable to process. He continues: 'I had to work it all out, how I was going to get over here without any of you noticing. I wasn't going to come at first; I was going to drop the whole thing and walk away. I almost chickened out the night before we came, remember? I tried to tell you how much I didn't want to be here – but you refused to let me change my mind, didn't you? Then, I thought, where better to end this than here?' He waves his hand around. 'There was all this stuff going on behind the scenes while you moped around looking pathetic. Those emails I sent really did the trick, didn't they?'

My head jolts up to him and he smirks. 'It was you.' The words come out in a tremble. I shake my head in disbelief, my mind a mess of questions. 'But you handed in a passport at the hotel check-in. I saw it – it said Luke Speed.'

'A fakey. Pretty shit one at that. I knew it would be useless if I tried to fly with it. I decided, if I got found out, I'd grab a bag, get a taxi to the airport, walk away. The damage was done – I just waited to see how far I could take it, and what I could get away with.' He grins. 'And look where we've ended up, Cassidy.'

'Reggie – you pretended that you heard someone so you could get rid of him, didn't you? There isn't a man out here – there isn't anyone but us.'

He looks at me with pride and shrugs. 'You thought this trip would end with an interview. Instead, you're getting the scene of your life. You think I care about dying out here?' He laughs. 'I think it would be a pretty good finale, don't you?'

'Connor. Are you really going to leave me here?' I say, my

308

voice small. I think back to the hostage training I did while filming in Afghanistan: rehumanise your captor. 'I'll die. Do you really want that on your conscience? That's rather a different prospect than just ruining my career,' I say quietly. My eyes trying to find his.

He resists. 'I don't care about that any more. Things evolve.'

I stagger up. Hobbling with pathetic limps. 'Connor. I thought . . .' I bite my lip. 'I thought you really cared for me.' I look him straight in the eye. His jaw clenches. And then he sniggers. Watching me try to walk. 'There is no point. You can't get out of here without me.' He's thrilled.

'Do you really want to hurt me? Did I mean nothing to you?' I try to swallow the memory of the other night down. 'The way you kissed me . . . the way you . . . you . . . That wasn't all fake . . .'

'Shut the fuck up,' he roars, and my mouth slams shut. I look around for something to help me. We are surrounded by glistening forest. All damp and sparkling. Still recovering from its dousing. The sun glimmers, I squint. I peer over the rocks, and at the gushing water, splashing into the pool below. It looks deep. I wonder. Could I jump?

I sit on the rock and shift myself backwards. I don't want to lose my phone. I know it doesn't work out here, but it connects me, and I want it. I feel around my neck for the strap of the Ziploc bag and slip it into the pouch, tracing the clasp shut with one hand. It should survive in there. I tighten the strap around my neck, so it doesn't fling off during the fall.

I watch as Connor marches to and fro, muttering to himself.

And swallow a gag, feeling physically sick. Violated. Used. Raped. That's what it is, isn't it? I was lured under false pretences so my feelings towards him would counter any doubts that might have crept in. I can't believe I fell for it. I was manipulated.

I wasn't ever really loved, after all.

This is all my fault.

I inch back further on the rock.

'All I ever wanted to do was embarrass you. Shame you. Make your life as pointless as mine, and as my father's. Take away the one thing you love. Your career. I think I've made a roaring success of that, don't you?'

I sit back further on the rock as he rants, inching back. Can I do this? Will I survive the fall?

'But then you had to take it further, didn't you?' he snips, words full of hatred.

'You wanted to come out here. Make Luke relive something that no one ever should.' He begins to walk towards me. 'You're sick!'

'That's not right, Connor. I wanted to find Mari. I wanted you' – I shake my head, that isn't right – '*him* to have closure. I wanted to give him what he wanted. The chance to finally tell his truth. I thought he wanted to tell his story!'

'Well, you're getting mine instead,' he sneers.

'You broke the camera, and hid the satellite phone, didn't you?' I ask. 'Reggie,' I whisper. Wondering what became of him, lovely Reggie. How Connor did it. Someone is probably dead and it's all my fault. I was so desperate for it all to be real.

310

'It wasn't ever my plan to hurt you, Cassidy.' He pauses looking over at me. Eyes tracing up my legs, my breasts, a sly side smile on his lips. 'But now we're here, I don't really have a choice, do I?'

It's my only chance, who knows if I'll get another? And there is no way in hell I'm ever going to be held captive by anyone again. I'm taking back control. I feel the straps of my backpack, and firm them up tightly. I close my eyes and hold my breath and roll back. The fall takes for ever, before – *smash!* The water throws up around me.

48

For a moment I am completely submerged. Ignoring the pain in my ankle, I kick furiously, looking towards the undulating light. As soon as air hits my face I take in a huge gulp. Shouts echo from above. 'Cassidy! You bitch!' I'm swiftly caught up by the current and dragged into the spooling river. My backpack causes friction and, in a frantic struggle, I unhook myself, pushing it to my front to use as a float.

As I turn the next corner, I hear a cry followed by a huge splash. Connor is coming. My kicking thrusts become desperate as I'm pulled further down the causeway. The messy cacophony of jungle dances around, with its convulsing chorus of chatter.

'Cassidy! I'm coming for you!' I hear as I'm drawn around a corner. White crests of spitting water force me on. Then I hear an agonised cry of pain. Maybe he's hit something. I hope he has. Let him drown.

The current pulls me down, down, down. Bending every hundred metres or so. Water hits my mouth and goes up my nose and I choke and splutter.

Around a sharp bend of rocks, the pace slows. The ground grazes my feet and I realise I can just about stand. Then another shout. 'Cassidy!' I turn, panting. He must be close. I need to hide, the current no longer my helpful guide. 'Cassidy!' I look towards the bend. Any moment now, he'll emerge. I need to get out of here quick.

I wade as fast as my injury will allow, stifling my cries of pain as I limp into the mass of mangroves. Concealing my bag between the roots, I wait. As soon as he emerges, I gulp a last breath and go under.

My lungs burn as I hold myself longer than I ever have underwater. My heart beats into my ears. As I moan little bubbles drift past my face to the surface. I flap about involuntarily in the desperation to go back up. Finally, once it's too much to bear, I burst out, gasping.

Heaving, I see him further away down the river. Looking around wildly, an angry roar of, 'Cassidy!' which echoes into the rocky valley. I lower my face into the water and take another breath before sinking to my hiding place.

The next time I come up, all I can see is his back in the distance as he wades out the river far along on the other side.

I wait for him to disappear before coming up entirely. The milky water around the mangroves is stagnant and smells, and I'm elated to collect my bag and pick my way through the roots to safety. They cling on to the fabric of my clothes like desperate hands of fans.

Once out of the water, on dry land, I collapse onto the ground, coughing – hacking away, exhausted. Vomiting white bile as I heave. Taking deep breaths, I try to regain a sense of reality. Luke . . . Connor . . . how can this be?

I feel an alien sensation on my thigh, and when I realise I've not imagined it, I quickly rush off my trousers. A leech is stuck, happily contracting as it sucks. What am I meant to do? *Think, Cassidy, think.* I'm sure I've heard you shouldn't rip them off. I cry helplessly, as I dare to touch its slimy skin. I wish I could google the best thing to do. 'Urg!' I scream through my teeth in frustration. My eyes fall on a nearby stick. I just want this thing off me. I jam the point of the stick under its body and flick. It stubbornly clings on, and I try again with more force. It pings off. Its contorting body lies in the dirt in shock. A red sore is left from its teeth, and I look at the ugly mark. I lie on my back and pull my drenched trousers back on. Forcing the damp material up my legs. I hold my ankle, pressing it with both hands as it throbs. Then I let out a sob, putting my head in my hands, allowing myself a moment to process the last hour.

The world has imploded on itself. Luke isn't Luke. The film. Mari. My heart. All of it broken into a thousand pieces. Everything has gone. And now I'm here, alone in the jungle. And even if I get out of here, what is waiting for me at home? My whole identity is my work. Connor has succeeded. Even if he doesn't get to me, he's won.

I sob and bite the inside of my lip.

Come on, Cassidy. You are stronger than this.

I pull over my bag and place it in front of me, deciding to perform an inventory. My water bottle: a few inches. Three

314

protein bars, and an apple I took from the guest house – that feels like a thousand years ago. I hold up the map. It's drenched through and falls apart in my hands. I hop up and lay it in the sunshine to dry. Next, I tentatively remove my phone from the Ziploc bag. I press on the side button and the screen lights up. I sigh with relief. I shuffle out the memory cards with all the footage we've shot out here, they are also bone dry. Then I realise that the external battery pack isn't in the Ziploc bag but in my backpack, loose. I hold it up. Water drips. I find the end of the wire and connect it to my phone, but it doesn't work. I have about three-quarters left from its charge overnight. I just need to be careful not to drain it too much. I click the button to check my pocket torch, but it has also succumbed to the river. I look up at the sky. I doubt I will get out of here before nightfall. If ever. I shake the thought away.

I scoop my T-shirt up and wipe my face. Waving away the buzzing mosquitos humming around my ears. I flip the camera on my phone around and press record. I must capture this. Whatever I am in the middle of will have an end. If I die here, I want it documented somewhere – what happened. It gives me comfort, even though there is a chance no one will ever see it. I think of Mari's diary and wonder if she felt the same.

'Hi,' I whisper, sniffing. 'Cassidy Chambers here. I . . . I can't believe I'm saying this. But Luke . . . the man I was with is not Luke Speed.' My shaking hand moves a strand of hair from my face. I stifle a tear. 'His name is Connor. Connor Barber. He's . . . he's . . . Max Barber's son. He's approached me under false pretences to get revenge for what he thinks

315

is a miscarriage of justice,' I say, finding it difficult to believe. 'Now I'm here – in the same jungle Mari and Luke were lost in. All on my own, with no idea where I am. My ankle . . . I've twisted it badly.' Although my voice shakes, recording this is giving me some comfort. 'I'm going to follow the river down, hopefully hitting the main causeway we arrived through. And wait for someone to pass . . .'

I hear something and shut my mouth. I turn the camera in the direction of the sound. I stand up. My ankle roars in pain as I move. I hold my breath as a bush rattles, and a chicken hops out. Bucking its head. I almost laugh. It sees me and startles, before running in the other direction.

I put the phone away carefully into the waterproof casing. I stand as the jungle hovers around me, like a vulture circling dying prey.

I can't quite believe that the story I was trying to tell will end by finishing me.

49

Before I head off, I limp back into the river, and wade out to the flowing current to collect more drinking water. I gulp it down and refill it again. Back on the bank I retrieve the damp map. There is a muddle of blue lines, and I've no idea where I am. My only option is to head downriver and hope I don't come across Connor. Hoisting my backpack on, I clip the front. By the treeline is a long bulky stick, and I use it to shift my weight onto as I walk, helping me stagger. I wonder how far I must navigate this wilderness. And once I arrive, how will I know I'm at the right place? What if, during my fast-paced ride down, I joined a connecting waterway, and I'm heading in the wrong direction entirely?

I can't let these fears engulf me. I need to hang on to all the hope I have, otherwise I'll be paralysed by fear, and never get through this.

I head through the treeline, making sure the river is always in my eyeline on my left, as I don't dare show myself beside it. One foot in front of the other. That's all I've got to do. The squark of birds. The jangle of branches. Hoots and chatter as I'm tailed by anonymous bystanders.

Sweat trickles down my sunburnt face. A cackling monkey jumps across the vista. Vines like ropes dangle from above. Fear reverberates through me. This nightmare has to have an end point, I think, pivoting on the spot. Why did we come here? So stupid and reckless. I'm going to be eaten up by this place. By the sun, or by whatever terrifying beasts are out there. Or by *him*. The boars or white-handed gibbons will chat happily as they munch through my bones and flesh. Red dripping from their hairy chins. A bloody hand offering their young a bite. I remember someone telling me about the Malayan sun bears and thinking what a friendly name. But now, as I twist and turn, vulnerable in my stinking clothes – I wonder if beady eyes are watching me through the thick undergrowth. Will my last moment be the terror of realisation just before a pounce?

Behind me, I hear a snivelling noise, which stops me in my tracks. My breath scant as I slowly turn to face it. A huge wild boar. Stocky and stout. Bigger than I ever imagined. I think of running but remember Reggie said they can charge at thirty miles per hour. Its tusks are large and pointy. Its pithy eyes zoned in on me, and its hooves tracing back and forth in the dirt with delight. I back away slowly, my hands out in front, palms faced forward. My back hits the trunk of a tree. I look up – it has low branches shooting off in every direction.

I try to temper my breathing as I look across at the animal.

Drool slopping from the corners of its mouth with a low-level raspy noise. Then it steps back a few paces as if about to take a running jump. I have but seconds to make an escape.

Stay calm, I tell myself. The disgusting noise gets louder and more acute as if gearing up for a lunge. *One, two, three . . .* I count in my head before I launch into a turn and throw myself up the tree and onto the first branch. Tucking my legs up and over, not daring to look back.

I pull myself up, again, onto the next level of branches. But something has a hold on me, stopping my advance. I twist my neck to see. My bag is caught. My only option to escape is to untether from it. And let my precious belongings fall to the ground. I undo the clip on my chest and one by one, I let my hands go, using all my might to hold my weight with the other as I untangle myself from the straps.

The bag collapses onto the ground, and I heave myself up another branch to safety. Up high I watch as the boar growls over to investigate the package. Sniffing at it.

I watch miserably as it uses its teeth to tear at the fabric, stabbing with its hooves. I hear the crackling sound of plastic wrappers and watch on as it crunches through my only remaining food. My plastic water bottle is next to emerge from the guts. The boar rolls it around on the ground with its snout. *Please, no.* It crunches down on it with its hoof, causing liquid to spill from the gaping hole. Instead of useless watching, I take out my phone and record my new plight in action. The boar munches through the garish wrappers and my precious

319

apple. I lean my forehead on the slimy bark of the tree, waiting for it to be over.

It's hours before I feel safe to come down. The boar depleted my stash and unceremoniously waddled back into the under-growth. I get as low as I can on the ladder of branches before hopping down, biting my teeth together as pain shoots up my ankle. I roll down my sock. It's all red and swollen. I cry out in frustration. If only I was fully fit, I'd be much more able to deal with this.

I kneel by my bag and hold it up. All rags. Light flickers through the torn material. It is useless now, all slashed and chewed. The broken water bottle crackles in my hand. I didn't realise how precious it was before it was destroyed. My mouth is already dry. I put it above my head and let the small pool of water still congregating in the bottom of the vessel into my mouth. I let the liquid hang there for a pleasurable moment before it falls down my dry throat. The tease of it fills me with terror. You only know what you've got when it's gone. How true that is here. At least I am by a body of water, but it scares me to think what I'll have to risk each time I need to drink.

I hop along, continuing my pathetically slow journey. What will happen if Connor gets to base camp first? Will he try and delay them getting help somehow? Send them off in the wrong direction? Or is his sole focus finding me and making me pay?

I think about the satellite phone. He must have it – that's why he wasn't worried about pulling me away from the path and getting us lost. He's had that safety net this whole time. I wonder if it survived the river.

I mull his plan over. He must have known the truth would come out eventually. The film could never go out. Eventually, something would crop up and he'd be found out. Maybe that's why he decided to finish it here. Once I revealed I knew something he hadn't covered with his own research, it was game over.

I think of Raef's disappointment when he finds out I've completely botched his project. The film that has been bought and paid for doesn't exist. This huge production, international travel, involving months of shooting and pre-payment for post-production.

How am I going to tell him the film never existed? The channel and advertisers' money – gone. Songbird – a fledgling company just finding its feet. It will be ruined by this. Whose fault? Mine.

Connor has won.

But does any of that even matter? I will mostly probably die out here. Never having got anywhere near the truth of what happened to Mari. All that wasted time. How will I bear to explain this to Mr and Mrs Castle? That is surely the worst thing in all of this. They wanted answers before they died. And now they'll never find out. Guilt and shame rain down.

I should have known. All the clues were there. I was just so focused on the prize, and the fact he'd chosen me – *me* – to tell his story. That only happens to the best. Usually men, who've reached the pinnacle of their career. I wanted to reach that too. But all I'm going to be is a laughing stock. Pride before a fall. And this is one almighty crash.

I hear something close. I stop. That boar had better not be coming back. I ain't got nothing else to give you, mate, you got it all. I quickly search around for a tree to scamper up. I'm already learning how to survive here. My heart quickens. But nothing materialises and I breathe a sigh of relief. I continue. My stomach gurgles with hunger. It must be mid-afternoon. Cleo and the others will be incredibly worried by now. They'll be talking about calling for help. There'll be a helicopter in the air before I know it.

I decide to head out of the treeline to the river and drink to quell the gnawing thirst. I wade out slowly. Dipping my hands into the cool pooling water. I stand straight and look around me. In better times I would look out in wonder across the achingly beautiful valley. But now, all I see is darkness and the multitude of causes for my demise.

A movement further down the river, on the other side, catches my eye. Adrenalin pumps, preparing me to run.

My eyes bulge in terror. My blood drains. No. It can't be.

He just stands there watching. My legs plead with me to get going. But I am so shocked I can't move an inch.

50

All I hear is my panting breath as we stare. He is far in the distance, but I can see his knotted hair jutting out in every direction. His face and body sludged with mud. In one hand he holds a long knobbled stick a foot taller than his height. His waist is adorned with torn rags.

Is he a mirage? Am I imagining it?

He doesn't make a move towards me and is very still. Statue-like. So, shaking, I get out my phone, and film. Focusing on him standing with self-assurance on the rock. Then, he slowly turns and walks trance-like between two tall trees, into the thick jungle. I swiftly replay the recording, to make sure he's real, and the jungle hasn't turned me into a malfunctioning wreck. Blinking, I take in what I shot. There he is. *He* exists.

Everyone was wrong. No one believed Luke. I think of the pages and pages of police interview where Luke begged them to listen. He was telling the truth the whole time.

There is a man in the jungle.

And now I'm lost out here with two men on my tail.

I wade back onto the riverbank. Periodically checking he's

not behind. What madness is this? I need all my senses to get out of this predicament. But all I want to do is curl up in a ball and give up. I'm not strong enough. I'm not. I push a tear away. *Come on, Cassidy. You can't let any of them win. I'm a fighter. I've got out before. I can do it again.*

I limp into the bush, my ankle so sore I can't help but moan as I struggle. I check the time. Late afternoon. I swallow a grimace, thinking of being out here at night with no tarpaulin or hut, fire or food. I think of the survival clips I've watched online of people rubbing sticks to create a spark. Does that actually work?

I decide to keep going as far as I can push the day. I stumble far enough away from the river to evade any eyes, but close enough to hear it, in case my thirst becomes unbearable.

I stop, leaning on a trunk. Heaving in pain. I look at my hand placed there, and something beside it comes into focus. A carving. I move my hand away quickly. Shocked.

It takes my mind a while to compute the strange carving – a simple line drawing of a bird. I run my finger around it. The cuts aren't fresh, but I look around in case I'm being watched. The mere thought that someone was here once, carving this tree, makes it more probable I am not alone, somehow.

I look ahead. A smaller version of the bird, this time in a tree a few metres ahead. I begin to film, limping from one trunk to the next, my body tingling with sickly adrenalin. Another. And another. I follow them further into the dark underbelly of the jungle. Stumbling towards whatever they are leading me to. My head telling me to run, but my heart wanting to see. Needing to know: what are these markings doing here? There must be a reason someone did this.

After about twenty, I come to a clearing. My insides go cold. Hanging from nearly every branch are twisted sticks and hand-made string. Like baubles in a Christmas nightmare. A noise! I turn but realise it's coming from a windchime. I touch the hard coconut shell it's fashioned from. Evening light breaks into the circular space. Shaking, I move my phone around, recording the strange lair that could only have been created by obsessive insanity. The trees around the edge all have their own intricate carvings. Different shapes cut into the wood.

In the centre, a mound.

Then it dawns on me – this is a burial site.

My throat feels sore as my eyes well up. I limp towards the grave and collapse by it. Sobbing. My phone drops out of my hands and onto the ground.

I've found Mari.

51

I lift my knees to my chest and hug myself. 'Mari?' I whisper. 'Is that you?' The *clop-clop* sound of the chimes knocks around me. I feel as though I've stumbled on something primeval – haunted. I pick up my phone and begin a new recording, flipping the camera so my haggard tear-stained face is in view.

'Hi,' I cough, surprised by the croak in my voice. 'I found some strange carvings in the jungle and followed them here. I think I've found a burial site. And I think it might be Mari Castle's.' Tears well up in my eyes, and I continue in a shaky rasp. 'I saw a man on the other side of the river. He looked just like the man Luke described to the police. I know it sounds crazy. I can't believe it . . . all the rumours about someone up here – they're true. Luke was telling the truth. He's innocent.' I think of Luke, hidden away from society – terrified to return to the real world for fear he won't be accepted. He tried everything to get people to listen, and no one did. Even me. I never thought the strange apparition could be true. I bought into Dr Ackerman's story – that Luke could have been through something so ghastly up here, he created him to deal with the ugly reality. But I never really thought this man could be real. The footprints by the fire, the sounds I heard that first night, the rope hanging from the tree. Rumours Reggie told us about – I was an idiot to quash the possibility so readily.

I feel a swell of action inside – I need to get out of here so I can set Luke Speed free once and for all. Show everyone what's really going on here.

'Neither of those teenagers that got on a plane twenty years ago came back, not really,' I tell the camera as the sad thought permeates through me. 'They had their whole lives ahead of them. And this man, whoever he is, took it away.' I put my phone down and stare around in devastation at this strange shrine for his kill. I'm not dealing with a sane person. I've no idea what he's capable of.

The light shifts. It will be dark soon. I need to find somewhere to hide, and I certainly don't want to be anywhere near this place. I should get back to the river for a last drink before I find cover for the night.

I get up, wincing in pain. I'm exhausted. Tears threaten. I order myself to stop. If I'm going to get out of this, I can't waste energy crying. Flies congregate around my head as I walk. The low-level shrieking hums frustrate me and I try waving them away, but they follow.

I hear the river and limp faster, grimacing. My knees bang in the dirt as I cup water into my hands and drink feverishly, taking more and more into my palms, fending off the unquenchable dehydration this moist heat seems to impart.

Then I hear a noise.

327

A whirring. Like a lawnmower, but up in the sky. My heart leaps. The drone! They're looking for me. I stand and shout, waving my arms, trying to locate it in the sky.

My head darts around as I search, but to my horror, it's already turned and is flying off into the distance. 'No!' I shout. 'Come back! I'm here. I'm here!' Even though I know it can't possibly hear me. I watch as it zigzags out of sight. 'Fuck!' I scream into the valley. The noise reverberates against the rocks, ending in eerie silence.

Then I remember. I'm not alone. I snap my mouth shut and turn slowly. Looking for signs I'm being watched. A tingle of fear slides through me as I imagine who could be observing this. An unhinged man who's lived in the jungle for decades, or one who's just arrived, both equally hell-bent on seeing me off.

I leave the bank of the river, searching for a safe place to hunker down for the night. It will be dark soon and I don't want to drain my phone battery using the torch. I hear a call and look up, panicking, as I see a large hunting bird crowing as it circles above. Dark omens. I think of all the creatures that will try to attack as I dream and shudder.

I'm going to die here, aren't I? Stop it, Cassidy.

I wander aimlessly, looking for somewhere with natural protection from the elements. Every rustle makes my insides jump. My mind begins to ask strange questions. *What would you rather? Be eaten alive by a wild boar? Be bashed to death by Mari's killer? Or succumb to whatever sicko Connor wants to do to get his own back . . .*

Nausea circles me and I wipe sludgy sweat from my forehead. I feel dizzy and grotesque. This isn't just exhaustion; it is something else. I grasp a tree as I bend over and vomit.

All that precious liquid in my system – gone. I look at the drenched ground, river water and bile. *Come on, Cassidy. One more day. They're searching for you – you saw the drone!* I cling to the tiny morsel of hope.

I notice a mound of rocks and limp towards it. It is a large system of boulders, hunched against one another. To one side is a small entrance point. A cave. I lower myself to the ground and get on all fours, crawling inside the tight space. It's small but cool. It will do. There is only enough room for me to sit, knees to my chest. The sound of the jungle is muffled, and I feel separated from its dangers. I bite my teeth together as I prise my boot off the blistered foot. Rolling down my sock, I point the torch at the area. The plaster Connor carefully attached to my heel has come off and the wound is red and ugly, full of pus and raw. Infected. A new worry. I knew this churning sickness was attached to something bad.

I lean back against the rock, sighing with relief that I've found a solution for tonight. If I just get some sleep, tomorrow is a new day. The search party will find me. I will survive this.

329

52

I've been sitting here for hours, half asleep, petrified by every sound. My lips move with eclipses of thought that stumble through my consciousness. The hard rock I'm leaning on forces me into an uncomfortable half-slumped position. My ankle throbs. There is the taste of vomit in my mouth that I haven't been able to swallow away.

A noise and I jolt upright.

Fear and dread so overwhelming it simmers in every pore.

I ball my fists, listening. Footsteps. '*No*,' I mouth. I hear the snap of twigs. A tapping noise. Like a stick striking rock.

Is he out there?

My whole being seizes. I close my eyes tightly, willing it out of my imagination. *Please let this all be in my head.* Then a tapping again. *Oh god.* He's out there. Is he going to kill me, and dig a shallow grave next to Mari? Where I'll lie for eternity listening to the dull thud of chimes? The knocking gets louder as it approaches. I pull my arms around myself and inch my feet as far as possible from the entrance. Making myself as small as I can. *Please help me. Somebody help*, my mind screams. But there is no one who can. I am all alone.

I press my teeth together and a cold sweat sweeps through me as a shadow passes over the lip of the cave. I blink and stare in disbelief at the dirty bare feet positioned there.

It's him. He's found me.

I hold my breath. *Please don't notice me. Please.* Can something, anything, save me? My safe little haven has become a trap. Fishing in my pocket for my knife, I take it out, extending the blade and gripping the handle. I expect a hand to come in and yank me out, and I squeeze the handle tighter – I've never hurt anyone before, but I will.

After a few seconds the feet simply move on.

And he's gone.

My whole body slackens with relief.

Finally, light creeps towards my toes. I didn't sleep a wink. Too scared to move an inch after my night visitor. It takes me a while to get the courage to force my tight, aching body out of the space. I bite my teeth together as I put weight on my ankle and stand up, leaning against the rocks. *Argh.* It feels worse than yesterday. And my heel is throbbing on the other foot. I look down at it, lifting my trouser leg. The blister is oozing. I need antibiotics. What will happen if I don't get the medicine I desperately need? How long can I survive? Will my death be agony? *Cassidy, stop. Focus. Stop delaying your only way out.* Wallowing isn't going to fix anything. I need to get moving. No matter how slowly.

'Do the next right thing,' I whisper to myself. *Next right thing, next right thing*, plays over in my head like a sick tune. Turning into the nursery rhyme over time. I limp along on hyper alert. I know he's in the vicinity. Maybe he's watching me as I shuffle along, waiting for me to give in. I imagine him slitting my throat and dragging me by my hair back to that disturbing site. No – I will not go. I will fight.

I'm desperate to get back to the river for more water, but scared to leave the relative safety, hidden within the jungle. My cracked lips mutter as I walk. About the case. About Connor. About all my bruising mistakes. I think of his eyes that seemed to twinkle when he laughed, and the dark black void of indifference they were replaced with. I try not to think of our night together. The overwhelming feelings which were unjust and untrue. All that was light and magical is now dark and putrid and rotten.

How stupid I have been.

I think of the dolls then. All the dolls I played happily with. Sort of pleased I'd got one over on my mum and found somewhere better to be. *Let her worry*, my six-year-old brain had thought as I pulled at their clothes and plaited their hair. The sound of the nursery music tinkling in my ears. How shameful I felt later when I realised what I'd done and the danger I was in. But it wasn't my shame. It was hers. She gave it to me.

I'm delirious as I hobble near the river just inside the treeline. Eight hours. That's how far we walked on that first day with Reggie. Was that yesterday? The day before? No – longer? I feel like I've been here weeks.

I must have come down the river at least a few miles after the jump. Surely I should make it down by the end of the day? I must. Because what is the alternative? Another night out here alone. With that man in the dark. How long could I survive out here in the state I'm in? I think of Luke trapped for weeks. How terrifying it must have been for that poor boy – practically a child. Running away from this man, only to come home to find hostility and anger. I must get out of here and tell them the truth. If I can do that, this wasn't all for nothing.

I hobble out of the bush to the river to drink. I'm insatiable for it. The river is now in an incline, rushing faster. Could I possibly throw myself into it and let the current take me the rest of the way?

I think of the others – they will have got help by now and Duncan will be searching with the drone. I imagine him with the remote control in his hand, carefully searching the monitor for signs of us. They'll be looking for three people. Reggie. I blink. Lovely Reggie. What did Connor do to him? Or was it the man after all?

After drinking some more, I sit under a tree to rest. I feel like a wrung-out cloth, with not much left in me. I close my eyes. Calmness overcomes me. Maybe this is the moment I simply give up. I am two opposing people – one minute overwhelmed with fear, the next completely calm, like the sea, on a listless day. I think of the teal blue of the Deal seafront, with Rebecca, the last time I saw her. We'd strolled along the pier with seagulls dipping. Her hair had rushed in front of her face as the wind rattled past. Her smile as her hands comforted her small stomach, yet to pop. My cracked lips smile at the memory. Will I ever get to meet that baby?

A noise. *Thonk*. Something has fallen out the tree and landed on the ground to my right. I blink my blurred vision away and watch as a coconut rolls towards me. I don't believe it at first – and must physically pick it up and hold it in wonder. I shake it. Liquid sloshes inside. Sugary water and food.

I get out the penknife and place the coconut on the ground, firmly, so it won't roll away, and begin to stab it over and over. Tearing off the smooth green outer layer, I get to the furry brown part. I don't want to break it in half and lose the sweet liquid. I'm also worried I'll end up cutting myself and I could certainly do without another gaping wound.

I smack it with the knife, near the tip where three little dots reside. An edge snaps off, much to my pleasure. I hold it above my head and let the water into my mouth. Once I've exhausted the fluid I pull at the edges, snapping off pieces of shell and biting down on the waxy flesh. Just having something in my stomach makes me feel less despairing.

As I munch, I weigh up my options. Crawl through the jungle or take my chances in the river. The latter is tempting. But I don't know where it could take me – there could easily be a sharp drop down a waterfall. It's a risk.

I think about home. What I'll do if I ever get back. My whole career I've been chasing something. Running ahead, trying to 'arrive', but really, what does that mean? In ten years, if I survive this, where do I see myself? Alone, surrounded by awards. And cats. And no one else? Is that really what I want?

Did I let Connor manipulate me because really, I'm missing something I need to let in? Connection. Closeness.

Then I hear the whizzing sound of the drone and stand. The remains of the coconut fall from my lap and I run towards the river. *Whizz . . . whizz.* It's there. It is right above my head. I jump around, waving my arms like a maniac. It hovers and then moves up and down, as if nodding. They've seen me. They know where I am.

A smile as wide as my face. Happy tears of relief. I'm going home.

I wave at it, grinning cheerfully. I imagine Duncan and Cleo cheering over at base, calling one of the rescue team over to show them. I wave at it and try to mouth, 'Luke isn't Luke. Max Barber. His son!' Accentuating my lips, so they can read them. I doubt they understand. The information is too extraordinary. The drone hovers before zipping up again. I watch helplessly as it flies down the river and over the jungle out of sight.

I feel giddy. All my worries lift off my shoulders in an instant. This is the beginning of the end of this. Relief.

'Hello, Cassidy.'

I whip around.

Connor.

53

Connor is covered in sweat and dirt. His T-shirt, which should be a light green, is dank and patchy. He still has his backpack and seems to have survived the jungle far better than me. He takes a swig from his water bottle and grins, confident he's snared me. I back away, towards the rocks. But he strides over and catches my wrist, holding it tightly. 'You think I'm falling for that again?' he sneers.

'Connor, they know where I am. They're on their way to rescue me. It's over. Can't you see that? They know who you are. I told them.'

'Lies, Cassidy, all lies,' he replies arrogantly.

'They heard me on the drone.'

He smirks again. 'Those things don't record sound. Don't you remember? You told me.'

'I got it wrong, the replacement is a different model,' I say, the agitation in my voice giving me away. He shakes his head with macabre pity. 'We both know that's not true, Cassidy.' But he cautiously looks around and yanks me towards the line of trees, away from the open valley.

He shoves me onto a rock. 'Sit there,' he says, pacing, the machete in his hand. 'I'm amazed you're alive. I thought one of those giant pigs got you. Kept expecting to come across a pile of bones.' He looks over at me with an expression I cannot distinguish. Is it relief I am alive, or displeasure? There must be part of him that cares for me. I know there is. I need to tap into that.

'Do you really want to hurt me, Connor? You've got your revenge, okay? My life is ruined, my career – I'll never work in film again. Isn't that what you wanted? Isn't this the end of the line? Come on, Connor, you're not a murderer . . .'

Hidden under that bravado he's conflicted, I can tell. 'Maybe it's not enough. Maybe it would be better this way.' I can tell he's trying to square this off in his mind, and he's undecided. I still have a chance.

'Connor, you couldn't. Look at me, Connor.' His eyes flit towards mine but move quickly, as if he can't bear it. 'Don't you remember? You must have . . . you must have liked me a bit too . . . I felt it. You must have,' I whisper.

'Shut up,' he snaps, scratching his head in frustration. Does he really want to take his revenge all the way – to death? A charge of murder is far worse than fraud. But a neat accident would rid him of that. What happens in the jungle rarely makes it out. We've seen that before.

'It felt real to me.' I stand up, daring a few limping steps towards him. 'When you touched me, held me, you—'

'Shut up,' he says again with more urgency. Have I hit a nerve? He's confused. I've complicated things. I tentatively

337

look around for an escape. I need to run past him and jump into the river. I'm incapacitated with my injuries. He's bigger, fitter. Everything is stacked against me.

I carefully put my hand in my pocket, fishing out my pocket knife. My thumb brushes the elephant carving and I offer it a little prayer of hope. What had Reggie said about elephants? Was it strength? Longevity? I hold the handle in my fist, with the blade sticking out, hiding it behind my leg. 'Can I have . . . can I have some of your water, Connor?' I ask.

He glances at me, annoyed. 'No,' is his simple reply.

'Please, Connor. Just a sip. I've not drunk all day.' He gives me a cursory look and his shoulders relax slightly, a small nod. Walking over, he unscrews the cap.

This is my chance. I need to pounce and run. A hard hammer hit and then the fastest run of my life, bad ankle or not. This is about survival. Chop it off for all I care, I just want to get out of this.

As he walks towards me, the pressure of the moment heightens. He sidles up. Holding out the bottle. 'Connor,' I say, raising my chin. 'Just one last kiss . . .' He looks startled by the suggestion, and I take the moment with all I have. One, two, three . . . I stand up.

Bang!

The force of it causes him to cry out in shock. I'd closed my eyes for that split second, and when I open them, damn, the handle of the knife sticks out of his shoulder and he looks down at it in disbelief. The machete dropped to the ground.

I take my chance.

I run from the treeline and out into the valley. He roars and I feel his presence behind me. My ankle is agony, but I ignore it. Focusing instead on the rocks and the water below.

But I'm too slow. I scream as he grabs the back of my shirt and hauls me to the ground. I try to crawl away, but he flips me over and sits on top of me, his weight pinning me to the spot. He grapples, getting a handle on my arms and jamming them against the ground above my head. I wriggle, trying to break free, but he's too strong, even injured. If I'd struck just an inch lower, he'd be bleeding out on the floor of the jungle.

My one chance, gone.

His hands find my throat and squeeze. I grab at his fingers, trying to prise them off. But his grip is like cement. I stare at the sky. Willing for a helicopter. A flock of birds dart across my vista. Blood rushes to my face. 'Please . . .' I choke. 'Please.'

'It was never meant to go this far,' he pants. 'You did this. You did this. I . . . I . . .' he cries, spit landing on my face. 'You fucking bitch,' he roars. And then tenderness takes over. 'I . . . I . . .' There is something that looks like love in his eyes as he tries to kill me.

I feel light-headed. The view of his face blurs. My kicking legs quietly give up.

I am going to die.

Just as I feel myself fading, the pressure around my neck suddenly evaporates. Am I dead? Connor's weight on my body – gone. He groans. I grasp at my sore, tender neck and twist to one side, gagging. What's happened? What's going on? I pull myself up and look around, light-headed and dizzy.

I see him.

The man covered in dirt. Knotted hair. Bare feet. I watch aghast as he yanks Connor's body away. He's untying some sort of rope around his waist. It looks handmade, thin, but strong. Like the rope we found hanging by the huts, and the hanging twisted sticks by the grave. He ties Connor's wrists behind his back, quick and efficient, like a seasoned sailor mooring a boat. He then lets Connor go, and he slumps, passed out.

'Thank you,' I gasp. Every word and swallow hurts. Should I run? The man doesn't seem aggressive. In fact, the opposite. He is calm, unbothered by my presence. Besides, he just saved my life, and I don't feel threatened. If anything, I feel protected.

My eyes track his lean body. His shape is different to Connor's who is all thick muscle. This man is trim. Small even. I can't age him. He could be thirty or fifty. It's impossible to tell.

'Thank you,' I croak again, in case he didn't hear me.

He ignores me. Spitting on the ground. He crouches down, forearms resting on knees, in thought. Before turning to the river. His hand spoons the surface, before sucking up the liquid silently.

'*Sawadee kha?*' I try, in case he doesn't speak English.

He stands and begins to walk away. I don't want him to go. 'Wait!' I call, getting out my phone. I need to film him,

340

for Luke. I need to get as much proof as I can that he exists. I press record, holding it indifferently to my side, so he doesn't know what I'm doing.

'Do you . . . do you speak English?' I ask. 'What happened when those two backpackers came here a long, long time ago? Was there an accident?' I ask, my voice laced with compassion. He stops in his tracks; he must have understood. 'You didn't mean to. Did you? The grave – the care you've taken. You wouldn't have done all that if you didn't care.' This is the interview of a lifetime. This man was never meant to exist. Yet here he is in front of me. I can exonerate Luke. Free him and Mari's parents of the pain of never knowing what happened to their daughter.

This interview is why I came to the jungle.

The only person who can unlock the truth is standing in front of me.

'Who . . . who are you?' I ask. He remains silent. 'I found the grave. Did you make it for the girl, Mari?' I ask quietly. He stands there, motionless. 'Do you . . . understand?'

He very slowly turns around. His eyes downcast.

Then he looks up and I see his eyes properly for the first time.

Dazzling blue.

He opens his mouth. 'You shouldn't have come here.' I blink a few times. The sound of his British accent cuts through the fetid air like glass. No. It can't be. It doesn't make any sense.

I step towards him. 'Luke?'

341

54

He tears apart a leaf and throws it, watches a piece float into the river, calmly observing as it drifts downstream. 'Who are you?' he asks, quietly. 'Why did you have all that camera equipment?' He glances up at the sky. 'And the drone.'

I rest back on a rock, taking the weight off my various ailments. 'I was making a documentary about Mari.'

He nods, in thought. 'I assumed that.' He gestures over to Connor, all trussed up on the ground. 'Who's he?' He shoots me a look. 'I thought you were together or something . . . Is it not working out?' I smile softly at the joke.

'Something like that. Were you watching us the whole time?' I think of the footsteps below the hut on the first night.

He nods, throwing another piece of torn leaf into the water. 'I saw the fire,' he replies simply. His words are measured, and his sentences sparse. I look at Connor, passed out on the ground. The bleeding on his shoulder has calmed. I'm sure he'll recover. I have a flash of a memory – his breath on the scoop of my neck – and I shudder. My eyes trace his big, rugged body. He never made sense out here, he never seemed to fit. I now realise why. He never spent months out here surviving. I look over at Luke. Bare-chested. Only raggedy material across his waist which I realise used to be cargo shorts.

There is so much I want to know. Where do I even start?

'How long have you been here?' I ask tentatively.

He looks over, frowning. 'I left in twenty-seventeen.' He looks up at the sky. A bird calls from above and he cups his hands around his mouth and mimics the noise perfectly.

'Five years,' I tell him softly. I'm mesmerised by him. He has absolute self-assurance in this unruly place.

'Was he a cameraman or something?' he asks, nodding over at Connor again.

'I don't think he's very well,' I respond quietly, unsure this is the right moment to divulge who he really is, and why he was ever here. 'Did you do something to our guide? Reggie?'

His eyes narrow. 'I don't hurt people. Unless . . .' He nods at Connor.

'I wasn't accusing you . . .' I start. He views me with suspicion. 'I'm just worried about him.'

He points up the mountain. 'He's up on the ridge, quite near the second camp. He's been bashed in the face, hurt his leg. He managed to find some yucca and a water source nearby. He'll be fine until you get to him.'

'Thank you.' I am so relieved.

Then he raises his arms in the air, and like a dart, he dives into the water. It is the most perfect shallow dive I've ever seen. He comes up and slicks his hair back. Water flings backwards. His hands firm against the rocks as he pulls himself out.

The mud that had covered his shoulders and chest has been washed away. He notices me observing. 'The mud, it protects from the sun,' he explains. He sits on the edge of the river, his feet submerged. He's so calm. So unrushed. Leisured. Not one ounce of panic or stress. This environment has been all terror for me, but he obviously thrives in this ecosystem.

'Is it Mari?' I ask.

He wrings out his hair. And nods. 'Took me a while. I had time.' He stares into the valley.

'Why . . . why did you come back?'

He gives me another side glance. 'You interviewing me for your documentary? Because I haven't signed one of your silly forms.'

I shuffle. I'm still secretly recording him. I can't not record this. One of the most explosive pieces of film ever captured, and my hand shakes with adrenalin. I'll have to work out the logistics of getting him to let me use it later.

'I guess . . . I guess I wanted to find out what happened to her. Tell her story. Your story. Tell a truth about something that has been re-hashed by the press without much rigorous exploration.'

His eyebrow rises. 'That line usually work?' He sighs. 'I've heard it all before.' He looks uncomfortable. 'You know, one newspaper offered me one hundred thousand pounds to talk? When I said no, they went and took all this stuff I'd said to "close sources" completely out of context and made me look insane.' He looks down sorrowfully. 'But I suppose I was, to a degree.'

'Have you been here this whole time?'

'Why should I tell you? Because of you – causing this scene – I'll have to leave.'

'Don't you want to come home?'

'*Home?*' He says the word viscerally. 'Strange of you to presume where my home is. I'm not sure you know me well enough to make that judgement.'

It's strange, I feel like I know him. But he's right – I don't know him at all. Maybe I should be afraid, he could be a murderer. I think of the Luke in Mari's emails, and the much-loved version that Mr Castle, Alice and Dr Ackerman talked about. This is him.

'Sorry,' I state.

He sighs and puts his head in his hands. He can't have spoken to another human all the time he's been here.

And then it's as if he just gives in. 'I'd been living on this rehab for a few years in the countryside. It was run by this old priest. More of a commune really. After a while, when I was better – clearer – I started getting involved with working on the land. Being outside. Making things with my hands.' He stares down at his open palms before continuing. 'I found it therapeutic. Being back in nature, it quietened all the stuff up there.' He taps the side of his head. 'I got into survival, camping in the woods. Hunting. It was cathartic after being lost out here, something about taking back control, I suppose. Last time I was here I had no idea how to survive, so I was completely vulnerable.' He sighs, and gets up, staring out into

345

the valley. 'I haven't spoken to anyone else for a long time.' He looks emotional then. Like he's completely conflicted – wanting to disclose everything, but terrified to.

'It's okay, Luke. I'm . . . I'm listening.' I grip my recording phone and swallow. I suddenly feel terrible for recording this and wish I hadn't started now. This feels too special, too intimate. But if I stop, he may notice, and the moment will be lost for ever. 'Why did you come back, Luke?' I gently guide.

After a pause, he replies. 'I wanted to come back and find Mari's body. Prove I didn't carve her up like they all secretly think I did. I thought maybe if I could show them, and they could do their forensics or whatever, then I'd finally be free.'

'You mean DNA? Prove that man . . . ?' I ask.

If it wasn't Luke, could there have been someone else? He grits his jaw – a sharp intake of breath, wondering if he should go on. Swallowing thickly, he continues.

'You must understand. I was under a lot of stress when they found me. They kept jabbering at me. *Where is she? What happened to your girlfriend, man? What did you do to her?* And I . . . I made him up.'

'You made him up?' I gasp. A confession.

He walks towards me, his finger pointed out. 'You have to understand. I only did it because they thought I was this terrible person, who went out of his way to . . . hurt her. I was eighteen – I panicked. I couldn't explain how I just woke up one day and she was gone. They were hostile towards me from the off.' His voice cracks. 'So yes . . . I made him up.'

346

'He never existed,' I whisper.

'I lied. They knew I lied. I couldn't backtrack. It would only confirm what they thought.'

I think of the burial site. 'But you found her?'

He nods. 'I spent a year before I left researching the area. Then I spent the first few years here searching. I found her pink bag first. Quite unbelievable the police missed it. But they didn't try very hard once they found me. And this.' He walks over to the pouch he'd been carrying before he dived into the water. He takes out something square. Dusty. Scratched. The other disposable camera.

'I found it near her body. I think she must have been holding it when she jumped.'

'Jumped?'

He looks at me and nods. 'Her bag and remains were at the bottom of a cliff.' He pauses, grimacing at the memory. 'I thought that was all I needed. To bring her home. At least her parents would be able to have peace, even if I couldn't. But after I found her, I couldn't bear to leave her. And I got caught up in the terror that I'd go back, and history would repeat itself.' He walks up to the lip of the river and looks out into the valley. 'I like it here. I understand who I am here.' He begins to cry, shaking. 'And I've been too scared to come back and tell anyone what I found in case they didn't believe me. So, I buried her here, with me.'

'Luke – I'm so sorry.' I think of Mari, the girl in the emails. How troubled and scared she'd sounded. How on the edge.

'Every morning I wake up and say tomorrow, tomorrow I'll

347

go. But here . . . here I know the rules. And if I stick to them, I'm okay. But back there. Back there . . . it's harder. It's a much harder system to fight.' He looks out. 'I have to constantly apologise, or explain myself all the time. Deal with people's accusatory looks. Here I can just *be*.'

I look at the disposable camera he's holding. The secret. I didn't get a chance to finish the diary. To find out what happened between the couple they'd been clinging to so tightly when they came here. I open my mouth to ask him but Connor moans. I turn to see him squirming on the ground. He settles back again, still unconscious.

I glance over at Luke tentatively. Now isn't the right time for that question. 'How have you survived out here on your own for five years?'

He sniffs. 'I prepared. Got fit. Researched everything I could find on jungle survival. Took me two years to find the courage to do it. I walked in through Laos and hitched through Europe – took months. I didn't want anyone to know I was here.' He leans forward and picks a flower, putting it in his mouth and chewing. He hands one to me and I do the same. It is sweet. The petals dissolve on my tongue. 'I just wanted to disappear into the wilderness. No one even missed me, I bet. Even my own mother disowned me, after all my antics when I was using. I wasn't sure I was ever going back.' He dusts his hands together. 'I'll walk you back down to base. It's only an hour away.'

'What about . . . ?' I gesture to Connor.

'He could do with a bit of time to simmer down, don't you think?'

I nod, agreeing. 'Are we really that close?' I say, amazed. 'I was going in the right direction?' I slip my phone into my pocket.

He nods. 'I've been tracking you. I was hoping I wouldn't have to intervene. But then that guy tried to kill you, so I thought I'd better . . .'

'It was you last night, while I was in the cave?' I ask, and he nods.

'You scared the shit out of me.'

He laughs. 'Sorry about that. But yes – you would have hit camp. Pretty impressive for a first timer . . .' He helps me up and pulls my arm around his shoulder, so he can take the weight off my ankle while we walk. 'What's your name?' he asks.

'Cassidy. My name is Cassidy. Nice to meet you, Luke.'

55

Luke cuts and turns through the bush, barely leaving a mark, sauntering with the distinction of someone who knows where they're going. He tells me where to watch my footing and pauses to listen, nodding to himself when he's recognised each rustle and hoot. Light glimmers as we pick our way through. His footsteps silent and lithe, and I feel like a demolition truck in comparison.

We come to a large tree, with hulking visible roots that splurge out like spiders' legs. We pause and I limp around it, taking in its ancient majesty. 'It's a dipterocarp tree,' Luke explains. 'It's the biggest one around here. I sleep next to it sometimes,' he says, pointing out a comfy dip.

'It's like something from a fantasy film,' I muse, stroking it. He leans against a section of trunk, crossing his arms. God knows how much time I have alone with him before the noise of other people tramples over it. I bite my lip. 'You told the police that you woke up one morning and she was gone. Why do you think she left you, Luke?'

He picks up a stick and begins to peel back the bark in

perfect straight lines as he considers his answer. 'How well have you got to know Mari? Do you still buy into the propaganda?' he asks, peering over to me. 'I understand why they did it. Wanted to keep her perfect for ever. Immortalise her as this flawless person. Keep her in the nation's hearts.' He sighs. 'But to play along, I had to deny myself.'

Now, Cassidy – ask him now. 'What happened before you left Cambridge? It was something big, wasn't it?'

He looks surprised, and I let the silence settle while he decides how to reply, and whether to trust me. Finally, he glances up. 'Did you know that Mari had eight siblings?'

I frown. 'No.' I thought she was an only child.

'Miscarriages. Elsie is very religious, more than Charles. I remember Mari telling me her mother always thought it was a punishment and a lesson – the reason she had to work so hard for her. And because Mari was the only one, and her parents were older and desperate for a child, they were overly protective. But on the flip side – they were also very lenient towards her behaviour. Overlooked things. There were a lot of strange boundaries going on which I didn't really understand at the time. I was only eighteen. Her dad especially didn't want to upset her. Even when she was caught out being terrible, he turned a blind eye. He wanted to keep up the pretence their only child was special, somehow. I think he even lied to himself, about what she was really like. Now I've been through what I have, I can see she really needed some sort of therapy. She was spiralling, and I couldn't cope with the responsibility. They were the grown-ups; they should have got

351

her some sort of help. But they didn't want to accept she was broken, I suppose.' I nod, thinking of the elderly couple and the conversation we had in the garden. 'They're all buried in their back garden. Did you know that? You can name your own species of rose, so they named each flower after a child. Mari told me that once.'

I think of the perfectly manicured garden and the gorgeous flowers, all hues of pastel immaculately pruned and tended to. Graves.

'It must have been why Mari was obsessed with death. She talked about it a lot. More than anyone I'd ever known. I think her parents' anxiety had impressed on her. Elsie was a nervous wreck about everything. Understandable, really.' He looks uncomfortable before continuing. 'When my dad's cancer came back, and it looked like he wasn't going to make it, Mari was devastated. She really got on with my dad. My mum was always wary of her, but not Dad. Mari became pre-occupied with being near him. With helping care for him. Especially at the end. She was more affected by it than even me, I think. After he died, I found myself comforting her, rather than the other way around. It was overwhelming. But there was another reason it hit so hard.'

He stops.

'What, Luke?' I whisper. 'What happened?'

He looks over at me again, unsure, before deciding to continue. 'Towards the end he was in a lot of pain. Mari couldn't take it. She couldn't sit still. Then one day she came to me saying we should put him out of his misery. She said it wasn't right – he shouldn't be hurting so much when death was inevitable.'

Oh my god.

'I refused. Saying she was crazy. We couldn't do that. I could never physically do that to my dad. He was my . . . my . . . everything.' His chin buckles at the memories. 'But she wouldn't let up about it. Going on and on about how much pain he was in. How we loved him and couldn't let him suffer one more day. He was at home, having palliative care, with days to go, the doctors said. His distressed moans at night were too much to take. And she . . . she offered to do it.' He gasps a breath. 'In the dead of night, while Mum slept. We heard him cry out in pain. And we went into his room. We lit a candle, and I held his hand and kissed his face. I told him I loved him. And she . . . she . . . she did it with a pillow. He struggled and then went still. He was gone.'

He looks up at me. Pulling a tear across his face with his hand. 'You see. Maybe I don't belong in society.' He cries into his hand. 'No one ever questioned how he died, because he was on the road to it. Mum never had a clue. The guilt was crushing. She should have been there when . . .'

I feel a surge of sadness. 'I'm so sorry, Luke,' is all I can muster. Thinking of him having to navigate all of that on his own at such a young age. A young boy overwhelmed, dealing with his girlfriend's inherited trauma, along with his father's death. The secret. The event that was the precursor for all of this: the death of his dad, under the guise of a sort of messed-up euthanasia.

'Mari was the only girl I'd ever loved. When we first started going out, people tried to warn me off. She was like no one else I'd ever met. Like an asteroid had hit the planet and she'd emerged. Every single day she fascinated me. If she decided something was wrong, that was it – you couldn't change her mind. She was uncontrollable. I used to think that was heroic. But then after my dad died, I saw the danger, and what she was turning me into. There was a connection to reality missing somewhere. Like she was just passing through. And she was never going to stay long.' He's been venting wistfully, like he's forgotten I'm here. 'When I was rescued, I had all these mixed feelings about her. Anger, resentment – love. I felt it was my duty to keep who she really was a secret. For Elsie and Charles. They wanted everyone to see her as this perfect untroubled daughter. Charles was convinced it was how to keep her story in the press. And I was cowering under the weight of my lie about the man stalking us, and what happened to my dad. So, I started taking drugs to numb it all. But Mari was always there. Following me in the darkness of addiction. Whispering to me, asking me to find her. Because that's what I'd always done, I'd always protected her, and I'd failed. I had to come back. I still . . . I still loved her.'

I nod. Shocked at all these revelations.

A bird calls, breaking the intimate moment, and he re-adjusts, wiping the tears away, sniffing. 'We should get going,' he says, before helping me back up.

'Not much longer,' Luke mutters. I can feel nervous energy

pouring off him. My head is crammed full: Connor and falling in love, Mari's diary, and then finding Luke and hearing his side. We are coming to the end of the story. The puzzle is almost solved. But how can I believe anything he tells me?

'What happened when you last saw her?' I ask the question I have been waiting to hear the answer to since the beginning of this.

He sighs. He's said so much already. 'We'd been lost for about three weeks. Wasting away. Delirious. Mari got it in her head that we'd die together in a suicide pact before it became more horrific than it already was. Take control of our destiny, she kept saying. I tried to talk her out of it. Asking her to give it more time, saying we'd find a way out. But I could see in her eyes she'd already decided. At each of my refusals she became more agitated and frustrated. She gave up, refusing to even try and get out of here. In the end I told her straight. I wasn't ever going to do it. And I woke up one morning and she was gone. In the ground she'd written: *Sorry*. She'd gone into my bag – taken the camera. I thought that was strange.' We stop walking and he removes it from the pouch. 'You see, there aren't any more photos to take.' He touches the dial. 'The last five photos. They will be her last moments, I'm sure. She had this obsession with documenting everything.' He hands it to me. 'Here, take it. Get it developed when we get out. If what I think is on there, take it to the police, fight for me.' His kind eyes plead into mine. I nod and slip the camera into my pocket. 'I promise I will.'

He coughs. 'You know something? I never saw the snake.'

I frown. 'What?'

'The snake when she ran into the bush, away from the path. She screamed, legged it. I had no choice but to follow her. I never saw it myself. I often wonder if she saw one at all. If she actually wanted us to get lost out here, together.'

I blink. Thinking of Mari's diary imprinted on my brain. *We can't be together when we touch down in Heathrow . . . The thought of him with anyone else makes my insides shrivel and squeeze together . . . Sometimes I surprise myself with what I am capable of.*

Was the pact something she had in mind, before they lost their group? Could it have even been . . . her intention?

In the distance I hear voices and the whizzing sound of the drone. We are close.

Luke looks towards the sound, and then up and around this pocket of jungle, ruminating. Taking in his last few minutes being safe. Any lightness has evaporated, and he seems drawn down by the weight of what may happen when the cavalry takes over. Will history repeat itself? Will he be shot down once more or carried to safety when he comes out of his solitude?

My part in all this hurts. The recording in my pocket burns a giant, ungainly hole. I realise I don't want to be the one dragging him into the limelight. I don't want him to leave his precious jungle if he's not ready to.

I think back to when I asked if he wanted to go home. And I feel it. Really feel it. This is his home. I don't want to be the one to take that away and thrust him into the limelight and into another media circus. I don't want that on my conscience. This has to be what he wants.

356

He begins to walk towards the noise of people. I don't follow.

'Stop,' I call.

He turns and glances back at me. 'What?'

'You . . . you could stay.' He tilts his head in confusion. 'Hear me out. I'm the only one who knows you're here. I filmed you when we saw each other across the river that time. It's shaky and out of focus and you look . . . you look just like the man you described to the police. Connor – he'll think it was the man too. He never heard you speak, he doesn't know who you are. I could show them that as proof there really is a man out here. I could say he buried Mari. And no one will ever have to know our secret.' I'll delete this whole conversation. I don't want it any more, it's wrong. I've stolen it. 'Stay if you want – or reappear once your name is cleared.' I gesture to the camera. 'I'll say I found it.'

This plan goes against everything I believe in – it isn't the truth after all. But after everything he's gone through, and everything I've learnt about Mari and Luke . . . I just want him to have the future he wants. At least one of them deserves that. He saved my life and if this jungle really is his home, he should be able to stay.

He looks staggered. 'You'd do that . . . for me?' he coughs out in surprise.

'If you want me to, I will.'

357

56

We stand there in silence.

'Okay,' he croaks, stunned at my offer.

I nod, holding out my hand.

'It was . . . it was a great privilege to meet you, Luke.'

He takes my hand; we look directly at one another, the gravity of the moment unshakable. He squeezes my palm and we let go. Then he backs away slowly, moving into a shard of light. He has the look of an ethereal spirit bathed in green-laced sunlight. I turn and walk towards the voices.

'Cassidy,' he calls, and I stop and turn back to face him. 'Thank you.'

I smile at him. 'Thanks for telling me what happened out here.'

He turns and begins to slide between the green backdrop. I limp towards camp. Gritting my teeth in pain, glad to know I will soon have the medical attention I desperately need, but apprehensive to be part of civilisation again. Part of me is jealous of what Luke has here. The simplicity once you've harnessed control of it.

Just as I'm about to hit the edge of the treeline, I take a deep breath, preparing myself to rejoin the others. I look at my hands; they are shaking. Before I step out, I hear something and turn. He hasn't disappeared after all. He is standing right there. 'I'm coming with you,' he says.

'What?' I breathe.

'I needed to come back to find her – and myself. I've done that now.' He coughs. 'I . . . I need to end it. Tell everyone what I lied about. Tell the truth. Otherwise, all it will be is a story in my head that never stops replaying. I did what I came to do.'

'But Luke, what if they don't believe you? What if there isn't anything on the camera?'

He nods, thinking. 'I'm ready to face it.' I can see he's made up his mind.

I nod and he takes my hand.

'Are you ready?' I ask, and he nods. 'As I'll ever be.'

Gripping each other's palms tightly, we step out of the depths of the jungle, and into the next chapter of this journey.

The first thing I hear is Cleo scream my name.

I wake up, feeling like I've had my first good sleep for months. My gaze settles on the window, where bright light streams through and palm leaves scratch at the glass. I look around the small private room, remembering where I am. Hospital. Yesterday – the fraught helicopter ride. A silent Luke grimacing at the thought of an onslaught from photographers, journalists, onlookers – people he'd spent years running from. A cursing Connor, screaming in agony; a uniformed policeman

359

tackling him down as he tried to get away. The chaos as we landed, and the ambulances and police cars with their whirring lights that met us as we disembarked.

I raise my arm to push my hair from my face, feeling a tug, and I see an IV drip. My legs throb and it hurts to swallow. I turn to see Cleo asleep in the chair next to my bed.

'Cleo,' I try, my voice hoarse.

Her eyes flit open, and she reaches out for my hand, clutching it tightly. 'Cass.' She begins to cry.

'It's okay. It's okay,' I tell her. 'I'm fine. How long have I been asleep?'

'About twelve hours. You must have been exhausted.'

'Where is everyone? Reggie?'

She smiles. 'He's fine – he's in another room. He'll be fine, he made a fire – the helicopter found him quickly because of the smoke.' She shakes her head in disbelief. 'I can't believe Luke . . . Connor . . .'

'Where are they?'

'Connor is here, on another floor. He tried to kill you, Cass. I can't believe . . . I knew there was something about him, I just had no idea it could have been this.' She nods to my neck. 'I doubt he's getting back to the UK anytime soon. They've got two guards on his door.'

'Luke?' I ask, concerned.

'He's at the police station. They've sent a team up to exhume the body. It's not looking great for him, I'm afraid. They want to talk to you again, properly at the station this time. I'm holding them off as long as I can.'

'Cleo?' I sit up. My heart beats a little faster thinking of what I'd bundled to her before I was besieged by the authorities wanting to know what had happened. Her lips curl into a soft smile. She checks the door is clear before removing something from her pocket. The camera. She hands it to me, and I grip it to my chest tightly, relieved. I promised Luke we wouldn't let whatever is on there get lost in all this.

She stands up. 'I'll go fetch some water.' I grab her wrist before she has a chance to walk away. 'My phone?' She reaches to the plug by the floor and pulls out the wire and leaves it on the sheet next to me.

'We found Mari,' I whisper, not quite able to compute.

'Yes. Yes, we did.' Her eyes sparkling with emotion.

'Connor led us here,' I realise.

'It was you, Cass, all you.' She squeezes my hand. 'Go back to sleep, rest, okay? I'll be back as soon as I can.'

I nod, lying back on the pillow, taking a moment to let the relief that it's over settle. Then I take my phone, unlock the screen, and read Mari's final email.

Hi Mari,

So, we're about to enter the jungle. We've just got off the train and I'm in an internet café just before the bus takes us to the boat. I think this might be the last time I write to you, so I wanted to say goodbye.

I feel different. I know it's over. I thought I would come away and be free from myself. But I'm still here. I'm still me.

I've been so depressed since the full moon party. Luke thinks I'm on a comedown from the drugs. But it isn't that. All I can hear are voices in my head telling me my time's up. I know that's selfish, but I want Luke to come with me. We are meant to get this life over with so we can try again. With a clean slate.

I can't go back and live with what I did to Luke's dad. It's never going to go away, is it?

I don't know much about this place. All I know is the end of my story is here, in the jungle. I'm not brave enough to do it alone. Sorry, Luke, you'll have to come with me.

EPILOGUE

FINDING MARI: A SEMINAL PIECE OF FILMMAKING
EVERYONE NEEDS TO WATCH

★ ★ ★ ★ ★

By Sarah Blake

The complex saga of the highly anticipated true crime series *Finding Mari* begins with a phone call, cleverly reimagined and told by a surprising central player in this extraordinary tale: Cassidy Chambers, the filmmaker herself. You'd have to be living under a rock for this to be a spoiler, but that phone call is the prologue to finding the body of much-loved but troubled teenage girl Marigold Castle. Chambers is always careful to keep the victim central to the story, even though the narrative lingers at times on her own abduction as a child, confirming this isn't your usual cold case retelling.

Woven through the story we all remember from 2002 is the making of the film itself. Chambers makes the brave decision to tell the whole truth: her affair with the imposter, Connor Barber, who sought revenge for his father being found guilty of a heinous crime. He comes across surprisingly sympathetically in the interviews conducted over the phone from jail in Bangkok, where he is to spend the next ten years for attempted murder, especially when the film meanders into his difficult childhood with a bullish patriarch.

Chambers is pragmatic in her self-shot narration, having been dragged into the story herself. She explains that the need to contextualise her history of abduction was important, because she sees this as the reason she was so vulnerable to Connor's manipulations and why the harrowing emails he sent took her back to her dark past, causing her great distress and clouding her judgement.

I was affected by the Castles, whose interviews are relatable to anyone who has loved a child, the loss of whom is any parent's greatest fear. The fact the elderly couple were finally able to bury their daughter brings a crack of light to this tale. The moment when Mrs Castle places roses on her daughter's grave will leave you in tears.

And then there's Luke Speed. Another victim in all of this. The photographs from the camera effectively became Mari's suicide note. The series suggests she took a photo of Luke asleep on the jungle floor before she crept away to the edge of the cliff. The last shot is of a picture of a lone bird in the incandescent morning light. Together with her diary entries and a post-mortem confirming her cause of death, these photos have cemented Luke's freedom from suspicion. Once the authorities established she'd died by suicide, the Thai authorities made the decision it wasn't in the public interest to charge him with moving her body, and let him come home. Luke is currently working on a memoir – allegedly being fought over by the top five publishing houses – and a survival TV show is on the cards. As you watch his journey through this epic tale, you can't help but root for a better future for him.

How to sum up in a pithy one-liner? Watch the film. Truth is hard to come by – and you do feel touched by it in this.

Khao Soon National Park

September 2002

'Hey!' The flash of light wakes him, and he lunges at the camera. She laughs, a high-pitched deranged laugh she's adopted over the last few days. It rings in his head and pools in his gut, hatred surging. 'Fuck's sake, Mari.' He wipes his eyes. Sleep isn't easy to find. The hunger takes it, strips it from your insides, *tap-tap-tapping* like tinnitus through your whole being. An ever-present reminder that you are lost.

'Chill out, Luke,' she says.

It's been three weeks, if they've counted the days right. Time went out the window once their phones died. Luke's been trying to work it out from the position of the sun but isn't sure he can call it right, yet. He looks over at his girlfriend. Eyes glazed; her cheeks concave, instead of the honey-dew wholesome mounds that were there before. Her shoulder blades bony, like bats' wings.

Some days they walk. Others it is too hard to face. She would happily lie there, staring at the dirt floor all day long. He feels as though he is dragging her every inch they cover. And he has no idea if the way they are going is right anyway.

He often thinks of the story Mr Arnold, his inspiring history teacher, told them of the *Terror*, the ship that disappeared in the Arctic en route to finding the Northwest Passage in 1845. One hypothesis is that the boat got stuck in the ice, leaving the crew to wander the barren land, crazed with scurvy, until they ate each other to survive.

'Go back to sleep then,' she says, sat with her knees hunched to her chest. Two lines of mud have found their way onto her face, and she looks like an emancipated Rambo.

'No, let's get going. We're almost there,' he says, standing up, dazed. She shrugs.

The day before he thought he'd seen a vantage point through the gaps in the evergreen. A rocky edge, high above, with a flat precipice. Luke is sure, if they can find a path to it, they'll be able to view the landscape and spot something in the vista that will help them decide on a new course of action. A fire burning, or the point of a temple, anything that looks even vaguely man-made in the distance.

Silently they pack up.

'I don't know why we are even bothering,' Mari mutters. She has become the noose that will finish them. All his energy goes into keeping her afloat. Keeping her walking, keeping her motivated to get out of here. If he were alone, this would be

367

easier. Every time that thought has passed through his mind, he's felt sick.

They trudge silently. The morning dew gummy on their insect-bitten skin. He stops and waits for her to catch up. The adrenalin in his body mounting as they get closer, wanting to break into a run to get to the top and see what is below. But he waits for her slow ascent.

Finally, they break onto the plateau, and he rushes ahead, blinking as he takes in this vast sea of rainforest. His head jolting around as he searches.

Nothing. Fucking nothing. Just jungle. More and more of it as far as the eye can see. He begins to cry. He puts his head in his hands and sobs.

He feels her hand ride up his back. He jerks away and walks from her. The anger and resentment rising. 'What?' she demands, almost bemused at his reaction.

'You don't even care that we're never getting out,' he says, cutting the air with his hand in frustration.

She stares out at the view. 'I told you, Luke. Things happen for a reason.'

'What if it's never over?' he says, almost to himself. Terror and hopelessness engulf him.

'Let's end it then,' she says, with an air of confidence he hasn't heard from her for weeks.

He peers around. She has stepped closer to the edge of the cliff. A bird soars and hovers in front of them. The camera still in her hand, she winds the thumb wheel and snaps a photograph.

'Don't waste them,' he says roughly.

She chuckles. 'What are you saving them for?'

'I wanted to take the last photo when we finally get out.'

She knows this, he's told her many times. She looks down at the dial. 'All gone.' She shrugs. 'Whoops.'

A burning surge of anger in the pit of his stomach. His nostrils flare as the hatred flows through him. 'Was there a snake, Mari?' he asks, for the millionth time. 'Was. There. A. Snake?' She doesn't reply. Just lifts her chin, goading him. Could she really have made the snake up, to get them out here alone, on purpose?

He storms towards her, hands clamping over each shoulder. He shakes her, trying to get her to look at him. She won't. 'I hate you,' he says through gritted teeth. 'You are the worst thing that ever happened to me. I wish I never met you,' he spits, wanting her to react for once. To finally cave and tell him what she's really thinking, feeling. But she doesn't say a word. 'Because of you, I can't even think about my father, the good things, without that night, and what I let you do. I can't even look my mum in the face. And now I'm putting her through this, too.' He lets go of her and crouches down, winded. And she just stands above him. Motionless.

'Okay, Luke. I'll tell you.'

He looks up at her, amazed. Breeze catches on hanging rats' tails of her limp, damp hair. Her eyes devoid of emotion as she enjoys the lull, biting her bottom lip. Everything goes quiet as he watches in slow motion her mouth beginning to form the first word.

'There. Wasn't. A. Snake.'

A clash of cymbals as the anger rips through him. And he charges up at her, pushing her back, towards the cliff edge. She screams and tries to hold on to his T-shirt but loses her grip and he collapses to the ground as she falls off the lip. Her scream stops abruptly as her body hits the ground below with a thud.

And all is quiet again.

ACKNOWLEDGEMENTS

Firstly, thank you for picking up this book and reading it. Three books in, I am still in awe that people actually buy and read my novels.

Thank you so much to everyone at Quercus for all your support. My editor Kat Burdon, who was so very enthusiastic about this story from the off, I've loved working on this with you. Also thanks wholeheartedly to Stef Bierwerth, Joe Christie on publicity, David Murphy and Isobel Smith on sales, Charlotte Gill on marketing and Lorraine Green for your excellent copyediting skills. Lisa Brewster, for another incredibe cover. Getting a book to market is a massive team effort, and I appreciate everything you all do. Thank you also to Graham Bartlett, for helping me with all the police procedural and legal elements of the story; any errors are my own.

My agent, Teresa Chris, thank you for all your guidance and passion. It is rare to meet someone as fanatical about charity shop clothes as I am.

The inspiration for this book comes from various sources, including a memorable backpacking trip to Thailand in 2002 with my friend Emma Spike (hi, Emma!). Our adventurous escapades, our ability to miss every ferry (due to a rather rigorous exploration of those buckets mentioned in the book), boys and arguments about said boys – ah, to be nineteen again! The sense of freedom was exhilarating and terrifying, and I hope I managed to encompass that here. Thailand is one of the most beautiful countries I've been to, and I'd love to return someday.

Due to my television career, I'd always wanted to tell a story from the point of view of someone else trying to tell a story. And here it is! In 2016 I made a series in the Amazon jungle. The experience left quite a mark, and I knew I wanted to try and get it into a book somehow. I want to thank the fixers on that shoot without whom I would have crumbled – Paola Toapanta and Roberto Aguirre, thank you! I used my filmmaking knowledge to create Cassidy's character and weave the story through a production, but artistic licence was liberally used.

My parents, who have always encouraged me in this pursuit – thank you for everything, most importantly for the methodical beta reads. One of my aims was to finally catch my dad out with a twist, and three books in, I am pleased to report I managed it. As always to my sister Juliet, for always being so excited to get her hands on my next book. I'd like to also thank various family members who are so kind to read early copies: Ida Fairbairn, Caroline Penney, Elizabeth Savidge, Jennifer Semple.

Also, to my wonderfully encouraging non-book friends – Lottie Dominiczak, Lucy Francis, Kate Hubert, Sophie Nevin, Candice O'Brien, Bridie Woodward.

My author friends who have been vital to keeping up momentum and spirits, especially the Drafty Writers' Club, Katie Khan and Kate Maxwell. And, of course, Lizzy Barber, Charlotte Duckworth, Liv Matthews – I think I would have given up without our water cooler WhatsApp group. Charlotte Philby, massively thankful our paths crossed at secondary school, and we can now loiter around book festivals together. Thank you to all the authors who took time to read an early copy of *Her Last Summer*.

My husband and kids. Dan: we've been together a decade, married for seven, which is a shock to us both as we always seem to forget our anniversary. Your positive outlook aways gets me through the darker days of writing. Thank you for always reminding me, 'You always say that' when I tell you I'll never be able to write another book, which is exactly what I need to hear every time.

I've dedicated this book to my daughter because it was her turn, but also because Cassidy is such a strong female lead. I hope that she'll find the courage to be the strong female lead in her own story one day.

Most importantly, thank you to all the booksellers, book bloggers, and champions of books who've spent time selling, writing reviews and posting my books online. It means the world to me; thank you. If you enjoyed this book, please consider leaving a review. I love reading them; it spurs me on for whatever I write next!